"STAY BACK!" LEN WARNED.
"JUST STAY THE HELL BACK!"

"But Len," Harry said, "if I stay back, how can I savage you? How can I tear your throat out and feed your entrails to the wild things that scurry through the woods behind your sorry excuse for a house?"

His tone was more matter-of-fact than questioning, as if the act itself were a foregone conclusion.

"You got one minute, pal. That's how long it's gonna take me to get my gun."

Harry took a step toward him, and Len took an unconscious step backwards. Fear was beside him now, but even fear could not keep Len from looking into those eyes. And as he did, he felt a hushed sweet stillness. . . .

Trapped by those eyes, Len didn't notice the sallowness of the skin or even the redness of the eyes. Nor, finally, did he see the smile on Harry's face just before he turned the stake toward Len, just before he shoved it into Len's buttery gut.

Minutes later, after Len had been blooded, Harry Matheson stood over the body and produced a match from his pocket. "That's two," he said. . . .

BLOOD BROTHERS

T. Lucien Wright

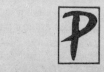

PINNACLE BOOKS
WINDSOR PUBLISHING CORP.

Dedicated with love
for my daughters—Patricia and Jennifer.
To brothers everywhere—
be they vampires or not.

This is a work of fiction. Any similarity to persons living or dead is purely unintentional.

PINNACLE BOOKS

are published by

Windsor Publishing Corp.
475 Park Avenue South
New York, NY 10016

First printing: January, 1992

Printed in the United States of America

Prologue

THE PAST

"She's been gone three days now," said Emily Cartwright, a friend of the family, and an even better friend of the deceased. She paused, thinking of her own mortality. Would she be the next to go? There were signs: the pains in her chest, deceased relatives that propped themselves on the foot of her bed in the wee hours. Signs. Damnable signs.

"Three days," she continued with a modest shake of her head, her eyes red from tears, tears that, again owing to the severity of the pain in her chest, were not being shed entirely for her dead friend.

Emily leaned a little left, giving her a view of the back bedrooms. "The boys ready yet?" she asked their mother, a tall, lithe, beautiful woman who was also the deceased's daughter and who seemed to be taking this death better than Emily.

Shanna Matheson smiled lightly at Emily, said, "I'll see," and left the room. A minute or so later she returned, her twin boys flanking her and looking for all the world like lifesize, childhood photographs of herself.

They stood reverently by, understanding, even at the age of six, the gravity and solemnity of the proceedings.

And they were, as many a relative had mentioned, as alike as bookends; both blonde, both tall, both thin and straight, their features almost femininely delicate. Emily regarded them with a warm smile, a smile neither bothered to return. They had been, Emily knew, the apples of their grandmother's eyes: And didn't they look handsome in their dark blue suits, white shirts and black ties? Studying them, she wondered if they yet knew what had really happened—not the usual soft soap, the "God has taken her to his bosom" garbage, but the truth. Did they know that during the days and weeks and months to come the earth would inexorably reclaim their Nana? Did they know that, during that time, mindless minions of insects, who were only just part of the life and death cycle and therefore blameless, would steal into her vault and enjoy a mighty feast? She thought not. But, she allowed as she tried to see past their youthful, innocent eyes, perhaps six was not the proper age to know of life, or more precisely, the end of it.

"We're going to put Nana to rest now," she told them in hushed tones. She regarded them a while longer, pondering the robotlike immobility of their gaze, and added in less hushed tones, "You both look very nice. Nana would be proud. Very, very proud." At that, Harry, who stood to the left of his mother, smiled.

At the request of the family Emily sat with the boys during the ceremonies. Through it all, the reading of a poem written by the deceased just for the occasion and speeches immortalizing the deceased, the boys remained calm. Well, Emily noted, they are putting up a brave front. A very brave front. They might not know what would happen to their Nana, but Emily wagered they did know they'd never see her again. She took Jerry's hand first, then Harry's, and each looked at her momentarily, their eyes somewhat questioning her action. Again they looked at their Uncle George, the last of the speakers, a bear of a man with catcher's mitts for hands, the fingers

6

of which hung over the front of the podium in "Kilroy was here" fashion while he talked. The boys had heard horror stories about their Uncle George, that he wouldn't hesitate to wallop you a good one if you stepped out of line, and both boys shuddered in unison, as the vision of one of those huge hands blistering down onto their bare backsides drew sharper focus.

Emily, however, didn't know a thing about what the boys had just envisioned and mistook their reaction as being chilled by the presence of death. She squeezed their hands lightly in what she hoped was a comforting gesture.

After Uncle George's lengthy remarks, Father Simmons, who had given their Nana her last rites, said a few more words, and offered a final prayer. In short order the room was empty of everyone except Nana, most mourners mingling in the hallway and on the front steps to await the loading of the hearse, some remarking that it was a lovely day, that Nana would have probably picked a day just like this to go to her reward. Jerry, upon hearing this, thought, they give you a reward for dying? and turned toward his brother to question him about it. But Harry, to Jerry's quiet horror, was gone. He had, for some reason, left him alone in a place that was, to Jerry, more than a little frightening.

With an indrawn gasp he tried to wade through the forest of humans, leaving Emily behind, unaware that her charges were now gone.

Tiny beads of sweat began to appear on Jerry's forehead as he blindly searched for his brother. This was, after all, a place where dead people went before they were put into the ground. What if they thought, what if they mistook . . .

But as he searched, his mind's eye suddenly flashed a shadowy glimpse of his Nana in her coffin and he knew instantly where he could find his brother. With one last push through a forest of legs, he stepped into the room where his Nana was being kept, and stopped.

Harry, who knew he was there, turned slowly, looked at him and said, "Isn't she pretty?"

Jerry, somewhat puzzled, walked slowly across the room, looked in at his dead Nana and searched for the beauty of which his brother spoke.

Chapter One

Thomas Jefferson Smith clutched reflexively at his thin and suddenly pain-filled chest. "Damn!" he said, both agitated and frustrated. The pain receded and he shuffled onto the bridge that overlooked Naples Falls. About halfway across he stopped and leaned against the railing. Naples Falls was frothy and quick here. White water slapped onto pylons and boulders. Mesmerized by the music of the creek, Tom visualized his body falling slowly and dreamily through space, toward the rocks that shouldered past the surface of the choppy water. "Death, now there's a thought," he said aloud. "Leave your worries at the door, folks, no need for worries here." He shrugged. What the hell did he know about death? Not much, not much at all; just the sour stench that fogged the air for a while and then dissipated, leaving no trace at all of the person responsible. He spat, brought up a little blood. "Shit," he said as he wiped his mouth with his sleeve. "Since when did I have the guts to kill myself?" He smiled feebly. "Scared of death and just as scared of life. Isn't that a scream, isn't that just a scream?"

He walked on, past Cosmo's Restaurant, past Trither's Photographic Studio, Rover's Retreat, the Silver Spoon and then finally the small, white Catholic church that signalled the edge of town. A few minutes later, after he had passed a dozen or so private homes beyond the limits

9

of town, he found himself in the empty parking lot of a 7-11 two thirds of the way up a rise. He looked back toward town and winked back at the blinking yellow caution light, its signal weakened by a gathering fog.

From here he could hear the falls but he couldn't see them. Beyond the blinking, fuzzy yellow of the Route 5 caution light, he saw nothing. Just to his left, where the road turned gently right at the beginning of a slope, the fog appeared almost solid, its arrival more reminiscent of dragon's smoke than the padding of little cat's feet.

As Tom stared vacantly toward the falls, he detected movement out of the corner of his eye, on the road to his left. He turned, squinted, and saw the girl-woman Charlene riding her bicycle at a slow, constant speed. Girl-woman was Tom's description. Her fifty-year-old eyes were still those of a young, vulnerable, simpleminded girl.

Probably headed home, he thought, wherever that is. He had seen her up there before, on that hill behind the 7-11. He had lain in the bushes and watched her go through some strange ritual.

Like a blind person in familiar surroundings, Charlene pedaled steadily into the fog; the rhythmic squeak of an unoiled bicycle chain faded and was gone.

"Crazy old broad," he said.

A short time later, while he contemplated where he might spend the night, Tom watched two people step from the fog where the road dipped, just as if the fog had suddenly heaved and moaned and given them birth. The sight of two people stepping from a middle of the night fog momentarily startled him. Sometimes he saw someone jogging at this time of night, and, of course, there was Charlene, but he rarely saw two people. Most townfolk were in bed before Johnny Carson's monologue.

They were, he decided, walking toward him. And wasn't it strange the way they appeared to glide rather

10

than walk? But maybe it's just the fog, he decided, that and the dark—makes them look like that, like they're gliding. Now he could see that one of them was a woman, a slim, but well-endowed woman, while the other was a large, very well-developed man.

Maybe they wanted to talk, ask him directions or something. Car could be broke down at the bottom of the hill. Thousand different things.

Tom stood as they drew to within twenty yards, raised his hand slightly and nodded. "Evening," he said companionably.

No answer, just that steady, slow glide.

"You folks lost?" he continued, forcing a smile.

Still no answer.

Although Jerry Matheson knew very well that he was sleeping, he was still able to question himself. Why am I dreaming about some guy standing next to a 7-11? he wondered. His dreams were usually more convoluted, with unexplainable twists and bends and dead ends. But this dream was detailed, precise, without the usual fuzziness and black backwash. He could almost feel the cool night air bite into his lungs and the slithering fog passing over his body. He drew closer to the man who was obviously the focus of his attention, a tall but very slight and shabbily dressed man. As he stepped to within a few feet and stopped, he saw that his mouth was quivering and that tears had gathered at the corners of his small eyes. The terror in them was like that of a small, cornered child awaiting the strap. And while he watched, the man's terror became even more profound, and the word "murder," which had been standing idly by in a dark corner of his thoughts, just as suddenly shoved its way to the fore. This little man, this dream conjured character, was about to be killed and as far as he could tell, he was going to do it.

He stepped closer still, and out of the corner of his eye

he saw someone else—a woman, he thought. But he saw her only briefly, and then only the top of her head, only her long hair defining her gender. The little man held up a long fingered hand and said something, something Jerry couldn't make out—yet another oddity. Dream conversation was the norm, not deafness. He tried to lip read, but even awake he couldn't do that. Still, he was able to make out the word "please" as it ushered through wet, fissured, sharply slanted lips. "Please, don't kill me!" Was that what he was trying to say? Was he begging for his life?

That question went unanswered, for suddenly Jerry felt the outer edges of consciousness tug at him, followed immediately by a momentary distortion of detail, which seemed to indicate that he was trying to wake up, and also seemed to indicate that he didn't want to see this little man die. Even a dream death.

He waited, fully expecting consciousness to overtake him. It didn't. The man drew closer, close enough to detail the pallid, stubbled face, the pleading eyes . . . and now, the corded, roosterlike neck as it inexplicably became the focus of his attention. He leaned to the man, closer still, until his pores seemed cavernous.

But then the little man began to blur and the words, "Wake up, Jerry!" slipped almost unheard into his thoughts.

"Honey, please!" the voice continued.

Jerry snapped his eyes open, effectively releasing the man to whatever fate awaited him. Then he sat up and stared at the dark wall in front of him.

His wife, Maria, put a hand on his shoulder. "God, honey, you scared the hell out of me! You were yelling, Jerry. Do you know that? You were yelling!"

He turned, sat on the side of the bed, scrubbed his hands over his face. "Jesus," he mumbled, "what a dream!"

Maria, who had distinctly heard Jerry say the word

"kill," moved her hand in a circular motion over his bare back.

"There was this guy, a bum . . ."

He thought about the man, and for a fleeting second he seemed familiar, long ago familiar. And strangely, the dream rekindled, actually following him into consciousness. The action continued as the characters became transparent, which allowed him a view of both worlds. To a writer it was a godsend.

Seconds later, their son, Tad, stepped into the doorway, his small body framed by a stack of boxes. Tomorrow was moving day.

"What's wrong?" he asked, his voice ragged with sleep.

Maria got out of bed and went to him, kneeling to his height. "Your dad just had a dream," she said soothingly. "Just a silly dream."

"A nightmare?" Tad asked.

Leaving Tad's question unanswered, Jerry hurried out of bed and shrugged into his bathrobe. "Look," he said as he stepped toward the door, "I won't be able to sleep for a while; think I'll do some work. Why don't you keep your mom company, son?"

"Okay."

"I won't be long." He closed the door behind him.

By the time Jerry reached the top of the stairs sentences were quickly ballooning into whole paragraphs, their clarity obviously attributable to the mindplay he was being offered.

"Holy shit!" he said aloud.

Vaguely he heard Maria ask him if everything was all right.

"Yeah, fine," he answered. His voice quavered excitedly.

"You're sure?"

"Yeah, go to sleep. I'm okay. In fact, I'm great!"

His body suddenly oily with sweat, he hurried to his

13

study and snapped on his word processor.

Name, he almost yelled, he needed a name. The name Thomas slipped into his thoughts. Yeah, he thought, Thomas.

Thomas Jefferson Smith's hollowing veins collapsed as his blood roared toward newly opened exits. And as he drank, Harry Matheson could feel Christine's gaze upon him, the core of her existence being tested by her overwhelming need. Her thirst. But tonight they would not share; at least not this victim. Thomas shook as if electrified; his sightless eyes bulged, almost threatening to splinter the surrounding bone, all of which caused Christine to move closer to this victim, her sharklike skin tingling with anticipation.

Harry drank noisily, aware of Christine's closing proximity. But she knew about Thomas Jefferson Smith, knew very well. This one was not just for food, this one was for revenge. And revenge, strengthened by immortality, was far more important than a mere quenching of thirst.

When he was done, Harry wiped his mouth with his sleeve and smiled at Christine, smiled because the taste of revenge was very sweet.

She regarded him coldly. "Why?" she asked, her voice raspy with anger.

With an imperturbable air Harry let his gaze wander over her. It was a pleasant journey. Her long, dark hair fell lightly over her shoulders and curled ever so delicately there, almost cupping breasts that seemed fuller when accented by a slim, girlish waist. And when she moved she did so with an undulating sensuality that, even now, was neither self-conscious nor vulgar. What a shame, Harry thought, that immortality has removed the innocence from those flashing green eyes.

"Why?" she repeated through clenched teeth.

Harry didn't bother to answer her question. He simply

14

reached into his jeans pocket, pulled out a long, wooden match and struck it on a dumpster beside the 7-11. "See you in hell," he said as he flipped it onto Thomas's body. Cremation didn't concern him, only symbolism. The flame leaped momentarily then died under the assault of a capricious wind.

Moments later, Harry hoisted Thomas over his head and threw him into the dumpster, the sound muffled by a thick accummulation of trash, as if an exhausted Thomas had simply fallen heavily into bed.

"One down, five to go," Harry said as he looked into Christine's angry, questioning eyes.

Chapter Two

MOVING DAY

Jerry hadn't said a word for the last twenty miles or so, ever since WCMF had reported that a body had been found inside a dumpster beside a 7-11 in Naples Falls. Maria shot a glance at her husband, who was too busy guiding the five-year-old Custom Cruiser down the rain-slicked dirt back road to notice. As she turned to check on their sleeping son, the front left tire thudded into a mud-filled pothole and sprayed the windshield with a thick wash of mud. The rear tires suddenly lost traction. "Shit!" Jerry whispered as he jerked the wheel and lightly pumped the brakes to regain control, fumbling for the wiper switch after he had. Well, Maria thought, you do have a tongue after all—somewhat venomous, but still capable of the spoken word.

Jerry hadn't counted on this. The weatherman had called for partly to mostly sunny. Partly to mostly sunny would have been ideal—no, not simply ideal—perfect. Just perfect. Now the sky was that godawful, somber-looking gray and the temperature had fallen into the low sixties. Hell, they'd probably move in during a goddamn downpour! Weather like this was usually reserved for funerals. Gray and drizzly—just perfect to stick someone in the ground. He sucked in a huge volume of air, let it

16

out and, in so doing, released the tremendous coincidence from his thoughts. So he had dreamt about some guy getting killed at a 7-11; so they had heard a news report that mirrored his dream. So what? Dwelling on it for much longer wasn't going to do any good. Maria hadn't wanted to move in the first place. An extended sulk on his part wouldn't help matters much.

He looked into his rearview mirror at the blue and green FOLEY BROS. moving van about a hundred yards back, the sum total of their worldly possessions imprisoned within. Getting Maria to say yes to this move had been about as difficult as convincing her that his last novel would sell (it had, maybe not as well as either had hoped, or as well as his brother's second, but they had made money, and making money, after all, was what it was all about). She hadn't wanted to leave the city: her mother, her career. But after at least a million fights he had finally managed to convince her that this move would be beneficial to their somewhat deteriorating relationship. Besides, he told her, he could support them well enough now, in the manner to which she had become accustomed. He had made damn good money last year, and this year would be even better, he could feel it. And although writing was certainly speculative, as Maria had told him more than once, in the long run all you had to do was sell a few books and get yourself a following. It was all downhill from there; one long, greasy slope. His masterpiece was taking shape anyway, and, out here in God's country, it would solidify. And besides, his brother had written a few best sellers out here, before he packed up and left for Hollywood.

Harry had said that United Artists wanted the movie rights to one of his books, one of his first, but the only way they could get their hands on it was if they gave him complete artistic control. "Hell," he'd added, "I don't want my work to suffer the same fate that some of Stephen's has." United Artists had grudgingly agreed, but agreed they had, and Harry, Jerry thought, was more than likely sequestered in some dimly lit room right now, working like a madman. Harry had said that he was probably going to stay in California, too, which was why he'd offered Jerry the house.

"Even if I do come back," he'd informed Jerry over the phone, "I'll find something else. Something newer, I think. And listen, don't worry too much about making payments until you start making a decent buck." That last sentence had been spiked with a generous helping of sarcasm. Jerry, unaccustomed to such generosity from his brother, if not the sarcasm, forgave him his spiked tongue, but at the same time allowed the very real possibility that Harry might be harboring an ulterior motive. Still, Harry was showing him and his a kindness; actions that were certainly inexplicable, but actions that were also very much appreciated. And if Harry had an ulterior motive, Jerry sure couldn't figure out what that ulterior motive might be. Someday, after he started making a "decent buck," maybe he'd get the chance to reciprocate.

Just before that telephone conversation ended he wished Harry good luck with the script and told him to knock em' dead. Harry said he would.

In the back seat, Tad Matheson snapped his eyes open. Sweat dripped down his thin, freckled face, a face similar to his mother's, although Tad's hair was more red than blond, and his freckles were much more plentiful.

"Hey, sleepyhead," she said, smiling.

No answer.

"Tad?"

"Huh?"

With furrowed brow, she studied him more closely. What little light there was glinted dully off rolling droplets of sweat. And, she determined, his eyes were definitely glassy. With motherly efficiency she felt his forehead with the back of her hand, then lightly pressed his cheek. She sighed with relief. No fever, thank God. Just a dream, just another dream.

"We there yet?" Tad asked as Maria opened the glove

18

box, pulled out a Handi-Wipe and mopped his brow.

"Just another three or four miles," Jerry Matheson said, forcing a better mood than the one he had displayed for the last half hour or so. "Bet you can't wait, huh?"

"Yeah, can't wait, Dad."

Well, that wasn't very convincing, Jerry thought. "And wait'll you see the surprise, son," he added. "Just wait'll you see."

Maria smiled at her son knowingly and dropped the Handi-Wipe into a McDonald's litter bag under the dash.

"You wanta talk about it?" she asked.

"What?"

"Your dream, Tad, your nightmare."

Tad only shrugged, which surprised Maria. They had made an agreement. Bad dreams were best brought out into the open, kind of like throwing up bad food. Once out—talked out—that particular nightmare would never return. She had promised.

"You really should talk about it, son," Jerry coaxed.

Tad stared at his father's half-troubled reflection, the thinning, wavy blonde hair, the heavy, black-rimmed glasses and pasty skin; the hard blue eyes that always seemed to look right through him.

"Son?"

"What?"

"You wanta talk about it?"

"It was nothin', Dad, it's okay."

"You're sure?"

"Yeah, it's okay, Dad."

Tad watched as his parents eyes briefly touched. They knew he was lying. They always knew. But he certainly didn't want to tell them what he had dreamed. His mother would only accuse him of having an overactive imagination, just like his dad. And that would probably ruin his dad's day. His dad's big day.

The dirt road—thankfully—turned paved within a mile of town. Tad looked out his side window at the surrounding hills. Scudding black clouds scraped across the tops of miles-away evergreens like huge, dark gray

19

chisels. To their right now was Hunt's Hollow ski area, a private slope, just one long, almost vertical drop. Naples Falls, renowned for its wine grapes, was New York State's answer to California's Napa Valley. The townfolk consisted primarily of vineyard employees and retirees who had opted for the slower pace of country life. Even the town's newspaper, the *Naples Falls Gazette,* printed only hunting news and town gossip. Rarely did they feature world events.

In a few days, the town would hold a mile-long flea market and festival along both sides of Route 5. The festival customarily brought a horde of tourists into town, summer visitors intent on snapping up anything that could be passed off as either quaint or rustic. Grape pie—although neither quaint nor rustic—was a favorite, and usually sold for seven bucks a tin. It didn't really taste any better than store-bought grape pie, but the fact that it was bought from the source seemed to validate the inflated price. No one seemed to care that grapes weren't quite in season yet and that the pies had been carefully frozen, then thawed for the festival; the fact that grapes were out of season only seemed to support the price (country living, as more than one observer had come to note, did not, necessarily make one a country bumpkin). But there were those who had begun to wonder mightily about the theme of the festival, the "vulgar sensationalism" as a few of the more learned townfolk were wont to say. But still, it was a theme that had been time tested and hardened, and a sudden and dramatic switch toward what some might construe as normalcy might just cause some of those tourists to look elsewhere for their 'bizarre' fun. And how many festivals started when the sun went down? Jerry, whose family had lived here during his senior year, had been away the week of the festival. He had, however, heard a few things. If nothing else, he thought, the festival was certainly unique.

The Matheson's new house was on the outskirts of town and about a third of the way up a heavily wooded hillside, hidden from view from everyone except motorists who were usually well past before they realized the house was there. A Red and White supermarket, about a quarter of a mile down the road, signalled the edge of town. Between the house and the market was the town cemetery, smallish as cemeteries went, but pin neat and through which many a couple wandered aimlessly. Since the town was founded by Colonel Nathaniel Carson, a revolutionary war veteran, the Naples Falls dead had been, for the most part, interred here. It was not unusual to see a two-hundred-year-old tombstone neighboring a fresh one, which also left many a wanderer with a very real sense of mortality.

Across the road from their new house, and at the bottom of the hill, was a very old and very run down, pale yellow ranch house, the thickly weeded yard littered with used tires and a couple of ramshackle dog houses. Two mongrels, a house each, their heads wedged boringly between their forepaws, lay inside. Their respective names, Heidi and King, had been scrawled in runny black paint over each semi-circled entrance. Behind them plumes of gray-blue smoke rose sinuously from the gray tentacle of a wood-burning stove. A rusting, whale-like, dark green '73 Plymouth Fury straddled the lawn and stone driveway. It wasn't much of a place—almost reminiscent of Appalachia, Jerry thought—but out here, he didn't much care.

He threw on his right turn signal, prompting Tad to lean forward, eyes round with anticipation. The car started up the inclined, stone driveway. In front of them was a deep, two-car detached garage bordered on the left by the cemetery. The garage and the house—a large, well-kept, turn-of-the-century colonial to the right and further up the hill—were both painted white with light blue trim. The house was large enough to someday fulfill Maria's dream of owning and operating a bed-and-breakfast inn—one of the reasons she had consented to this move, despite her initial objections. Conditions in

21

the area were favorable, too. There were a number of ski slopes, and of course tourists were easy prey for the casualness and charm of a bed-and-breakfast inn.

Jerry turned right as the driveway took a ninety degree turn just in front of the garage, drove on for another sixty feet or so and then stopped at the edge of the yard. To the left was a flat stone path that led to the enclosed front porch. The path veered off to the right and then butted up against the enclosed side porch. There was a huge, gnarly, Halloween-type oak in the front yard, a hole midtrunk, octopuslike branches stretching in all directions. A swing tire hung by a thick rope from one of the high branches. Tad eyed it with wonder—a ride on that thing would be a real heart stopper. (The slope of the yard left a fearless rider at least twelve feet off the ground at the apex of the ride.) Were it not for the boneyard right next door, Tad would have been deliciously happy.

The FOLEY BROS. moving van inched up the driveway and squealed to a stop some ten feet back. The driver, a large, potbellied man dressed in a red and black flannel shirt and jeans, drew back the emergency brake, cut the engine, and got out. His help, a very bored looking, wiry man in his twenties who wore a Montreal Expos cap shoved back off his forehead, waited in the cab, his attention focused on the threatening sky.

Jerry got out and met the potbellied man between vehicles while Tad and Maria anxiously exited the car, hurried up the pathway and walked up the steps to the enclosed porch. They had intended to go into the house, but Tad stopped and watched with mild concern as his dad threw up his arms, leaned forward a little and then planted his hands on his hips while the other man glared at him.

The other man was not only tall, like his dad, but almost as big, too. Tad was half afraid that the other man would just reach out and pop his dad a good one. Then they'd have a real mess, even though his dad could probably whip him. Tad strained to hear the two men but the enclosed porch muffled their words beyond comprehension. Finally, and much to Tad's relief, his dad waved at the potbellied moving man like he might a swarm of flies and huffed off, talking to himself as he walked up the flat stone pathway. He threw open the door and sent it clanging against the outer railings. His eyes filled with rage, he glanced at Tad then said to Maria, "They want a hundred bucks more to unload—can you believe it? A hundred bucks!"

"They can't do that—can they?" Maria asked. "Did they give you a reason?"

"Oh, yeah, sure, flimsy as hell, but a reason. They said because it's wet out and they gotta carry our stuff up an incline."

"You're kidding!" Maria interposed.

"Wish to hell I was," Jerry answered.

"Well, what did you tell them?"

Jerry looked at his wife, a small but somewhat derisive smile on his face. "Well, Maria, what could I tell them? We sure can't leave our stuff in the yard!"

A smile slowly blossomed on her face.

"What's so funny?" Jerry asked.

"You. And me, too."

"Maria—this is not funny!"

She touched her fingers to his lips. "Jerry. We've got the money. A hundred bucks is not going to bankrupt us. A couple of years ago, maybe, but not now."

Jerry returned her smile. "Habit, I guess. I suppose I'll never change."

Jerry usually shifted moods as dramatically as a half-load of cement shifts in a speeding truck taking a sweeping turn—thuddingly, so this slow turn very much pleased Maria.

"C'mon, kiddo. Follow me," he said, taking Tad by the hand. "You, too," he said to Maria, his smile almost jack-in-the-box size. "Let's take our son on a tour of this place."

Jerry assumed the role of the self-assured realtor as he

took his family into the large dining room off the kitchen. Maria and Tad had seen it all before, but she stood patiently by as he spoke primarily to his son, who hadn't seen the house for a long while. He stopped near the large bowed window that looked onto the side yard.

"The view, Mr. Matheson, as you can plainly see, is uncluttered by long lines of four-bedroom colonials. And from what I understand, zoning clearly states that it never will be. Just acre after acre of tombstones. You know, those people that were dead when I lived here are still dead?" He ran his hand reverently along the cherry wood window seat. "Real wood, too, sir, just like the beamed ceiling."

Tad listened, but he simply couldn't understand how his dad could make fun of the fact that they lived right next to a graveyard. You were just asking for it then. You might as well go out in the yard with a nine-iron during a thunderstorm.

"Of course," Jerry continued, "this wallpaper will have to go. But then, redecorating is just part of the fun of owning a new place, isn't that right, Mr. Matheson?"

Tad studied the wallpaper more closely. It wasn't that bad, he decided. But when he imagined himself walking through the house in the middle of the night and seeing these large red and blue flowers by moonlight, a chill scampered up his back. "Yep," he said with conviction, "it's gotta go!"

Jerry grinned. "Glad you agree, Mr. Matheson!"

"Me, too," Maria added at a whisper.

The family let go with a collective laugh, each having decided that this paper was, indeed, close to hideous.

They left the dining room and went into what at one time had been the parlor, separated from the living room by an open double doorway. It was more library than parlor. Floor-to-ceiling bookcases covered the three full walls, and Jerry certainly had collected enough books over the years to accommodate the shelf space. The floor in here, as in both the dining room and the living room, was a highly polished, unstained oak. The bookcase against the outside wall covered the only window in the room, other than the door that led to the front porch. As Tad looked around, he was positive he detected a musty smell, like that of old, soggy, confined-to-the-basement newspaper. He mentally envisioned these bookcases filled with all kinds of books, (although it was definitely hard to imagine that many books) and felt somewhat awestruck.

"This, Mr. Matheson," Jerry said, "would make an excellent study. Don't you think?"

Tad supposed that it probably would. What else could it be?

They went into the living room, a considerably brighter room than the parlor/library/study. A long picture window that looked out onto the main road had been installed here. The family stood nearby and watched the movers as they wrestled with a long, white sleeper sofa. Maria silently hoped they'd be careful with it. It was fairly new and still unsoiled.

Across the road then, and framed by the back of the station wagon and the front of the truck, they saw a short, thin old man dressed in a green and black flannel shirt, his thick gray hair dampened by mist. He was feeding one of the dogs. They watched while the dog raised its head for a moment, lazily pushed itself up, and sniffed at the food. As the dog lay back down, the couch moved across their field of vision, effectively assuming the role of the on-off knob on a TV.

Jerry turned. "As you can see, Mr. Matheson," he continued, "the fireplace is good size, and, I might add, workable. Some people, in their decorative haste, paint their fireplaces. I would, however, recommend a good pair of doors. The winters are as cold as a puppy's nose out here and an uncovered fireplace opening will suck your heat like a leech on a pig!"

"Jerry!" Maria scolded, "you're going to give him nightmares!"

"Naw," Jerry responded. "He's a big boy now. Bloodsucking leeches aren't about to give him nightmares. Isn't that right, sport?"

"No way!" Tad said.

The room, easily the largest in the house, thirty feet long by twenty feet wide, still managed to exude a feeling of warmth. It was, Maria thought, a room in which she would spend a lot of time, and would thoroughly enjoy decorating. The walls here were covered by the same hideous paper that adorned the dining room, although here, because of the room's size, the effect was not overwhelming. The mantel over the fireplace, thick and unscratched, had been brought to a mirror gloss by layers of varnish. Appraising the wall above the mantel, Maria remembered that a picture had hung there for a very long time. The paper was considerably brighter and fresher in an area approximately two feet tall by three feet wide. On either side were brass candle holders affixed to the wall, sans candles. Those, she thought, would definitely stay. Maintaining the nineteenth century feel of this place would be essential to its popularity as a bed-and-breakfast inn. The candle holders, as well as the ornate light fixtures, glass doorknobs and solid, gleaming wood doors fairly screamed "old world charm."

"I like this room," Jerry said with a smile, his eyes panning left to right then back again. He looked at Maria. "I can just picture it—me in there spitting out a best seller, you in here . . . doing whatever you please."

She forced a smile.

"C'mon," Jerry said, taking his son by the hand. "Let's check out the upstairs."

At the same time, the movers stepped into the doorway between the parlor and the living room, the white, sleeper couch in tow.

"You coming, hon?" Jerry asked.

She thought a moment, then, "Why don't you two go on ahead. I'm going to show these guys where to put things."

Jerry turned, saw the fat man smiling falsely at him, turned back, said, "Okay, hon," then squeezed past the fat man and the doorframe, Tad right behind.

"In here?" the thin man asked as Jerry and Tad disappeared up the stairs.

"Yes, against the south wall, please," Maria said.

"Lady," the large man said tiredly, "we don't decorate, we just move."

Maria glared at him—they were giving these clowns a hundred bucks over and above—they had damn well better 'decorate'.

"Sure, south wall," the fat man said grudgingly.

Maria thanked them and went into the kitchen.

The antiquated gas stove and a tiny white refrigerator, about her height, would probably have to be replaced, especially if they went into business as a bed-and-breakfast inn. To the left of the refrigerator a grouping of three large windows looked onto what had been a vegetable garden. She remembered how astonished she had been at Harry's disinterest in the small plot. The dirt, although thick with rock and stone, was fantastically mucky and therefore great for growing things. Harry, a dyed-in-the-wool vegetarian, had grown some very large yet tasty vegetables in the city. She remembered his pleased smile as he held up a foot long cuke or a softball size tomato. I wonder why he really did what he did, she thought. Sure, he's not a Scrooge, but he never has been so unabashedly generous either. His suspect behavior even made her wonder about her brother-in-law's well-being, although she had absolutely nothing to base those thoughts on. She had even mentioned her fears to Jerry, who only smiled as though he were humoring her. He had always believed that if anything ever happened to his brother, he would know it; had something to do with their being identical twins and all that hocus pocus garbage. "We share things," he had told her. "If something happens to him, I feel it, and if something happens to me, he feels it. That's the way it is, and always

27

will be. When he dies, I'll know. Believe me, I'll know."

But there had been the one time, just before Harry moved to Naples Falls, when Jerry had scared the hell out of her by popping up in bed in a cold sweat, his face white with fear, an episode that had been somehow different than the yelling of the previous night. When she asked him what was wrong, he just smiled and said, "For a minute there . . . I don't know, for a minute there, I thought something had happened to Harry. I thought he had . . . died." Then he had simply shrugged it off, adding, "But he's not dead. Maybe his heart skipped a few beats or something, but he's certainly not dead." At the time she had marveled at how very aware one was of the other, especially if one could detect a slight malfunction in the other's heartbeat. But that, she knew, was probably impossible. Jerry had simply brought some deap seated fear for his brother's welfare to the surface via a nightmare. He did love him very much, and living out here all alone, despite the fact that he was a grown man, only fueled Jerry's anxiety. Lost in her thoughts, Maria barely noticed the movers as they walked into the kitchen with their white formica dinette set and two of four Breuer chairs. She asked them to put it by the window.

"You got anything you want put in the basement?" the thin man asked.

Maria looked at the cellar door. She had been down there—once, and that was enough. The place was crawling with spiders and about as clammy as the inside of a spinning dryer.

"Not likely," she said.

"Good," the thin man answered.

After the movers had done as asked, she sat down and looked out into what was now a misty rain and watched as a chattering squirrel scurried up a nearby tree. A vague loneliness drifted into her. She was here, in the country, her only neighbors, outside of a little old man with a rundown house and a pair of lazy hounds, were a graveyard full of dead folks. She smiled. Least she'd be able to get a word in edgewise with them. But they were here because Jerry very much wanted to live where his brother had lived, because he hadn't been as "inspired" as he thought necessary in the city. Well, she sure couldn't see how anyone could be inspired out here. People inspired her—crowds of them, and people were what she thought should inspire good writing—not this . . . wilderness.

Jerry hurried into the bathroom off the master bedroom and flushed the toilet. Instantly the quiet house was filled with the sound of gurgling water. Grinning at his son, he said, "And never again will you stand outside a closed bathroom door, your eyes floating. Won't that be a treat, Mr. Matheson?"

Tad laughed.

To the right, at the top of the stairs, was a large sitting area and yet another picture window, this one against the west wall. The view from here, to the right, showed them all of the garage and the edge of the cemetery, a short forty or so feet beyond that. There were five large bedrooms up here, two behind the stairs, one to the left and the other two in the front of the stairs, each remarkably well-appointed, with matching curtains and wallpaper and complementary carpeting, which left very little to do, other than some bathroom modernizing.

Jerry put his hand on Tad's shoulder as he suddenly remembered the surprise. Dropping to one knee, he cupped his son's shoulders. "Hey, didn't you forget something, sport?" he said.

Tad's face squinched up. "Huh?" he said.

Jerry shrugged, got up. "Well, if you can't remember . . ."

Tad's face brightened. "The surprise," he squealed. "Yeah! The surprise!"

Jerry walked over to the picture window and looked toward the garage, mock confusion mapping his face.

"Now where'd I put that?" he teased.

Tad took him by the hand and anxiously led him to the stairs.

A raft of stale, musty air greeted them as they entered the garage through the side door. Fully forty feet deep, the garage was more warehouse than anything. Stored in here were the tools needed to keep the large yard in shape; things left behind by his brother or bought outright by Jerry beforehand. A red, K-mart Mastercut riding mower had been pushed against the far wall, the shelf above it home to four gasoline cans in varying stages of rusting decay. An assortment of rakes, shovels, hedge and grass trimmers leaned against the near wall.

The murkiness created by small, dirty windows was somewhat diluted when Jerry flipped the light switch, flooding the area with conical shafts of light from a row of seventy-five watt bulbs encased in white, metal tents. As if on cue, the delighted soprano yelp of a puppy echoed through the garage. Tad let go of his dad's hand and ran in the direction of the yelp, toward the back and behind a stack of cardboard boxes about thirty feet from the side entrance and on the right hand side.

Of course, Tad knew it was a dog, even before they walked down here. He had heard his dad and mom talking about it. But such a dog—golden-haired with spindly legs splayed out to the side, his face dripping sweetness and love, his little tail sweeping along the dirt floor as he eyed this little man. Behind him was a teepee-shaped doghouse made out of cedar with real shingles on the roof, just like the ones they had seen at 84 Lumber. Tad got onto one knee and ran his hand lightly along the dog's back as his new playmate licked and sniffed, obviously preferring his new master's mouth. Tad pet him gently, gladly accepting the dog's love and almost afraid to pick him up, just like his dad was afraid to pick up little babies.

Jerry rounded the boxed corner and smiled down at the

happy pair. "Golden retriever, son. Mucho dinero, too. What are you gonna name him?"

Tad looked into the dog's huge brown eyes. "I don't know, Dad. We can't name him just anything, you know. He's too special to name just anything."

"Well, son, just anything isn't much of a name anyway."

Tad smiled, genuinely amused by his dad's latest joke.

"You're right about that, though," Jerry continued. "I mean Spot or Fido or something like that just wouldn't do."

"Maybe something classy like Prince or Duke," Tad offered.

"Prince. Yeah, sure, that's a good name."

Tad turned his attention back to the dog, Prince, and said to him, "You're gonna love it here, Prince. There's all kinds of woods with all kinds of rabbits and things to chase. You're gonna be the happiest dog in the whole wide world! Right, Dad?"

No answer.

"Dad?"

Distant rumblings.

"Dad? Earth to Dad."

"Huh? D'you say something, son?"

"Where'd you go, Dad? You looked like you were thinking about something."

Jerry thought quickly—he sure couldn't tell him where he had gone, or what he had seen. How do you tell your son that his new, extremely lovable pet would probably make a great meal, that you saw yourself kneeling beside him sucking the blood right out of his tender, young throat. How do you tell your son that? You don't. Not in a million years. You lie. You lie heavy and you lie deep. You tell him something about his new name or how you thought it was going to be great that the two of them were going to grow up together. But you certainly don't tell him the truth.

Suddenly Prince started yapping as if a rabbit had

31

entered his field of vision. Tad turned to him, grabbed his ears gently and shook his head lovingly. Jerry smiled and thought about being saved by the proverbial bell.

A few seconds later Tad grinned broadly at his dad, hoisted his squirming puppy into his small arms and carried him into the house to show to his mother. Following close behind, Jerry tried to dismiss his vision. He failed.

Chapter Three

Charlene Philgras stepped off her blue three-speed, pulled out the kickstand with her sneakered foot, then reached into her saddlebag and took out a small, neatly folded blanket; a procedure she had followed every night for the last thirty-five years. The hill overlooked a town that had remained pretty much a time capsule, save for the new brick fire station and a clutch of sprawling suburban homes that blemished the landscape to the south. But although she did have a window onto the town, the spot was also reasonably secluded. A choke of scraggly bushes rimmed most of it, but a giant oak dominated.

Charlene unfolded her blanket, spread it out, and sat down, a procedure that prompted her to remember something her mother told her long ago, "You're not a bright girl, Charlene, but you are a very pretty girl. And loyal. Oh, how many times I told your father how loyal you were, how dedicated to your family. And loyalty matters just as much as anything. Maybe even more when you get right down to it." Charlene's dog had died in the seventies, but she still remembered his loyalty. Loyal was just as important as numbers adding up right or words meaning what they were supposed to. She thought

33

that she was as good at being loyal as anyone else was at being smart. So that was an even Steven. And loyalty, bold and etched in the hardest marble, was exactly why she was here tonight.

Over the years her enormous backside had carved out two large, spoon-shaped indentations in the ground beneath her threadbare, plaid blanket. Those indentations, she decided, further marked this spot as her very own private place, a place for her to think things that smart people thought; space things and death things and sex things. And over these so many years she had come to a great many conclusions. One of those conclusions—the very heaviest—remarked on the fact that life was pretty much it. Death was as final as any No Outlet street and you'd better get what you could while the gettin' was good. This mindset could never be altered. It had been fortified by thirty-five years of staring into the darkness at nothing but lightless buildings and empty skies. (Fortified because during that time nothing other-worldly, no spectre nor alien, no ghost nor goblin, had ever so much as even hinted at a visit.) And wasn't the county morgue right over there on the other side of the falls? Not to mention Holy Sepulchre Cemetery just behind the Catholic Church.

Her study of these vessels of death had been, of course, preconceived. In the winter of 1955 she had lost her mother to breast cancer. And she had suffered like no dog should suffer—mainly because she had forsaken modern medicine for the mercy of the saviour. Modern medicine, Charlene had long ago decided, probably would have been a smarter choice. And that wrong choice had troubled her a lot because her mother was smart, just like anyone that wasn't like her. So why had she done such a dumb thing as not let the doctor give her medicine?

Her mother had been a local woman so Holy Sepulchre had graciously accepted her, taking her into its gravelly bosom with the solemn promise that her eternal sleep would be as restful as any mortal sleep she had ever enjoyed. The church always kept a light on out back. Kind of like a night-light for the dead, Charlene often thought.

What brought Charlene up here these many years, what had made her forego any semblance of a normal life, was the fact that her mother told her that she would come back and that Charlene was to find a place to wait until she did. The headstone was large enough to be seen from any high hill in the area, which was also a constant reminder of just why she was here in the first place.

Love, in its customary fashion, and with loyalty for a foundation, had been her guide; a love that cancer had only succeeded in nurturing. But although her love remained strong, time, in its equally customary fashion, had put huge dents in her faith. Thirty-five years was a very long time to wait for someone to crawl out of their grave. (And even the emaciated, hollow-faced look of a progressing cancer would be preferable to whatever time had done to her mother.) "No, you sure as hell can't do a one-eighty once your heart stops," her uncle had said after the funeral, while everyone sat around drinking Black Label and eating pasta scooped from huge aluminum pans.

But by now Charlene realized that her mother was probably not coming back, that maybe even April 1st, when her mother told her to start, probably meant something, too.

At home this evening, before she packed her sandwich, she had decided that, well, in a week or so, she'd stop coming up here. She had a life to live, what was left of it, and wasn't it about time her mother let her live it? She'd understand. She'd have to. If her mother decided to keep her promise and come back after she stopped coming up here, that was okay, too.

The wind picked up and Charlene, who was unusually prone to the cold steel touch of night winds, wrapped her blanket around her.

She watched as the big elm near the church's back door

35

bobbed and weaved, its shadows darkening, then blurring. The wind had a sound now, too; like her mother's wail near the end, but then, lonely night sounds always reminded Charlene of her mother's pain-filled wails.

A sudden gust of wind caught her bike and tipped it over. The metallic rattle startled her. She got up and righted it again. This new view afforded her a glimpse of the rooftop at the 7-11, where they had found that body. "Blooded," she'd heard at the beauty parlor, while she was having her nails done. Charlene had taken that to mean that someone had used a very sharp knife. She had no way of knowing—nor did the woman who had uttered that word—that "Blooded" had meant that the body had been almost completely drained, that the embalmer's task had taken only half as long as normal.

But the coroner's job hadn't been so easy. She had grudgingly concluded that the blood had exited via puncture wounds in the carotid, wounds consistent with snake bite. The official cause of death had been blood loss. Just how that had happened, the coroner decided, would only be determined when, and if, the perpetrator was brought to trial. For reasons that were not totally explored, however, she wondered if that would ever happen.

Charlene felt real pity for the man as she pictured his body lying there in a tangle of milk cartons and soiled cling wraps. At least Momma had me there, she thought, at least she had that. That poor man had only his killer. Who would want their last sight to be the person that killed them? That's an awful thing, oh so awfully awful!

There was a faint rustling in the thick bushes behind her. She turned, squinted, and with her mind's eye saw her mother trying to fight her way into the clearing. The rustling stopped. She stared at the dark mass of the bushes a moment longer. "Momma? That you, Momma?" she said.

She really didn't think her momma was in there, but

she had been coming up here for so many nights, too many to count . . .

Another rustle, louder this time. Charlene stepped backwards. Momma would have answered, oh yes. She would have said, "And who else would it be? I told you I'd come back and a mother always keeps her promise!"

Then if it wasn't Momma in there . . .

She struck a rigid pose. Someone had trespassed onto her spot—the sheriff would probably have something to say about that. But she was afraid, too. She had seen a few of them slice-em-ups, enough to know that this was a pretty good spot to carve a heart as well as a tree.

She waited for what she thought was a very long time, then took a few halting steps toward her bike.

More rustling. She stopped, caught her breath.

The wind weaved through the giant oak and sent a flutter of weak leaves to the ground.

All those nights and nothing ever happened, not one thing. Maybe it's time, she thought. Maybe it's really time for something to happen.

"Mommmma!" Oh, God, is it you? Please, Momma, is it you?" she yelled.

Her voice travelled the night air. It groped at closed windows and probed bolted doors and Charlene was oh so sure that her very next breath would be her last, that at any second a very large knife sharpened to a razor's edge would whistle through the air and take her head off her shoulders just as slick as a chicken's at dinner time. But the air was not violated by any such knife, nor was her next breath her last, and what she saw then went a long ways toward calming her pounding heart.

There was someone in there all right, but he didn't look like no slice-em-up slasher. He fought his way into the clearing and she saw that he was just a tiny man, tall, yes, but as thin as a rail and awfully sick-looking. His eyes seemed too big and scared and he wore a white robe, just like the one she wore when she had her operation. She looked at his long, bony, bare feet and thought that he

37

must be cold, although he didn't look cold, just scared. She felt a sadness well up inside of her. She tried to look into his eyes, but they were moving too fast. And he was shaking so, like a skinny, wet, scared dog. Oh how scared he must be, she thought. How awful, awful scared! Her sadness blossomed to pity and she quickly wrapped him in her blanket, a kindness which he did not acknowledge.

"What are you doing up here?" she asked gently.

He thought a moment and said, "I don't know," as though she could somehow supply him with the right answer.

His breath was sour, she noticed, like gone bad roast beef.

"Do you live here? Are you sick?"

The man looked toward the 7-11 then back at Charlene. "Yes. . . . I mean, I don't know. I think so. Someone . . ."

"Someone what?"

". . . Eyes. His eyes."

"Whose eyes?"

He looked at the 7-11 again.

"I don't remember. There was food down there."

His chest suddenly heaved as though he were about to vomit, but he didn't.

Charlene stepped closer to the edge of the hill and said, "Well of course there was food down there, that's where they sell food. I bought food there once. Do you know that a man was killed there? With a knife, I think."

The man stared at her, his eyes questioning.

"You know, maybe you better go home," Charlene continued. "You don't look so good. You're very white. I was like that once and they put me in the hospital. Were you in the hospital, too?"

He seemed to study her. "I know you!" he said. "You're the lady that rides the bike up the hill. Every night you ride the bike up the hill."

Charlene suddenly felt anxious. He had been watching her. He knew her habits.

38

"All you do is sit and wait," he added.

A smile gathered at the corners of the man's mouth, followed by a papery thin chuckle. "Just sit and wait." He looked down at the blanket. "On this. Every night, you just sit on this and wait. What are you waiting for?"

Charlene looked at him. He wasn't right. Not at all. She thought about asking for her blanket but she didn't. He could have it if he wanted. She had to go, right away. She had to go. She was bigger than him, but he was a man, and he was crazy, and he had been watching her . . .

His grin turned into a frown, much too deep a frown. "Someone died and you *loved* them, didn't you?" he said with exaggerated sadness; the exaggeration eluded the simple-minded Charlene. She keyed on the word "loved"—a word that went a long way toward weakening her anxiety. And he had certainly had the chance to do something to her before now. "My momma," she said. "My momma died of cancer. She was very sick."

The man looked down at the 7-11 again. "Yes," he whispered, the words barely audible. "Someone died."

He looked back at her. "Are you waiting for your momma? If you are, you are on a fool's errand. The dead sleep the deepest sleep. They do not rise. Only the living dead rise. And your "momma" is not among their number. Believe me."

He had drawn closer, and as she looked into his eyes, eyes that were as flat and lifeless as coal, incapable of reflecting even a hint of light, she felt a sudden wash of comfort. She had always been somewhat high strung, a nervous Nellie, her aunt called her, but now she felt just like clear water in a summer stream, warm and rested, with no particular place to go, nothing in particular to do except flow and flow and flow. A sigh worked out of her. He was showing her a kindness by doing this. He probably knew how much of a nervous Nellie she was and wanted to be nice.

He moved closer, his dark eyes burning into hers, and as he did, she saw a vision of her mother, unfocused at

39

first, then remarkably detailed. She was as she had been during those years before she got sick. She was in the backyard, the spring wind playing through her shining hair as she hung her wash out to dry. She was smiling that strange smile, the smile that always seemed to mean she was thinking happy things. Charlene liked this thought. She watched as her mother took a clothespin from her mouth and slipped it over a white sheet. The wind blew and behind that sheet she saw herself as a child, all blonde curls and chubby-faced, her hands gathered together in front of her, her paisley dress catching the wind.

The man's mouth grew cavernously wide, his eyes round and mapped by veins and Charlene, flowing, ever flowing, suddenly hated herself for being afraid of such a scared, cold little man. She felt ashamed, so ashamed.

He inclined his head to her . . .

Charlene smiled, waited.

. . . and slowly backed away.

Within seconds his fangs receded and the menacing look on his face, a look that had escaped her, was replaced by the same confusion she had witnessed as he entered her private world. She looked at him. Her mother was gone now, only her memory left, which was almost pleasure enough.

"No," he said simply. "No. There are others. Not you. Not you. You are not for the taking. You are as pitiful as I."

Charlene, in the afterglow of fond memories, cocked her large head and smiled, which fashioned her ample cheeks into the shape of a broken heart. It suddenly occurred to her that he might be hungry. "Wait a minute," she said. "I've got a nice tuna sandwich. I put some celery in it, too. Why don't you eat it? I'm supposed to be on a diet. Uncle Henry said I should."

He just looked at her.

Taking that to mean yes, she walked quickly to her bike, unzipped the carrier behind the seat, rooted around for a moment and then pulled out the cellophane wrapped sandwich.

"Here you are," she said, holding it out as she turned.

She felt as though her whole body had been immersed in ice water. There was no one there.

He had disappeared with the quietness of thought.

She walked quickly to the edge of the hill and looked down at the roof of the 7-11. Nothing. She walked to the bike path and squinted into the darkness. Still nothing. It was as if he had never been there at all. She listened, but the only sound she heard was some lonely night creature as it weaved through the treetops.

The sky was clear and starlit and Charlene was glad for that. She had moved her blanket to the edge of the hill and because it was very late and she was thinking about leaving. She didn't know how long it had been since the man had been here, but she guessed at least an hour had passed. She couldn't clear her head of him, especially how good he had made her feel.

Earlier, after the man had left, she had tried to remember her mother again. But the vividness with which she had earlier appeared to her, while the man was there, was missing. Try as she may, her brain would not provide her the detail she so craved. Her mother came to her only in short glimpses, like someone hurrying by a frost-encrusted window. So, capable of only that, she had given up. Since then she had been thinking of what she would do with her nights, after she stopped coming up here. There was so much she could do. Uncle Henry had promised to help her with her reading, and Marjorie at the beauty parlor said she would show her how to do nails. So many things. It would be hard to choose.

A car drove by the 7-11, delivered reality back to the hilltop, then disappeared, leaving only the sound of its engine cleaving the night air like an invisible knife.

But Charlene was glad when quiet returned because for some reason she had rekindled thoughts of her mother.

The scene was the same. They were in the backyard and her mother was again removing a wooden clothespin from her mouth. And she was there, too, behind that flapping sheet, just staring back at herself.

Smile, Charlene. Poor little Charlene. Why don't you smile? Your momma's there and she's not dead anymore. No. Don't frown, Charlene, don't frown.

Silence, utter and complete, then, the flapping of wings.

Her mother dropped the sheet to the ground.

Why'd you do that, Momma? It will get dirty now. Your fresh, clean sheet will get all dirty.

And just as suddenly a horrid, cold wind came up, a wind so biting that her mother raised her hand against it, a wind so fierce that it vibrated cheek and jowl. Little Charlene, however, didn't seem to notice. She was too busy staring back at her grown-up counterpart.

Footfalls, so soft, so lightly taken that even insects were safe beneath them.

The wind chased her mother's dress high and left her hair tousled while a gathering storm rent the sky, tearing off huge, black, skittering clouds. And poor little Charlene. She was so very intent on staring. And frowning.

"Uh," Charlene said, somewhat startled by a sudden snap of pain, as if a pin had been pushed into her neck, into the side of her neck. She closed her eyes and her mother became even more focused.

Another pinprick, somewhat stronger this time, and a pain-pleasure surged into Charlene. She swayed with it, her large body displaying considerably more grace than it ever had, like a pendulum on a huge grandfather clock. And as she swayed, she saw another vision—her mother's teeth had grown. They flashed back at her, first covered by her wind blown dress, then not; an almost

42

pulsating action, like sucking, like sucking at her mother's nipple . . .

As the blood flowed out of her, she saw her mother reach out to her and smile with lupine clarity.

But it wasn't her mother looking back at her. No. It was the man, the skinny, sickly little man.

Some minutes later the night was again disturbed by the furious flapping of wings. But Charlene, who lay in a death sleep, a death-sleep that the morning sun would deepen, a death-sleep that even her mother could never overcome, heard nothing.

Harry smiled as he watched Thomas Jefferson's Smith's first kill—an indication that his transformation was complete. He thought about the time in the near future when he would have them all together, when the very large joke would be on them.

He put his arm around Christine, enjoying the cool stone feel of her, and laughed heartily, a laugh that complemented the rising wind. Christine shook loose and rushed toward Charlene, her eyes wild with feverish hunger and Harry said, "Welcome to hell, Tommy. Good to have you."

Chapter Four

Walker Norville dropped to one knee and coaxed his dog, Heidi, in a clear, even tenor. "C'mon, girl," he said, "I even put some tomato soup on top. You know how much you like tomato soup. What'd ya say?"

At a shade over five four, Walker Norville gave two inches away to the average woman. His hair, medium gray now, was still as thick as a twenty-year-old's and his face was still lean and smooth, the face of a man twenty years his junior. The skin was stretched drum tight over that face; in the cold, it looked as if his cheekbones could pop right through the skin without warning. His temples were thickly etched by veins and his gray eyes were a shade lighter than his hair.

Although he was still spry and clear-headed, Walker secretly believed that seventy-six was perilously close to dying age, and that kind of baggage grew heavy from time to time.

But whether he was close to death or not, Walker Norville had long ago subscribed to the notion that old age also meant comfortable rockers and peaceable afternoons spent with your butt firmly imprisoned within one. Try as he may, he could not figure out why he always had so much energy; he was old—he wasn't supposed to. Sometimes he would sit in his dead wife's rocker, draw in a deep breath and say to himself, now this is what it's all about. In truth, he couldn't stomach more than five minutes of inactivity. Maybe when I'm eighty or eighty-five, he often thought, maybe then I'll feel old. Given his physical and mental state, that wasn't at all likely.

He hadn't had reason to smile much lately, but when he did, during trips to town or when fleas found the dogs, prompting a run to the vets, he made sure he remembered to pop in his North Carolina-bought dentures. "Cheap, real cheap," his friend, Ollie had told him. "Got mine there. Do a real fine job, they do." So one brisk fall morning ten years earlier, he hit the south road, skeptical and hopeful at the same time. Hope had won. His new teeth looked just like real teeth, not glaringly white or overly perfect. He had snapped them in earlier, before he went outside. He thought he'd saunter on across the road and say hello to the new folks. But he hadn't. He had caught sight of Heidi and that had put an end to his neighborly intentions.

Heidi, her head once again propped between her paws, ignored him totally. She was, pardon the expression, dog tired. Her wanderings had taken her far and wide, in hot pursuit of whatever dared move before her old eyes, even though catching that daring creature would probably have invoked total confusion—kill it, play with it, let it go? She had, in a word, overdone it. Later she would eat, but for now all she wanted to do was sleep, content and warm in her little cocoon of a house, untouched by whatever nature might have to offer. But Walker had mistaken her lethargy for sickness. She was fifteen now, and large dogs like her didn't usually survive even that long. Walker attributed her longevity to the fact that she'd had another of her own kind to interact with in whatever ways dogs interacted. Loneliness, Walker believed, could kill, and beasts, who really didn't have the brain power to figure that out and maybe do something about it, were especially susceptible. He often thought that as soon as one dog went the other

45

would quickly follow. The problem then would be whether or not to replace them, a problem he only concerned himself with on a subconscious level.

The comforting effect of the old man's fingers pulling gently along her fur soon prompted Heidi to close her eyes and doze. Walker gave her one last stroke, got up, went into the house and brewed himself a cup of blackberry tea to wash down a generous slice of grape pie, sitting himself down in his wife's padded rocker in front of the fireplace to enjoy his midafternoon snack.

On the mantel were snapshots of most of the Norvilles, past and present, the age of the frames indicating which. A picture of his wife Harriet and his daughter, Christine, graced the center of the mantel, a position of high honor. The rest of the family flanked them, each frame purposely smaller. Christine had disappeared only a month or so earlier. Walker grieved for her, certainly, but because no body had been found, he still held out a somewhat thready hope—a hope that weakened daily, sure, but would never die until her body turned up, not until he could pull open a drawer at the morgue and tell some harried official that, yes, it was her, it was Christine. There had been a sufficient amount of official noise after her disappearance: dogs aplenty and hundreds of volunteers poking around the woods. They had even dragged Fourth Lake outside of town. So he hadn't had a complaint about that. Some suggested that she might have met her Prince Charming and simply left; she was, after all, approaching forty. Walker, of course, discounted that theory entirely, Christine had had her share of offers, but she had declined them all. An aneurysm had taken Harriet, and it had been her death that had prompted his daughter to come live with him. She got a job teaching at the high school in Naples Falls and generally took care of him.

He looked out the front window at the yard and thought that both Harriet and Christine would be a mite miffed at how he had let the place go. He smiled. They would be more than miffed, they'd be downright pissed off! He picked up his cup, let a small river of tea slide warmly down his throat, put the cup down. Tomorrow, he told himself, tomorrow I'll do everyone a favor and clean up the yard. Maybe even say hello to the new folks. But as he thought about that, he couldn't help but picture Harriet or even Christine standing beside him, helping him along with that chore. He really wasn't much good with people, not first off. He always got a bit flustered and then his tongue would cramp up.

His women, now, they had been the social butterflies. They could talk to anyone about anything. Christine had even struck up a friendship with that strange fella that used to live over there.

And wasn't it interesting how, at least from a distance, that new owner looked so much like Christine's old friend? There was probably some good explanation for that. Oh, sure, somewhere there was someone who looked just like you, but coincidence wouldn't stretch itself so far as to have that fella move in to the same place you used to live in. Chances were the old owner and this fella were cousins, maybe even brothers for that matter. Well, he thought finally, somewhat intrigued by the resemblance, tomorrow I guess I'll find that out, now won't I.

That night, his forearm resting on his forehead, Maria lying contentedly in the crook of his arm, Jerry stared at the dark ceiling. He couldn't sleep. He had no idea of the time, and he really didn't care. The day he'd ceased to be a slave to the eight-to-five routine, their alarm clock had become a three-dimensional, blaringly loud reminder of it. Ridding himself of the thing had involved more than a simple dunk into the trashcan. The night he learned that he was to be published, he removed the Big Ben to his basement workshop, placed it in the exact middle of the workbench and summarily condemned it to death. He

47

had even borrowed a neighbor's sledgehammer for the execution. He remembered its death throes, the way the thing gave off one final choked-off ring like a chicken who's had its neck wrung just as the hammer slammed down between bells. He smiled. Years of seat shining had preceded that glorious day; short stories, essays, tiny checks from tiny presses and newspaper magazines every couple months. All done to build himself a literary resume, something to show to an agent or editor once his first novel was completed.

He thought about the clock, its guts spread to hell and back, one of the bells flung the length of the basement, the hands twisted, the circular body squashed. He often wondered if maybe he might have put his own head in the clock's place if he had stayed at Kodak much longer, always deciding that if he had done that, then he would at least have had a first person account of the maiming process, then maybe descriptions of the grotesque and macabre wouldn't come so damn hard for him. He remembered Harry telling him how he had overcome an inability to properly describe pain. He had stomped his bare foot onto a rusty nail. The resulting pain, Harry told him, was very easily described. ("Try it, Jerry, you'll see.") But, of course, Harry was sometimes given to stretches of imagination; he was, after all, a horror writer, so Jerry simply filed that story under "Sure, bro," along with a million others, and forgot about it.

He felt Maria stir, heard her inhale then exhale. He remembered their lovemaking that night—after Tad had been in bed a reasonable amount of time, long enough to fall asleep. Easily distracted by images of others straining to hear the sounds of his lovemaking, Jerry routinely waited until he was sure that Tad, or anyone else in the house, was sound asleep. But the bed, he thought, the goddamned bed with its telltale, rhythmic squeaking was a dead giveaway (Say, what are you doin' in there, Jer? Knockin' one off? Buryin' the old bone? Hidin' the sausage?). He hated that side of him that was more

48

animal than human, that horny little bastard that raised its stiffening little head every half day or so, wanting to be fed. Sometimes, he thought, sex could be a real nuisance.

Maria sighed again and he thought he saw her smile in her sleep. She had little trouble accepting her demon and he envied her that. He remembered how she had climaxed that evening, in rollicking, convincing fashion. Like the goddamn bicentennial! He had almost put a hand over her mouth. (Can't you come quietly? Huh? Can't you?) But eventually he had convinced himself that Tad was, indeed, sleeping, and that their new neighbor probably couldn't hear, even though the richter-scale quality of her orgasm put that in question. So he had let her finish. And after she finished she rolled over and let go with a giant sigh of exhaustion and relief. For the longest time afterward he simply lay there and stared at her silhouette against the window, the curve of her back, the way her long hair spilled over her neck. He really did envy her ability to give herself completely over to passion.

It was during this late night perusal that he thought, I love this woman, and was surprised by his admission. He never thought that way. Rare were the times when he even spoke those words—only after considerable coaxing, actually. Love bloomed for many reasons; beauty, compatibility, etc, etc. But sometimes you loved someone simply because they loved you, because, by all appearances, they had given their life for the betterment of yours. Such was the case with Maria. She was his benefactor. She had, more or less, subsidized his career. It was, he thought, the most solid reason to love someone. Beauty faded, as did compatibility, but the giving of oneself would never fade. Its memory would only strengthen.

Tad tried, but he just couldn't breathe with the blanket

covering his head, so he finally got up the nerve to stick his nose out. Earlier, after his dad and mom had quieted down—finally—he had heard something, a kind of wailing, he thought. He really didn't know where it had come from, but some inner direction finder told him the basement. That's what had caused him to cover his head with his blanket. Thinking about it now, however, he wasn't sure. Basements were always likely candidates for that type of thing. Still, if he heard it again, he'd have no choice but to crawl in with his dad and mom. Just another nightmare, he could say, which was probably true.

Chapter Five

THE NEXT DAY

At a few minutes before nine the next morning, Walker Norville was cleaning up his front yard. He looked up from his chore and was a little mystified to see his new neighbor's car still in the driveway.

"Probably just took some days off to get settled," he mumbled as he hefted a bald tire into a makeshift wheelbarrow. He wasn't altogether sure of where he'd put it and the others, but he knew that the front yard was not the best of places for used tires, not anymore.

Before retiring the night before, he had taken a grape pie out of the freezer for use as a housewarming gift, positive that his new neighbors had never eaten grape pie this good and anxious to see the looks on their faces when they did. If all went as planned, the pie would be washed down with a cup of coffee and sweetened by neighborly conversation, a series of events that would make Christine and Harriet proud. He'd take it on over around noon. By then he'd be done picking up the yard and ready for a piece, anyway.

Jerry pulled the bedroom window shade back a few inches and looked across the quiet road at his neighbor,

51

who looked for all the world like someone who would want to get friendly—why else was he picking up the yard? Well, being friendly with neighbors was what Maria was for. She was the one who was kind to strays, animal or otherwise. He just didn't have the time to get friendly with an old man who probably had as many stories as wrinkles. His time was valuable—he wasn't about to waste it on someone who was probably ready to croak. He let the sheer drop and immediately wondered what had given rise to those thoughts. Probably just the rigors of the move, he thought. Hell, everyone was on edge.

That included Tad, who hadn't been himself at breakfast; he had been too quiet, too goddamn surly. Maria had felt for a fever again, her face taut with worry. But Tad, Jerry thought, wasn't sick, just unsure of things—the country school, playmates.

Jerry parted the sheers and watched as Walker Norville pushed his tire laden wheelbarrow out of sight, around to the back of the house. Looks better already, Jerry concluded. While he watched, the old man suddenly reappeared and, just as suddenly, looked in his direction. The sheer dropped lightly from his fingers and Jerry backed slowly away from the window. He imagined the old man smiling to himself, having caught him spying. That's one for you, he thought. Maria entered the room then, a box labeled "Master Bedroom" in large black letters cradled in her arms. With a gentlemanly flourish he took it from her and laid it on the bed.

"Thanks," she said and walked to the window.

As she parted the sheers, Jerry felt a compulsion to yell, "Don't, he'll see you! Get away from there!" But he stifled that compulsion and busied himself with flapping open the box and laying its contents onto the bed: toiletries, perfumes, a wide assortment of bedroom knickknacks, clutter mostly, the little stuff that takes longer to pack than move.

Maria studied the old man for a moment and said in

52

monotone, "Tad's outside."

"You told him to stay close, I hope?" Jerry asked, mildly concerned.

Maria dropped the sheer, turned and casually shoved her fingers into the pockets of her deliciously tight jeans. "I told him not to wander off," she answered.

"You did tell him to stay away from the road, didn't you?"

"Not specifically. I think he knows enough to stay out of the road."

Jerry shrugged and hastily clustered a handful of after shaves and colognes on his dresser, right next to an electric shaver. "Yeah, you're right," he said, throwing an empty bottle of English Leather into a trashcan. "That's not a real busy stretch of highway anyway. Probably a lot safer than most city streets as far as that goes."

That was more than likely true, Maria thought, but then again, everything was relative. If you wanted to take a stroll through snake country you might be wise to wear knee-high leather boots. But that didn't mean there weren't snakes elsewhere, where you would least expect to find them. She wasn't at all worried about the road, but in some ways she was more worried about her son here than she had been in the city. It was the isolation mainly, the feeling that a fire would be left to its own designs because all the volunteers were hunting, or broken arms would have to wait until the only doc in town had delivered Elvira Culpepper's tenth son. Consciously she realized the stupidity of such stereotypical assumptions, but, she well knew, exaggeration often did have a foundation in reality. In the back of her mind—and building—was the want of a corner store, maybe the thunder of heavy traffic. Something less removed, less barren. She had a sudden picture of Tad trying to find his way home in a killer blizzard, a vision she shoved quickly aside.

"So," she asked, a small measure of reproachfulness in

her voice, "what have you been up to—other than checking out our neighbor?"

He looked past her, out the window, then back again. "You think he'll come over?" he asked, mentally rebutting her scolding tone.

It was a question that gave her pause. "Well, I hope so," she said finally. "I mean, he is our only neighbor. We probably should get to know him."

Again Jerry shrugged. "Yeah, I suppose," he said, not bothering to disguise the disinterest in his voice.

She took a deep, calming breath, which effectively changed the topic. "Listen," she said, "I've put a stack of boxes near the attic door, you know, stuff that goes from house to house and never sees the light of day?"

He felt a smile begin. "You mean like your mother's artwork?"

She cut him off crisply. "There you go, making fun of my mother again. You know how I hate it when you do that!"

Her mother's idol was Andy Warhol, whose work she thought was both pretentious and unpretentious at the same time. *Just plain confusing*, Jerry thought, *lacking direction—and talent. Probably the most overrated "artist" who ever lived!* So Maria's mother, Loretta, had copied Warhol's style, offering her creations as Christmas gifts. Five years running they got them, ten by sixteen oil paintings of everything from cat food cans to toilets, each done in magnificent detail, an aspect of her work that, even Jerry had to agree, reflected a degree of talent. But despite that admission, he really did hate those paintings. They were romance novels on canvas, mind candy.

Two Christmases earlier, as she handed over her white porcelain "impressionistic" toilet, she looked at him with furrowed brow and said, "What do you get out of it, Jerry?" turning an appraising eye back to canvass.

Jerry, sometimes given to sudden outbursts of sarcasm, stifled the obvious urge, ("Well, I'll tell you,

Loretta, what I normally get out of a toilet is . . .") and lied to her, saying, "Again, it's reminiscent of Warhol, but not in a plagarizing way. It's quite good, actually."

She had accepted that, pleased with quite good, although she would have used more flattering phrasing. Jerry often thought that she praised his writing so he'd praise her paintings, just two "artisans" stroking each other. The whole scenario made him want to heave his guts. But at least here, forty or so miles away, he wouldn't have to keep her stuff close by, ready for hanging should she want to ruin his evening by dropping in for a visit. Maybe now he could remand the stuff to the attic, where broken furniture and bad artwork went to die. But as he looked at his wife, he knew her mother's artwork was not among the stuff that "did not see the light of day."

"Yeah, I'll get to it," he said tiredly.

"Thanks," she answered, disregarding his tone of voice. "Listen, I'm gonna take a walk across the street, see if I can't get our neighbor to join us for lunch. I think it would be better if we made the first overture. I'm sure he thinks we're too busy . . ."

"And we're not?" Jerry interjected, his tone dripping sarcasm.

She tried to mask a look of exasperation. "We've got plenty of time to get settled. Okay?"

"Well, don't force him. I mean if he doesn't want to, that's okay, too."

Jerry, she knew, had always harbored a secret dislike—fear—of old people. She wasn't sure why, but she had a good idea. The aged, although sometimes slow-witted, usually dished out plenty of wisdom and sage advice, advice that someone who hadn't lived for very long just couldn't give. Years earlier, one of their city neighbors, an old woman, had read one of Jerry's short stories and had had what Jerry called "the temerity" to criticize it. Her criticism, Maria thought, had been accurate and, if heeded, probably would have gotten the story published.

As it was, Jerry had sent the story off sans corrections and was rejected with criticism. Again.

Jerry, of course, thought himself beyond criticism from nonliterary fronts. God, Jerry had told her, the only advice that old woman could give probably had something to do with which dental creme had more hold. But in his next short story, Maria did notice that he had, indeed, heeded her earlier criticism. He had shown the published story to the woman afterwards, convinced that because it was now published that it was also beyond criticism. A smug, condescending look had crossed his face that day, a look that fanned in Maria the flames of revulsion. He had been a pompous, all-knowing ass. A real jerk. But the old lady simply smiled and told him the story was nice, her tone very much like that of a mother complimenting her fourth grader because he had aced the English test. The old woman knew what he was about, knew exactly. She couldn't remember where she'd put her glasses, but she knew exactly where Jerry Matheson was coming from.

Jerry had changed since then, not a lot, but at least now he could handle criticism. Now, Maria thought, if only he'd lose that unnatural dislike—fear—of old people.

Jerry, who suddenly envisioned his mother-in-law's artwork hung strategically throughout the house, said, "You're sure, now? I mean, that's a pretty big attic. Plenty of room for all kinds of stuff, including your mother's art . . ."

Before he could finish, Maria turned and stomped off, her heavy footfalls clattering on the stairs. He went to the window and watched her walk down the pathway, stop, wave Tad to her from the side yard and then walk hand in hand with him down the driveway. Her gait was still too fast, which was pretty much normal. When she got angry with him, at least for less than subtle remarks, it usually took more than a few minutes for her to cool down.

He watched her stop near the mailbox, look both ways,

and cross. Even from his vantage point, Jerry could see the old man's broad grin as Maria and Tad grew nearer. Jerry turned away before introductions and went into the hallway, the twelve boxes that Maria had neatly stacked in groups of threes reminding him of his next chore. He drew in a deep breath, let it out, then went outside. As he looked across the street, he saw that his wife and son were still talking with the old man. They had hit it off—so what else was new? He frowned slightly. Even though he had witnessed the old man's warm grin, he had half-hoped that he was just one of those curmudgeonly old farts who liked to keep to himself. Obviously, that was not true.

As he watched, and as though his frown had somehow wandered across the street and tapped her on the shoulder, Maria turned and almost furiously waved him over. Jerry hesitated initially but then went inside, put on a jacket and crossed the road. Walker Norville offered his small, thickly knuckled hand. "Hi there," he said with a smile. "Name's Walker, Walker Norville. Been talkin' with your wife and son here about how cold it gets out here, but the summer's are hot too, and real muggy."

Small talk, Jerry thought, whoopee!

Norville looked at him as if he were looking through a microscope, then smiled out of one corner.

Jerry returned the half smile. "Something wrong?" he asked.

Norville smiled again and shook his head in bewilderment. "You sure favor each other, sure do!" he said.

Now Jerry realized what the old man was talking about. "Oh, you mean my twin brother . . ."

"Twins is it?" Norville said. "Well, when I saw you comin' on over the road I thought that was what it was. Couldn't be nothin' else. Spittin' image. 'Cept, last I saw your brother, he was, well, didn't have quite as much meat on his bones. Tell me, you write books, too?"

Jerry told him he did, let go of the old man's hand and hoped that would be the last of it. Jerry watched as

Norville, who seemed to be reading his thoughts, stuck his hands deep into his pockets and glanced around, his eyes panning left to right like Geronimo surveying a hunting ground. "Yes, sir," he said, "won't be long before the whole town falls asleep. Bein' down in a valley like we are the heat kind of lays on you thick. But we got some nice swimmin' holes. The boy'll like that, won't you, boy?"

"You bet!" Tad said with unabashed enthusiasm.

"I've invited Mr. Norville to lunch," Maria said.

"And I thought that was real nice," Norville responded. "Yes, sir. Real nice."

"First time I ever been in this house," Walker Norville said as the side door closed behind him. "And I've lived across the street from it near all my life. Course, Christine came over . . . but just the once, near's as I can recall." His words trailed off. "She liked making friends. Ever since she was little." His head moved slowly, his old, failing eyes taking in what they could. "Bigger than I thought, on the inside," he added as Maria tried to open a can of tuna with a garage-sale-bought electric can opener. As usual, it didn't work. The blade was dull. She fished around in a drawer until she found the old-fashioned kind, one that never failed as long as muscle power was available.

On the way to the house, Norville had asked Jerry if he wrote the same kind of books his brother wrote, the scary stuff.

"Tell you what," Jerry had said, "I'll let you take one home with you. *In Memoriam*, my first. Good book to curl up with on a cold night. Get your blood pumpin'."

"Ain't that slice and dice stuff, is it?" Norville asked.

"No, not at all," Jerry had answered.

"Ain't gonna scare me, is it? I'm all alone over there. Gets a mite close some nights, if you get my drift."

Jerry had chuckled. "Well, if it doesn't scare you, I

guess I'm not doing my job, am I?"

Norville had allowed that with a shrug and a mumbled, "Guess that'd be true enough," and that had been the end of it, until now. Jerry went into the study, picked up a copy of *In Memoriam,* and returned. "Here, lest I forget," he said with a smile as he handed it over to the old man.

Norville took it from him and studied the cover, holding it at arm's length until he had fumbled out his glasses. He flipped through it and stopped momentarily to read a few lines, then flipped through whole chapters and stopped again. At four hundred and two pages, the book was a shade over average length, and Norville had to shake his head and sigh after he had finished his short perusal. "Never done that much readin' in my whole life, let alone put that many words down on paper," he said with a measure of awe.

Jerry felt an urge to intimately discuss the novel writing process, but decided against it. His in-depth explanations would probably be lost on this old geezer. He'd just stare at him vacantly, his eyes like marbles, his brain about as receptive as a water-filled balloon. Hell, he probably wouldn't get around to reading it until this time next year, if ever. Still, if there was an upper hand to be had in their young relationship, he'd just as soon take it. *In Memoriam* seemed to allow him to take that upper hand.

Norville put the book down on the counter, tapped it a couple of times and said something about "making sure he didn't forget it," by which time Maria had finished slicing a piece of celery to use in the tuna salad.

She put a half loaf of wheat bread and the tuna salad on the table, as well as a gallon of 2% milk and a fresh tomato, and then opened a can of vegetable soup, apologizing as she worked about the quality of the meal. Norville told her there was no reason at all to apologize and then suddenly remembered the grape pie he had intended to bring over.

"You folks'll have to excuse me a second," he said,

59

starting for the door. "Be back in the blink of an eye. Maybe sooner."

Before either Maria or Jerry could ask where it was he was going, he was gone. Tad ran into the living room and watched as Norville glanced only casually left and right before he crossed the road, while Prince, still clutched by the clumsiness of puppydom, vainly attempted to climb onto the couch with his master. Norville reappeared a short time later.

"He's got somethin' wrapped in newspaper," Tad yelled into the kitchen, a fair amount of wonderment in his voice.

"What do you suppose that could be?" Maria asked.

Jerry raised his eyes, thought a moment, and said, "Probably grape pie," as if that were a foregone conclusion.

Maria thought a moment, then, "You know you're probably right. But how'd you know that?"

Jerry smiled like someone who's just found a quarter. "Don't ask me," he said. "Just all of a sudden it came to me. I mean, makes sense. This is wine country."

It was then that Walker Norville came back into their lives, grape pie in hand, a wide, neighborly grin on his face. He didn't need his women after all. This Maria and her boy were just warm and friendly enough to put an old man at ease. To make him feel just like one of the family.

Chapter Six

"You say you've lived here most of your life, Mr. Norville?" Maria asked.

They had just finished eating what was, indeed, exceptional grape pie. Mugs of steaming coffee sat before them.

Walker smiled and Jerry seemed to know what was coming next. He was right.

"I'd like it if you'd call me Walker," Norville said gently.

Maria, who had always referred to older people as Mr. or Mrs. felt a bit uncomfortable with that, but Norville insisted.

"Sure," she said warmly.

Norville smiled appreciatively. "Almost all my life," he said in answer to her question. "My family moved into that house across the road when I was fourteen years old. Lived there ever since, 'cept for a brief stint in the Navy."

What followed was an hour-long account about his and his family's life together, just across the road. The Mathesons' learned enough about Harriet and Christine Norville to consider them part of the family. And obviously, Walker Norville had loved them both very much. Every now and again he would stop talking and smile as a particularly fond memory rose up in the crowded theater of his mind, and it was during these "dead air" intervals that Maria began to feel a warmth rise unbidden within her. He had loved his daughter, certainly, but obviously his fondest memories were of his wife, Harriet. Maria had always had a fascination with "old" love, that is love that has withstood the onslaught of familiarity, the abuse of personal idiosynchrasies: "Please, dear, don't squeeze the toothpaste from the middle," or "Honey, when you're done using the toilet, put the seat down." That kind of thing, the grating, irritating little habits that are not unlike Chinese water torture over the long haul. She found herself wanting to blurt out questions like "Didn't you ever argue?" *Well of course they did,* she thought immediately. *Strong relationships are always predicated on healthy disagreements, on an airing of differences.* Or, "Did you take separate vacations," and even, "Did you have a favorite room to make love in?" although that particular question barely made it past the formulation stage, just far enough to redden her neckline, which in turn caused her to cover the abused area with her fingers. Always aware of a blush, she also felt the urge to hide them; a blush was, after all, simply the outward manifestation of private thoughts. Although she did blush often, and with gusto, Maria was not a romantic zealot; she rarely read romance novels, well, not as a habit, and she never grew particularly teary-eyed during three-hankie movies. But she was a sucker for a good, strong relationship, one that transcended time and space and, as was the case with Harriet and Walker Norville, even death. Listening to the old man, she found herself as spellbound by his memories as she had ever been by her husband's writing. And much to Maria's surprise, he had as much to say about his daughter, Christine, as he had said about his wife. Obviously he had loved both women very much.

But Norville did stop talking long enough to ask how Jerry's brother was doing.

"Well," Jerry said, "we haven't heard from him since he left for California. He sold one of his books to United

Artists and they hired him to write the screenplay. Tell me, did you ever get the urge to get away from here, live somewhere else? I was bored silly the year my family lived here."

Walker smiled. "Guess you like bein' bored silly, huh?" he said.

Jerry had no reply.

Walker thought a moment, then, "Oh, we sometimes wondered what it'd be like to live in the city, but we never made it past wonderin'."

"And it's so peaceful here," Maria added, discovering then and there, while they enjoyed what was essentially only small talk with this delightful old man—that the peacefulness was no longer cloying, no longer an invisible, smothering weight pressing in on her from all sides. Certainly she had not as yet fully come to accept the vicissitudes of her new life, but she was certainly more open to suggestions now. Later on, and after she had had time to think about it, she would tell herself that her newfound acceptance of the solitude probably had everything to do with Walker Norville. Here was a very well-adjusted, very likeable old man who had lived in these foothills and mountains all his life and appeared not to have suffered any dire consequences because of a self-imposed exile from what she had come to know as "civilization." Well, she further allowed, civilization was, after all, a nebulous word, very subjective. Simply requiring . . . adjustment. And later on she would also tell herself that she was glad Walker Norville lived across the road, and that they would be friends. Perhaps he, in his own small, ingratiating way could become for her the late hour traffic or the corner store she so craved. Perhaps for her, he could be a direct link with sanity.

"True enough," Walker said, "but still, takes some gettin' used to. I imagine for folks like yourself, havin' lived with city noise for a long time, that quiet nights like out here can kind of get on your nerves, leastways till you get used to them, which don't take long."

63

Again dead air as Walker took a long drink of lukewarm coffee, but this time, the silence was not uncomfortable.

Norville swallowed noisily, and, like someone who has just remembered a punch line, said, "But you know, just 'cause you're in the boonies don't mean nothin' ever happens. There was a time, forty or so years ago, when there was some trouble in town. I remember it made me wonder if maybe our little town wasn't turnin', you know, gettin' like the big city, people afraid to walk the streets at night or always keepin' one eye wide open, even when they were asleep. Oh, sure, forty years ago it wasn't as bad as now, but it was still pretty bad, least ways in the big cities like New York and Chicago. Miami wasn't so bad then, but drugs weren't near as bad then neither. Regular armed camp now, so my cousin writes. He's retired down there. Keeps his door locked day and night. Never know when some drugged up crazy might wanta steal your toaster so's he can buy drugs, not carin' a hoot whether he leaves you and yours alive or dead. Wouldn't catch me livin' in a place like that, no sir! And them drug dealers—hell, what good's it do them to make all that money? Just turn around and get themselves shot half the time! Yes, sir, you can't take it with you—no place to spend it."

Maria and Jerry nodded agreement, but Maria, her interest piqued, remembered Norville's opening sentence. She was somewhat of a history buff, and what he had to say about things that had happened almost half a century ago sparkled in her mind like a well-wrapped Christmas present. "You mentioned something about trouble?" she said.

Norville shrugged and smiled a little. "Yes, yes I did," he said. "Forgive an old man his ramblings. Brain gets so full it tends to overflow."

Jerry sat up slightly, which amounted to acknowledgement of what he thought was a casually interesting remark.

64

"Well," Norville began, "over the years there's been some trouble off and on, but nothin' like this. We had town gossip like most small towns, about things that did and didn't happen, but what made us sit up and take notice, did happen. Loud and clear." He looked at his host and hostess, casting a quick glance at Tad and Prince. "Of course, you bein' from the city, you'd probably not think much of it."

He waited for a response, got none, continued.

"Way I heard it," he began, "some tourist got himself shot during one of our festivals. They hold em' at night, you know."

"I didn't know that," Maria said, somewhat surprised. "Why do they have them at night?"

"Atmosphere, I guess. Anyway, what happened was, this guy just up and grabs a woman and as he's tryin' to carry her off to who knows where—and she's screamin' like all the banshees in hell are after her—Jess Purl, he was an off duty state trooper then, pulls out his gun and plugs the guy right 'tween the eyes. Right dead 'tween the eyes."

Jerry had pictured a group of local kids stealing into an orchard and chucking rotted apples onto the town's only police car, sending the local Barney Fife into a conniption fit as he tried to fumble out his only bullet, his eyes as big as pancakes. That, Jerry had thought, had been the kind of trouble Norville would be talking about. Just weak vanilla. But a would-be kidnapper getting plugged "right 'tween the eyes" was certainly not weak vanilla. Now Jerry realized that even a small town like Naples Falls was as prone to violence as anyplace else. Hell, he thought as he remembered a tired but accurate analogy, even a monkey with a quill pen could eventually write a symphony. "That's horrible," Maria said. "When did you say this happened?"

"Forty years ago, maybe a little longer. Made the papers up in Rochester. Biggest story we ever had. Oh, we had some other stuff, you know, mercy killings, well, just

65

the one; hunters shootin' each other up. But that happens all the time. Some of the fellas, not all of them, mind you, just a few, get all liquored up then go trampin' through the woods makin' deer sounds, or what they think a deer sounds like, you know, tryin' to decoy, like they was huntin' ducks? Couple fellas got their tickets punched doin' that. Guess some folks never learn.''

Jerry, however, didn't want to let the festival shootout die. There was some mileage there, some local history, and local history was definitely the stuff he needed for his novel. "Did anyone ever find out exactly why this guy tried to take the woman hostage?" he asked.

Yet another queer look from Norville. Jerry looked at Maria, then back at their guest. "I say something funny?" he asked.

Walker responded quickly. "No, no. Sorry I stared like that. I got driftin' again and left out what was so strange about what happened."

Norville hesitated.

"And?" Jerry prompted.

Norville looked at Tad, then back again. "Maybe the boy ought not to hear this," he whispered.

Maria felt a moment of discomfort. This old man was privy to something that just might impress her son the wrong way. Of course given a choice, Tad wasn't about to leave. But democracy in the Matheson family was only a part-time thing. And he was, after all, highly impressionable, his imagination easily as strong as his father's. Tad griped for a moment, as she knew he would, then grudgingly left the room, Prince trailing.

"Now everyone that was there," Norville started, "and there's some folks still livin' hereabouts that was there that night, swears it happened. Swears they saw it with their own eyes."

Again Norville hesitated.

"What?" Maria blurted, unable to control her anxiety.

Norville looked at her for what seemed like a very long time, then. "Man didn't die," he said with almost

66

absurd matter-of-factness.

Jerry smiled. "So, he didn't die," he said. "Not everyone dies from a gunshot wound."

Norville looked at Jerry, the light harshly delineating the sharp bone structure on the old man's face. "Not only did he not die," he said, "he didn't even flinch. He just takes the bullet in the forehead, looks at Jess Purly curious like and gets. Not too fast, not too slow. He just walks out and the night swallows him up. No one ever saw him again. Him or the woman." Jerry, not at all convinced, said, "Obviously he didn't get hit. Just because this, what did you say his name was, Jess Purly? well, just because he pointed his gun and pulled the trigger . . ."

"There was a hole," Norville interjected with the same matter-of-fact tone.

Jerry was temporarily lost for words.

"A nice, round hole. And when the man turned and left, the woman tucked like a sack of potatoes under his arm, arms flailin', some folks said they saw the exit hole, too. Three times as big. There was lots of blood, too, lots of it. Man trailed it on the way out. He just didn't die. Like I said, he didn't even flinch."

Maria now knew why Norville hadn't wanted Tad to hear this. With her mind's eye she could see it all very clearly, and it gave her mountains of prickly goose flesh.

But Jerry—ever the skeptic—still wasn't convinced. He wrote this kind of thing, which, somehow, gave him a different viewpoint. His mind wasn't as easily numbed as say, Maria's. He could maintain his objectivity. Obviously the incident had been handed down from generation to generation and, as time past, fantasy had replaced fact like cancer cells replace and devour good cells. A real snowball effect. This Jess Purly had more than likely missed his target entirely and those that were there had been too scared to realize that. When they got home they all just went over everything in their minds and filled in the blanks with miniscule shavings from a

67

recently read novel or something scanned on the front page of a tabloid while they stood in line at the Red and White. It was too bad the old guy lent credence to an incident obviously stimulated by mass hysteria.

Norville went on to further explain that Jess Purl had received a letter of commendation from the mayor of Naples Falls, even though they never did catch the guy. "But Jess," Norville continued, "well Jess was a religious man and he never even accepted that commendation. He knew he'd shot someone and he knew the man had probably run off to the woods and died. That ate at him for a long, long time, right up until the end."

The following silence seemed to indicate to Walker that it was time to go. He'd come over here and left them with a story that could very well give someone nightmares. He felt bad about that, real bad, but truth was truth, and they had asked. He smiled. The man, he thought, now he was going to be a tough nut to crack. He was kind of taken with himself, he was. But still, he was a decent man, it seemed, if the look on his face whenever he looked at the boy was any indication. Writers were more than likely that way anyway. Kind of overflowing with ego, out of necessity probably; carpenter had his hammer and T-square, writer types had their egos. Didn't make him bad, just hard to get along with, hard to look straight in the eye.

He picked up Jerry's loaned book, said, "I'll get to this straightaway," and then left.

As he walked down the stone pathway, Maria said, "Don't be a stranger, Walker. Okay?"

Norville turned and smiled, said, "Sure thing," waved and went home.

THAT NIGHT

Maria and Jerry didn't talk about it for the rest of the day, Maria because she just knew she wouldn't be able to

68

sleep that night if they did and Jerry because he had simply decided that it was a lot of bullshit, just a little truth layered with a healthy portion of fiction. What else could it be? People didn't get shot in the forehead and walk away. There were absolutes. Life was one. Death was another. And living required that a person religiously avoid all bullets in the forehead. He didn't even want to think about it, let alone talk about it. He thought maybe a little manual labor would do the trick—not too physical, just something to fill up the time. He decided to put away the twelve boxes Maria had stored outside the attic door, while Maria busied herself downstairs and Tad watched the movie, *Batman*, which had just started. Jerry could hear the opening music as he reached the top of the stairs.

The attic door wanted to swing shut, so he propped it open with an old floor lamp Maria had leaned against the boxes. After he had hefted a box of Christmas ornaments into his arms he climbed the stairs to the bare and unusually tall attic. The first thing he noticed was the decidedly dreary atmosphere. Layers of dust on the small windows at either end filtered only a feeble amount of moonlight. He felt as if he was in an old movie theater and someone was behind the screen shining a flashlight at him. He put the box down and searched for a light cord. He found one about in the middle, pulled. Nothing. No bulb. "Damn!" he mumbled, not at all pleased with having to hunt up a light bulb, not with the shape the house was in; only God knew where the spares were. But he sure couldn't do this without light, at least more than what this abysmally dreary evening and those filthy windows had to offer. He started for the door, and, as he did, the wind picked up, not to any great degree, only nominally, flicking leaves off the roof and sending them in a cascade across the small windows on either end of the attic. The thick accumulation of dirt obscured detail and made the leaves look like giant flakes of very early snow. He watched this effect for a moment. Every now and again he heard a small click as one of the leaves brushed a window

click . . . click.

and smiled faintly, appreciative of the atmosphere the wind had created, almost as if someone were tapping on those windows,

click . . . click.

some small, floating person trying to beg their way out of the darkness. He was reminded of *Head Games,* his vampire novel. Click . . . click . . . click . . .

and a sudden dizziness swept over him. He struggled for purchase, found it. But oddly enough, a residue remained, a lightheadedness that undermined his ability to stand. And with that lightheadedness his eyes glazed over, but only slightly, like vaseline smeared on a video camera. He could still see a fair amount of detail, but what was extemely odd was that now that detail was overlapped in places by a separate and swiftly emerging reality. There was a door there, sure, and bare wood attic walls, but as he looked at them, he could swear they were painted; he could swear the attic door and the wood that surrounded it had just received a fresh coat of glossy white paint. And it made him strangely anxious. It was like the time he had identified his Uncle Rick's drowned body. The uneasiness he had felt walking down the stairs to the morgue. And when the coroner pulled open the stainless steel drawer to reveal his uncle's remains he had felt a queer tightness behind his eyes, as if part of him wanted to see and part of him did not. He felt that way now. Now he was on those hospital stairs, now he was almost ready to have that stainless steel drawer opened for him. He didn't wait long.

Slowly but clearly a man materialized at the attic door, again as if he were peering through a vaseline-smeared lens. The man appeared to be inserting a key into the lock, almost as if he had somehow locked himself in the attic and wanted out; and he didn't seem at all concerned about Jerry. His only concern was the door and the

70

difficulty he had opening it. As Jerry watched, he withdrew the key, held it up, turned it, looked at it closely and then reinserted it into the door. As he turned to inspect the key, Jerry saw his profile. He was a large-featured man, his nose slightly hooked, and he wore a hat. He was dressed in a dark jacket and green work pants, the cuffs of which were caught in the back of his calf high boots. Seconds later the man turned the key, opened the door and then disappeared behind it like some nocturnal dimension traveler.

As he did, Jerry's normal vision returned and his body went suddenly cold. All he could do was simply stand and stare at where the man had been. It never occurred to him that he should run after him, because it never occurred to him that what he had seen had actually happened in his attic. But what had he seen? It played back to him. Despite the fact that the man had, apparently, opened a door and then closed it behind him, he seemed displaced. And he had been dressed casually, as if he'd just gotten out of work or something, his Red Man cap pushed back off his head. Red Man Cap? But how did he know that? How could he know that? The man had only turned sideways, not far enough to see the logo on his cap. He composed himself and tried to think that one out. Red Man hats were a dime a dozen out here. What he had seen—what he thought he had seen—hadn't been there at all. He had been giving his novel a great deal of thought lately, and because it would be populated with typical town folk, he had manufactured one of them—right down to his Red Man hat. He had done it before.

On his way down the stairs he overcame the urge to look behind him and mentally calculated how much wierdness had befallen him this last day or so. He attributed it all to stress: the move, getting the book started. And now there was this added weirdness, its outer fringes tinted by a kind of perverse excitement. He thought about that. During the incident he hadn't

71

recognized it, but now . . . He took a deep breath. Okay, so he had felt a . . . ribald excitement. An almost sexual tingling. Christ, seeing someone step into another time zone in your attic could do that to anybody.

He went into his study and sat down behind his word processor. He'd do the rest of the job he had barely started some other time, after he had managed to get a light bulb up there.

IN TOWN

Harry stepped out from behind the tree and appraised the house in front of him, the house that belonged to Lenny Griffin. He was especially fascinated by Lenny's picket fence. Obviously Lenny had spent a great deal of time fashioning each picket. Lenny, Harry remembered with a wry grin, had always had a fascination with stakes. He wondered about Christine, who had gone into Canandaigua to sit by the lake and wait for someone to stroll her way. Should he tell her of his plans—his final plans—or not? Oh, well, he thought, time would tell, time would certainly tell.

Chapter Seven

THE NEXT NIGHT—JERRY'S STUDY

The next night, Jerry's fingers moved over the keys with dizzying speed. It had happened again, he had awoken from a "dream" feeling an overwhelming urge to write, to release the flood of words within him.

IN TOWN

Len Griffin squinted at the fine newsprint and sipped at his coffee. The name staring back at him was vaguely familiar, although the name Tom Smith wasn't exactly lonely in the phone book. Still, he *had* known a Tom Smith in high school, back when dinosaurs roamed the athletic fields. Thomas Jefferson Smith. He read further. The age was about right; hoping to find a picture, he flipped to page seven, where the story continued. There was none. He scanned the story one more time, looking for cause of death. None mentioned. The body had, however, been found in a dumpster, which prompted Len to wonder just how that was possible. That highly repulsive vision floated before him momentarily. Chances were Tom Smith didn't die inside the dumpster. People didn't crawl inside dumpsters to die like elephants who instinctively knew it was time. Tom Smith was killed, *then* hidden inside the dumpster. Murdered. Len silently cursed the vagueness of the story. It would be nice to know whether someone you knew—had known—had been murdered. He shrugged, folded the newspaper and called the counter girl over. He smiled boyishly at her as he fished in his pocket for a few bucks, a smile she returned with polite indifference.

Len, a large man, his dark hair cut short, his face cratered by adolescent acne, wished there were more to do in Naples Falls. Sipping weak coffee in the Half Moon Cafe, hoping the waitress would bend over more often, was not his idea of a good time. And tomorrow was Saturday, his day off. Except for tours, the winery where he worked was closed on Saturdays.

On his way out, he stopped and asked Larry Culhaine about his son, Cory, who had just shipped off to Marine boot. Larry sat across from Ruth Connelly, his fingers laced lightly around a steaming cup of coffee. Larry and Ruth did little to hide the intimacy of their relationship, and Len privately envied Larry that intimacy. Ruth easily weakened a man's knees and when Len looked at the two of them, it was all he could do to keep his thoughts from drifting to the obscene. The rumor mill had it that the beautiful yet volatile Ruth had given Larry an ultimatum, his wife or her. He couldn't have both. Larry, Len knew, would drag the thing out for as long as he could. In his estimation, he could have both, at least until one of them "blew his brains out." Those were the words he whispered during a work break that day, and he'd probably only been half-joking.

After Larry had bent his ear with a lengthy dissertation about the "rigors and brutality" of boot camp, Len tipped his Red Man hat to Ruth and left.

His breath gave birth to tiny ghosts that, because of his quick pace, were quickly behind him. In deference to the unseasonal chill, he shoved his hands into his pants pockets. His steel-toed workboots clattered with a loud

74

and lonely sound on the empty sidewalk.

Within twenty seconds he had passed The Silver
Spoon, a luncheonette owned and run by his cousin, Al.
Rover's Retreat, a pet store recently opened next door,
was the reason he had lost his job at the Silver Spoon. No
one wanted to hear bored dogs barking, nor did they wish
to be assaulted by the nose-flogging stench of stale urine
that customarily drifted in around lunchtime. Originally,
Len had moved back to Naples Falls because Al had
offered him a job. But after a couple of months business
at the luncheonette, founded on the belief that barely
edible food at cut-rate prices would be popular with
country folk, declined. This, when coupled with the
problem of the pet store, cost Len his job. But Al, a
compassionate, understanding man, pulled a few strings
and got him the job at the winery. He had been there for
six months now and saw no reason why he wouldn't be
there for many years to come.

Len had no way of knowing that in actuality, his time
was down to minutes.

Len lived alone in a small, two-story frame house just
on the edge of town. His wife, Sharon, a childhood
sweetheart, had grown weary of small-town life and
small-town mentalities. She had left him two months
earlier. The town, she said, knew they'd had a fight
before she did, and Sharon, who very much valued her
privacy, just would not tolerate that kind of intrusion
into her affairs. But Len didn't mind sharing his private
life with townfolk. After all, they shared theirs with him.
Larry Culhaine and Ruth Connelly came to mind.

"Someday," Sharon told him the day she left, "there'll
be a new job opening in Naples Falls—town gossip,
prerequisite—low I.Q. and a mouth stuck in fifth gear!"
Len had laughed, but Sharon, who didn't at all like being
laughed at, threw open the door and stomped out.

She'll be back, Len thought as he stepped into the
darkness. Route 5 was behind him; the fog had started to
unravel. All she's got now is a cold bed. She'll be back. He

thought about that cold bed and envisioned another man in there warming it up for her, a vision that inspired yet another vision—Sharon prone at his feet, her face puffy and bruised—begging for mercy.

His frame house sat among a stand of evergreens, all but hidden from the road. A pocket of fog had settled neatly around it. The evergreens would have made a decent noise barrier had the road been well-travelled enough to be a problem.

Because Len liked to walk, his twelve-year-old Chrysler Newport had only twenty thousand miles on it. And it looked it. Even in the fog, moonlight glittered off its chrome bumpers and hand-rubbed finish. Only in inclement weather did Len park it in the garage, out of sight. Most of the time, it sat out front, as it did now near the mailbox, so as to be easily seen by passersby. But on his list of accomplishments, the Chrysler took second place to the fence that surrounded his well-manicured front lawn. Over the last year or so Len had painstakingly fashioned each picket and cross member with his Sears-bought tools, all stored neatly in the garage. Even Sharon, who passed out compliments with only lottery-winning frequency, had remarked on the nice job he had done. Given her remarks, and the remarks of others, that fence had become a source of great pride to Len. It showed the world, at least this small part of it, how capable he really was. And he had even gotten a few side jobs from admirers of his work, people like Bill and Sophia Langmuir who lived about a hundred yards south. But now, he saw, his handiwork had been tampered with; two vertical pieces had been broken, snapped off in the middle like kindling.

"Aww, shit!" he said. He dropped to one knee to examine the damage, his face reflecting the inner turmoil of a man who had just found the cold, dead body of a loved one. "Who'd do somethin' like this? Who the hell'd do somethin' like this?" After his very real grief had subsided enough to allow him a moment of rational reflection, he thought: *Sharon, that's who. She did this!* But why? Why would Sharon do something like this? She wouldn't, he finally decided. And she was in the city, anyway. So if Sharon hadn't been responsible . . . It was then when he noticed that one of the stakes further down was missing entirely, a yawning gap in its place. He squinted at the rest of the fence, what he could see of it on the far side of the lawn, and thanked the good Lord that the damage had been confined to this one small section. Luckily he had a few slats stored in the garage, fashioned for just such emergencies. He shrugged and went into the house—angry, certainly, but not irrationally so.

Some ten minutes later, as he sat in his favorite chair, a green Stratolounger with white lace doilies on the arms, he heard what sounded like someone running a tin cup against the bars of a cell. The drafty, poorly insulated house made it seem as if the sound were being generated from the radiator just to his right. He pushed himself out of his chair, walked to the front door and opened it cautiously. *Well now,* he observed with a strange inner calm, *what the hell's he think he's doing?* The tall, thickly muscled man stood about twenty feet away. Splattered across the front of his light colored shirt were stains that Len vaguely thought might be blood. His mind's eye replayed what might have happened. As it did, Len's inner calm disintegrated, and released in him a great surge of vengeful energy. With a lurch, he felt his legs propel him toward the steps. Adrenalin pumped them like gas-driven pistons, his face hot with rage. But because Len was not normally given to hastiness, his rage lasted only briefly, only until he had reached the bottom step. Then he began to think. A cold knot of fear tightened in his belly, he ran his hands along the thighs of his jeans, his body clammy with sweat. He thought about his Remington Over and Under stored in the bedroom closet, and the cold knot of fear receded slightly. "You got ten seconds to leave my property," he said after he had

77

summoned up just an ounce more courage. "Ten seconds!"

The man turned and walked to the end of the fence, the air alive with the wooden rattle of stake on stake, then turned and started back. Len felt a sudden and profound sense of protectiveness for what was rightfully his. He knew what he had to do. He would go inside and get his gun. He would protect his property, what the law said he could use lethal force to guard.

He backed up the steps but stopped when some vague sense of fair play prompted him to issue yet another warning. "I'm gonna call the cops! You hear me?" But his threat fell on deaf ears, and it was then, as Len reached the middle of five steps, that the man suddenly stopped and looked into his eyes. He ran a finger over the tip of the stake, and, in a controlled, melodic baritone, said, "Nice job, Lenny. Real nice job. Christ, you could kill a vampire with this thing."

Len felt his heart flutter. "What the hell are you talkin' about?" he said, a kind of frantic quality to his tone. "And how do you know my name?" he added almost as an afterthought.

The man took a step toward him and with a wry smile said, "Is that why you've surrounded your house with these things, Len? Are you a fearless vampire hunter?"

"Stay back!" Len warned. "Just stay the hell back!"

But this sudden confrontation demanded eye to eye contact, and in that regard, Lenny was not very well armed, at least not against this opponent. Staring into the other man's eyes made Len feel mildly drunk. His legs threatened to buckle.

"But Len," the man continued, "if I stay back, how can I savage you? How can I tear your throat out and feed your entrails to the wild things that scurry through the woods behind your sorry excuse for a house? If I stay back, Len, how can I do those things?"

His tone was more matter-of-fact than questioning, as if the act itself were a foregone conclusion and now all that remained was for Len to also realize this truth.

"You got one minute, pal, one goddamned minute," Len said in his best threatening voice. "That's how long it's gonna take me to go into the house and get my gun." He tried to stiffen his arm but his musculature had declined to rubbery at best. "And don't think I won't use it. Don't for one minute think that I won't blow your brains from here to Cohocton! You got that?" His words trembled with vibrato, a fact that was lost in his own growing fear.

The man simply stared, his face offering no clue about whether he "got that" or not, a stare that made Len feel like someone who's been arguing with their executioner about the proper voltage. But by now he certainly had had quite enough, thank you. He went into the house, shut the door behind him and somehow, despite legs of straw, went up the L-shaped stairs to the bedroom. Once there it took him about a half minute to reach into the closet, wrap his shaking hand around the barrel of the Remington Over and Under, pull it out and snap the barrels open. The sight of two slugs cozied into the chambers reassured him tremendously, but not for very long.

As he turned to go, weapon in hand, legs wobbling noticeably, Len felt a dreamily pleasant, almost sexual tingling. For a moment, and because he really had no choice, he simply basked in it, simply let it cascade over him. It was, after all, a step up from the stultifying weakness that he had felt since he first saw the man. Drugs, he thought remotely, a thin smile parting his lips, warmth streaming through him, this is probably what it feels like to do drugs. But balanced on the edge of this druglike state was a coiled, ready-to-strike paranoia, a feeling that there was somebody out there watching him, someone hidden by the fog, someone huge and tall. His eyes snapped wide open. The window, he thought, he's at the goddamn window. But that, he knew, was impossible. He was on the second floor. Twenty feet up. Don't even look, just leave the room. Don't even bother . . . But he would look. He knew that very well. Just like when he was a kid, the covers pulled over his eyes to keep nightmare monsters away.

Slowly, cautiously, while yet another cold, oily sweat spread from his pores, he turned his eyes toward the bare window. What he saw then—or more precisely, what he thought he saw—drew a quick yelp of fear out of him and made his blood rush headlong through his thinning veins. He was there, just beyond the window, partially obscured by the foggy mist, floating, simply floating, his head cocked crazily, his legs, from the knees down, drawn up behind him, his hands raised and clawed. Slowly yet relentlessly he pressed through the unraveling fog, strandy threads of it passing over him as he drew closer and closer to the window, the fog growing thinner and thinner until he had finally reached the window. He scratched on it with his long, obscenely pointed nails, all the while cocking his head from side to side and smiling wildly. And oh but his stare was the stare of a demon and it was so very difficult not to obey him when he mouthed the words, "Let me in! Let me in," over and over and over.

But Len had spent a year in Vietnam. He knew something about force of will. With some inner, nightmare-aroused defense mechanism, he stared back, daring what he saw to be real, daring it with some supernatural game of chicken; a game his opponent accepted and played out, right to the end. A game that, much to his surprise, Len eventually won. His opponent, it appeared, just gave up, just pulled back into the fog and gave up. And with this victory, Len was also able to siphon off the stream of warmth that had invaded his body along with the paranoia. He took a deep, lung-filling breath, choosing to stare at a photograph of he and Sharon on the nightstand, focusing in on it and only it until his courage had been refortified. When it had, he clicked the gun closed, left the bedroom and started down the stairs.

Halfway down, the paranoia returned and Len's stomach churned acidly. The blood pounded in his ears. He steadied himself, listened. He heard nothing, save for the steady electric drone of the refrigerator. Staring vacantly at the closed front door he took a few more steps.

But only a few.

The almost sexual warmth he had felt in the bedroom also returned. And this time he didn't have the will to fight it. God help him, he could not put those eyes out of his mind either—that was impossible. If ever anything was truly impossible . . .

He didn't want to, he knew that, but he did. He lowered his gun and let it thud to the floor. The closed front door was central to his world now, its three layers of white enamel and two inches of oak slowly losing consistency, slowly revealing what waited beyond.

While a tear rumbled unfelt down his cheek, he walked toward the door and, once there, hesitated only briefly.

The door swung open, and Len—as he knew he would, as some deep-seated intuition told him he would—looked dead into those eyes.

The man took a step toward him, and Len took an unconscious step backwards, as bewildered as he had ever been. Fear was beside him now, fear strengthened by the redolence of ruined meat and damp cellar, a combination that weighed heavily upon the cool night air. But even this assaulting pungency could not keep him from looking into those eyes. And as he did, he felt a hushed, sweet stillness not unlike, he thought remotely, that which probably fills a deer just before a bullet finds its heart, as it sights down the business end of a gun and looks into the eyes of its killer. And even though there was something terribly wrong and terribly final about that thought, he could not help but think it, could not help but feel overwhelming calm as it grew more detailed in his mind.

81

Harry said, "May I come in?" As he spoke, Len remembered all that was his: the pale green house with black shutters that sorely needed painting, the young evergreen to the left of center in the front yard that was doing so poorly. Out of the corner of his eye—and his thoughts—he saw his mailbox as the lights of a passing car glanced off the rusting metal. Len, remembering what the man had asked, stepped aside and said simply, "Yes."

Now in the foyer, the face of the man was well lit, but Len, trapped by those eyes, forever blinded to green shutters and dying evergreens and rusted mailboxes, didn't notice the sallowness of the skin or even the redness of the eyes. And, finally, Len didn't see the smile on the man's face just before he turned the stake toward him, just before he shoved it into Len's buttery gut.

For a few crazy seconds, Len simply stood there, still entranced, while Harry effortlessly turned the stake in a lazy circle, reducing the integrity of Len's digestive system to a quickly blending linkage of intestine and stomach and liver. But when the pain caused by his quickly disintegrating guts flooded through him, his trance weakened and his eyes grew round with the knowledge of his impending death. He stared wide-eyed at the stake as his glistening red blood fanned out over it, and with an indrawn gasp of horror he grabbed it with both hands and valiantly attempted to unseat it. But the pain of snapped wood rubbing against recently abused flesh was too much to bear, even for Len, who prided himself on his ability to suffer pain silently. It forced him to his knees where he hesitated only briefly, his gore, slippery and dripping, spilling out between his fingers while he futiley attempted to keep his inner workings where they belonged. Finally, he pitched straight forward at Harry's feet, the stake tickling his spine and then emerging out his back as the square end struck the carpeted foyer.

In a wilderness area of his memory, Len remembered those eyes before he died, remembered when dinosaurs roamed the athletic fields. But he didn't have enough time left to remember the name of his killer; very little time, indeed, just the space between heartbeats. He had done remarkably well to even make the connection. Oddly enough, and Len even thought as much at the time, the last thing he saw were the feet of a woman, just inches from his fogging eyes.

Minutes later, after Len had been blooded, Harry Matheson stood over the body and produced a match from his pocket. "That's two," he said.

Christine laughed.

IN JERRY'S STUDY

Again the words stopped flowing just as quickly as they had started. Jerry leaned back, exhausted. Minutes later he read what he had written, and as he read he recognized a degree of pleasure almost as strong as that which had surged through him while he wrote. And his writing was extraordinarily detailed, his analogies and metaphors unbelievably vivid, unbelievably well-drawn. These dreams, he thought wildly, are going to make me as famous as my brother.

Chapter Eight

This is what Tad saw: a young girl in a casket, surrounded by thick, gnarly roots, like a crown of thorns. While he watched, fascinated, one particularly thick root on the left slowly began to grow.

At first it was only a diversion, for his thoughts and attention were on the girl in the pellucid casket, but when he heard wood begin to splinter and crack, his eyes began to sparkle with this new reality. The root, as if possessed with a sense of purpose and even human intelligence, had pierced the casket and seemed intent on drawing nourishment from the young girl. Seeing this, Tad screamed at her, but she didn't move, she didn't hear and Tad knew that his teary-eyed pleas would go unheard. All he could do was watch while the root entwined her, rose up like a cobra, and pierced her chest with the speed of a lightning bolt. The girl's gentle, dead face contorted instantly, the mouth lengthening as if preparing to release the loudest of screams, the eyes growing twice their normal size, the skin of her face stretching and stretching, like a reflection in a funhouse mirror. Tad waited for her to scream, even winced in anticipation of it, but try as she may, she could not release it. As she turned and looked at him with her stretched, confused, funhouse mirror face, Tad woke up.

The first thing he saw when he opened his eyes was the

top thirty percent of the aforementioned tree, the part above ground, the part he had not seen in his dream. Seeing it now, upon awakening, only added to his horror. Now he could only stare at that tree, his eyes focused on it and only it—not the fragmented, black-keeled clouds gliding quickly overhead, not the morning sun reflecting faintly off tombstones, not the small car in the shadow of that tree, it and its grieving occupants just now cresting the hill. Just the tree. And as he stared, he again envisioned that one gutting root as it sought to relieve some hideous and probably unquenchable thirst. It was a' vision that sent a chill chasing through him as his pores released a cold, sticky sweat, the same kind of sweat he had experienced in the car on moving day. This time, however, he didn't have his mother to mop up his sweat. This time he, alone, would have to corral his imagination.

He drew in a deep breath and let it out. At the same time Prince walked around the side of the bed, his tail wagging. Seeing him, Tad returned to full consciousness. Seconds later, and aided by his dog's smiling face, Tad totally released the nightmare from his thoughts.

The Firebird cruised over the backroad quickly and effortlessly, and as far as Sharon Griffin was concerned, a reconciliation with her husband, Len, would not involve letting him use it whenever he pleased. Not this time. She had rehearsed her speech to him at least a hundred times. She would live with him, be his wife, cook his dinners— even have his children, if she was, indeed, capable of that this late in life. But she wouldn't do it in Naples Falls; not a town that seemed so damned preoccupied with everyone's business but their own. And she wouldn't let him talk her into it, either. She would give him a month; if he hadn't found another job in a month, then she was gone for good. Her lawyer would contact his and all that legal garbage. She hoped it wouldn't come to that—she still loved him—but love only went so far.

Unhappiness was pretty much the limit as far as she was concerned.

She glanced into the rearview mirror to get a quick look at herself, just in case Lenny was home. Her short, straight brown hair was just slightly mussed. She glanced quickly at the road, then looked into the rearview mirror again. Guiding the car with one hand, she fluffed her hair with the other, then smacked a kiss at the mirror. Her lips, full and pouting, were her best feature, at least according to Lenny.

Tad pulled the dog close. "You snore, you know that?" he said.

Prince licked him on the chin.

Tad withdrew slightly. "And you got morning breath, too. Let's go get you a milkbone."

Prince knew nothing of milkbones, but he did know inflection. Tad had said "milkbone" with just a slightly higher inflection, and high inflection—usually heard from the boy—meant he had done something right and would get a reward. A low inflection—so far associated with the words "bad dog!"—meant he had done something wrong. And doing something wrong—like messing in the dining room—meant a sharp smack on the rump. But Prince, as Tad had hoped, was one smart dog, as dogs went, and the future for him held many high inflections and only a few low ones. In some uncharted area of his brain Prince catalogued the word "milkbone," while yet another part of him couldn't wait to see what they were.

It didn't take Tad long to dress, grab a piece of raisin toast and chug a glass of orange juice—necessary overtures to a boy's summer day. After he had done these things, he pushed open the front door and stepped onto the porch. Prince followed, his tongue working furiously as he attempted to salvage as much milkbone flavor as he could.

Seconds later, while Tad stared through the screen at the cemetery, he whispered, "That's pretty damn stupid, Tad Matheson. Trees don't grow like that, they just don't! And if you're gonna live here you better not be afraid of that stupid old boneyard either!"

It was, he thought, an excellent speech: inspiring, worthwhile, adult. Now if only he had the guts to do something about it.

Behind him, unseen, Prince nosed at the screen, pushed it open, then slithered through, free at last. Within seconds he had crossed the yard, and by the time Tad saw him, he had raised his leg to one of the lower headstones.

Damn, Tad thought, Mom's gonna be pissed. He threw open the screen, bounded down the steps and ran after his dog.

Prince's morning squirt proved to be a solution to Tad's problem. Before he knew it, he had passed right into the cemetery itself, a fact he didn't have time to make mental note of either, because as he drew to within ten feet of his dog, Prince turned, looked at Tad playfully, then loped off at a leisurely, catch-me-if-you-can trot.

Sharon slowed down, looked both ways down Route 5, then took a right toward town. Seconds later, and in the cemetery off to her right, she saw a boy and a dog, obviously having a great time. But as she looked back at the road, the right rear tire, which had received precious little attention over the course of its 48,000-mile life, became intimate with a carelessly discarded ten penny nail. The sound precipitated by that intimacy—like a shotgun discharging—sent a surge of adrenalin charging through her. She held the wheel in a death grip, her knuckles white, her eyes glazing with fear as the car swerved first right then left then right again, its final destination known only to God. Much to Sharon's gasping relief, however, that final destination proved to be a right-side ditch. The backend spun out, miraculously jumped out of the ditch and then almost leaped to a halt onto the gravelly shoulder of the road.

Had the car flung itself in the other direction, toward a steep incline and a dead swampy area where the water was much deeper than it looked, she could have been trapped. And death inside an immersed car, her lungs straining for oxygen that wasn't there, was one of her nightmares.

She caught her breath, then banged the wheel in exasperation.

"Damn!" she said as she hurried out of the car, slamming the door behind her in anger. She slung her hands onto her hips as the extent of the damage revealed itself to her. The tire was shredded. With her luck, her spare would be flat, too. She opened the door, took out the keys, unlocked the trunk, raised the carpeted flap, and gazed in at the never-used "space saver" spare. It looked okay, but sometimes . . . She gave it a squeeze then thumped it with her fist. Rock hard. But, she thought, feeling somewhat foolish now, it really didn't matter if it was flat or not. She didn't know how to change the damn thing—oh, she'd been meaning to learn, but there was always something else to do, and she had never had a flat tire, so . . .

It was then when she heard a fragile male voice say, "You okay, lady? You need some help?"

She wheeled, her mind replaying the graveyard scene as she did, the boy and the dog. The boy looked back at her questioningly, his hands shoved deep into the pockets of his jeans. His dog stood beside him, his mouth open, his tongue lolled off to the side.

Sharon looked at them for a moment in an effort to regain control, then ran her fingers through her hair and smiled as best she could, given the circumstances. "I don't know. You know anything about changing a tire? Or maybe your dad—you live close by?"

Tad glanced behind him and pointed. "Yeah, we live

right over there. But I can change it for you if you want. My dad taught me." He took a few steps forward and pointed into the trunk. "You gotta jack her up first, but just a little. Then you take off the lug nuts." He gave the scene a onceover and matter-of-factly added, "Good thing you ended up on flat ground. Can't change a tire otherwise."

Sharon appraised him quickly and tried to imagine this puny kid hefting a tire. She couldn't, but at least he knew how.

"I'll tell you what," she said. "You supervise, and I'll change the tire. How about that?"

Tad shrugged. "If you want, but I can do it for you."

"That's okay," she answered. "Your mom might get mad if you came home all dirty."

Tad, who was more than willing to change the tire, considered that and thought it reasonable. Sure, he could supervise. Wasn't every day he got the chance to tell an adult what to do. He held out his hand. "My name's Tad and this is my dog, Prince. We were up there in the graveyard when we heard your tire blow. You were real lucky, lady. You could've gone off into that swamp."

"Yes, I know," Sharon replied, raising her eyebrows for emphasis. She took his hand in hers and shook it firmly, like she might someone twenty years his senior, then scratched Prince on the neck, a gesture that seemed to please him.

By now the front had rumbled through, leaving unobstructed sunshine in its wake, so the warmth that passed between Tad and Sharon was not entirely due to chemistry.

As Jerry watched Tad and the woman from the end of the driveway, a black hatred began to fester within him. He was sweating, too, and wasn't that odd. The source of his hatred, although he didn't fully realize as much, was the woman. That tall, pretty woman who did, in fact, look

89

somewhat familiar. But it was not an incapacitating hatred, not one he could not fight. Nor one he did not want to fight, although the swell of it inside of him was quite pleasureable.

With difficulty he pushed aside that festering hatred and walked down the road toward them.

Chapter Nine

Some time later, Sharon drove past the Red and White Market and, a little further on, Miller's Sunoco, a two-pumper. A hand-painted sign in the window offered a brake inspection for only $9.95 with a fill-up, offer good until the tenth. Seconds later she eased past Rover's Retreat and the Silver Spoon, both of which were open— *eased* because Guy Henry just loved to catch people doing even one mile over the legal limit, a leisurely 25 in town. Guy's office was two doors down from the Silver Spoon.

The low sun, as seen through a bright, storm-scrubbed sky, pounded mercilessly through the windshield and caused Sharon's thoughts to wander, which also caused her to miss the turn into her driveway. She pulled over to the side, stopped, looked toward the house. She didn't know if Lenny was at work or not, but it was okay if he was, she had a key. She'd just go on in. Maybe she'd go to the Red and White later and pick up everything she needed for lasagna, his favorite, and have it ready for him when he got home—if he came home, if he didn't go out boozing with his buddies. There was that possibility. Still, it didn't much matter when he got home. She had made a decision and she would honor it. Rarely, did she alter a decision after it had been thoughtfully reached.

As she eyed the Chrysler, the bumpers harshly reflecting the morning sun, she recalled her brief visit with Jerry Matheson. She had chosen not to talk of his brother—those memories were anything but pleasant—but Jerry, as he obligingly changed her tire, was more than willing to talk about his new career. She was happy for him. In school, she had known him only well enough to smile at between classes. He had always seemed nice enough. But during their conversation she had felt somewhat ill at ease, almost apprehensive. Somewhere behind that ready smile, his willingness to help, she sensed an underlying tension, almost as if he secretly wanted to reach out and smack her one. She had felt that tension while she drove off with Jerry and Tad in her rearview mirror. But as she thought about that tension now, she discounted it. She was edgy, a bit apprehensive—and why not? She had come crawling back to Lenny, which had, of itself, produced a great deal of anxiety, and then she had almost been killed. She had a right. She focused on the Chrysler. To her it had always looked like a child's overlarge toy. More than once she'd had the urge to kick in a door or run a key along the side, but she had always kept herself under total control. Hasty decisions, she knew, had a way of sneaking up on you later. "If you let your temper get the best of you, it will get your best," at least according to her father. She waited until a tractor trailer laden with sewer pipe lumbered past, then backed up and pulled into the driveway.

As she got out of her car, she noticed that one of the fence stakes was broken. "Shit," she muttered. He would probably blame her for that when he got home. Then they'd have a big fight. But Lenny did keep spares in the garage. Maybe, she thought, it would be wise to do some repairs. If he found his fence like that they'd really get off on the wrong foot.

She fumbled around in her purse for her key. Her search ended almost a half minute later, and then she walked onto the porch and pushed the key toward the lock.

Much to her surprise, the door was already open.

Guy Henry, a short, balding man with Popeye forearms and a face like a priest—or so he had been told by no fewer than three middle-aged women in town—lightly touched the side of a coffee pot that sat on a Grizzly wood stove. "Finally," he said, and picked up his mug.

Earlier, while he stood by the window waiting for the pot to boil, he had seen Sharon Griffin drive by in her Firebird, limping along on one of those space saver spares. He was a little surprised to see her back. She and Len had had a real barn burner of a squabble—a knock-down, drag-out, name-calling set-to. But that, he knew, was about normal. Most couples around here got into it on a regular basis. Leroy Irvin, who had taken a lot of psychology courses over to Canandaigua Community College, said it was because everyone was so bored. But it was good to see her again. There weren't many around here could stir up the loins like that one. Guy had been a tit man since puberty and he'd seen few sets as nice as hers.

He had just gotten back from a hunting trip, a highly successful, highly out of season—but what the hell did he care, he was the law—hunting trip that had bagged him a buck, a twelve pointer, a huge trophy that had—almost—eluded him.

He shook some creamer and a level spoon of sugar into his dark blue Buffalo Bills coffee mug, then filled the mug with steaming coffee.

But he had outsmarted that buck, he sure had. And now he would have his head in his den; in about a year or so. Taxidermy took forever and a day. But what the hell, at least he had the memories to hold him till then, the bragging rights, the ability to relate the entire experience. He smiled, sipped his coffee. The worst part was having to follow that buck until he finally dropped, ten

93

miles minimum, Guy calculated at the time, which stretched reality by about seventy percent. And dragging the carcass to the nearest road to wait for help had almost made his goddamn heart burst! He patted his bowling-ball-shaped stomach, dues paid for decades of entirely too much pasta and beer, and smiled again as he envisioned him and that buck lying on the side of the road, one dead and one damn close. A year, twelve long months, maybe longer until that buck's head was on the wall of his newly paneled den. Well, being sheriff never had impressed Gil Boatman enough to give him preferential treatment when it came to stuffing his trophies.

The phone rang, which somewhat startled him. The phone never rang until noon or so, when the second shift left the winery. Minor fender benders were almost a weekly routine, usually because some bored-silly employee snuck too many free samples of the grape.

With mug in hand, he walked to his desk and picked up the receiver. "Sheriff Henry. What's up?"

"Guy? That you, Guy?" a very old and raspy male voice responded.

"What is it, Bill?" Guy Henry said tiredly. He knew who it was. He pushed a stack of papers aside and sat on the side of the desk.

"Guy? That you, Guy?" Bill said again.

Guy Henry let the receiver drop onto his shoulder and smiled derisively. Bill Langmuir, a retired railroad worker with a bad case of old age, was on the other end. Talking with Bill was like trying to hold a conversation with a skipping record. "Okay, Bill, hold on, just hold on, slow down, take it easy. Just think about why you called."

As he waited for Bill to respond, Guy thought he heard a woman crying in the background, but questioning Bill about it would be an exercise in futility. He'd done well enough to dial the number. Questions about who was crying, or why, would only confuse him. He would just let him say what he had planned to say.

94

"Well, Guy, there's been some trouble," Bill said casually.

"What kind of trouble, Bill?"

The crying continued.

"Bad trouble?" Bill answered. His inflection made it seem like another question.

As the crying continued, Guy Henry decided to let Bill off the hook, literally. The best thing to do was to simply drive over there and talk to whomever was crying, if he could get them to stop.

"I'm gonna hang up, Bill. I'm gonna hang up and come over. You and the woman just stay there. Okay?"

"Wait a minute, sheriff, there's someone at the door," Bill said.

"Bill?."

No answer.

Guy hung up and hurried out the door.

Bill Langmuir pulled his blue, wool sweater tight to his frail chest and shuffled toward the crying woman, seated in his wife's padded chair. He tried to remember what this crying woman had said. *Oh, why did the old woman always leave him alone? She knew he couldn't cope.* He remembered something about someone being dead. But who? His brain did what it could to puzzle that out. Probably someone the woman knew, he finally decided. Probably. Else she wouldn't be crying. Bill smiled a little, gap toothed smile, pleased with his analysis but also vaguely realizing that at one time his carefully arrived at deduction would have been arrived at much more quickly and with very little thought at all, if any. He sat down next to her in his own padded chair and wiped a line of drool from his quivering chin with a large knuckled finger. His head and hands trembled mildly because of Parkinson's disease. The trembling was more pronounced than usual this morning because Bill had forgotten to take his Deprenyl.

Maria and Tad Matheson stood silently by. While driving to the vet's office on the other side of town, just to get Prince checked over, they had seen Sharon run out her front door, screaming hysterically. "Mom, that's her, that's the woman I told you about!" Tad had yelled. But before she could stop the car to help, Sharon had crossed the hundred or so yards between houses and had started banging on Bill Langmuir's screen door. A short while later she saw Bill Langmuir push the door open and let her in. She sat in her car for about five minutes before she decided to see what she could do to help. By the time she rang the doorbell, Bill Langmuir had already called the police. Right now, she wondered about what she had done. This woman had said something about murder, about a fence stake, about blood everywhere, hysterics that had left her on the edge of paranoia.

By now Sharon Griffin's uncontrollable sobs—caused not only for the fact of Lenny's death, but also for the fish-like gutting that had obviously caused it. And even now, consumed as she was by a fear-agitated grief, she realized that his killer had to be extremely strong. The stake hadn't simply entered his body, it had been revolved, as if someone had been stirring a cake mix. It wasn't even vertical. It lay on him from his stomach to his knees and had about as much chance of maintaining verticality as a spoon in a bowl of vegetable beef soup.

"Guy Henry said somethin' about comin' over," Bill said to everyone. A look of puzzlement came over his face, but it was quickly replaced by a smile of quiet victory. "Yep, sure did," he added.

By now Sharon was beginning to question her actions. Why hadn't she simply called Guy Henry from home? Why had she run the hundred yards to Bill Langmuir's house? She dabbed away her tears. Those questions were easily answered. The sight of Len's gutted body had made her panic. Normal enough. What if Len's killer had still been in the house? She could have easily joined her husband. And Bill Langmuir was her closest neighbor, even if he wasn't too much help. But at least he had managed to contact Guy Henry. At least he had done that. She looked at Sharon and Tad, then at the old man. Although his dark eyes were toneless and flat, she saw a genuine concern on his wrinkled, trembling face. He knew something was wrong, very wrong, and he was doing his best to tell her that.

Seconds later Tad left his mother's side and took Sharon's hand.

In his car Guy Henry wondered if perhaps Bill's wife hadn't witnessed some other minor crime, but he quickly dismissed that possibility. As had to be, because of Bill's frailty, Bill's wife was strong-minded, and she was not easily given to tears. Besides, that wasn't her car in the driveway. It had to belong to the crying woman.

His attention was drawn to the screen enclosed front porch. A slightly bent Bill Langmuir, his hands sifting furiously through his pants pockets, stood near the door. Sharon Griffin, her face puffy and red, stood to his right. Behind them he saw a woman and a boy who were unfamiliar. Sharon stepped hurriedly past Bill, which seemed to befuddle him. She opened the door and hurried down the steps. She spoke almost frantically.

"It's my husband, Sheriff," she said. "Someone's killed him. Someone's killed him dead as hell!"

Guy hadn't consciously expected this. Death in Naples Falls was a simple thing, most always natural and only every so often accidental. Murder was a once-every-decade happening, and then usually the cause was boredom. Sure, tourists had come up missing every now and again, but after a while, no one seemed to care much about missing tourists. He looked at her and hesitated to respond. The gravity of the situation had caught him somewhat unaware.

"Didn't you hear me?" she said, her inflection sneaking a little higher.

Finally, Guy Henry firmly grasped the situation. "Where?" he asked, enunciating perfectly, hoping to project a calm efficiency.

She pointed across the well-manicured Langmuir lawn, toward her own house, only partially visible through a row of evergreens, and said, "Over there, inside. He's right inside the front door."

Guy squinted through the trees. Right next door, he thought. He focused on the front door and remembered seeing the Chrysler, as well as the Firebird, as he drove by. He looked back at Sharon.

"Lenny?" he said.

"Yes, Lenny."

There were, he knew, very precise and proven ways to handle possible homicides. But because he had never actually investigated a homicide, including Tom Smith's, which was being handled by the state cops, he could only use common sense, that and whatever innate sleuthing ability he might have. Of course, she—everyone—would have to stay here. That much he knew.

He went back to the car, took out a shotgun, checked the chambers and said, "Stay here. No tellin . . . just stay here."

He chose a direct route, the most direct—a straight line, right through the evergreens. And as he walked, his apprehension about what he'd find grew almost uncontrollably. A buck was one thing. A man was quite another. "Right inside the front door," Sharon had said. The thought of pushing open a door and viewing a corpse was far from pleasant. Still, he was the law, the only law until he called in the state police, and he had a job to do. Today he would have to earn his $334.50 a week. And maybe today he would also learn a few things about himself as well.

Chapter Ten

With Sharon seated beside her, Tad and Prince in back, Maria pulled the car into the driveway and stopped to the left side of the front porch. Earlier, having decided it was the only decent thing to do, she had asked Sharon if she wanted to stay the night, or even longer if necessary. She had expected a polite yet firm refusal; relatives, Sharon would say, they'll want me to stay with them. But Sharon had nodded her acceptance and now it was up to her—and Jerry, hopefully—to see to her comfort. That was not going to be easy, especially now: In front of her was her mother's white Audi. She had obviously decided to surprise them.

Maria cut the engine and got out. From here, below the front porch, the tops of two wicker chairs were visible. The wind played through the screens and rocked them gently, giving the impression that unseen children or small adults were seated there.

Sharon looked behind her, toward the cemetery. It was well kept, but it was still a cemetery, and cemeteries always came with their own mystique, even those with the most fastidious caretakers. In fact, the most carefully preened boneyards were also the most atmospheric. It was the contrast. On the surface everything was neat and cut and orderly, but beneath, within the rectangular boxes, things got messy rather quickly.

Sharon thought of Tad. She knew they shared a secret fear of graveyards, although she hadn't confessed her fear to him, and he had only hinted at his. "Wasn't no one else up there," he had told her. "Just me and Prince." At that point she had seen Jerry Matheson coming down the road, effectively stifling any further conversation between her and the boy.

Maria started for the front door. "Coming?" she asked from the top step.

"Just let me get my bag," Sharon said.

She reached into the backseat, picked up her overnight bag then started up the steps. As she did, she felt a burning sensation at her throat. She stopped and with her free hand pulled the tiny, diamond-encrusted cross away from her neck and looked at it. That's strange, she thought. The cross was almost hot to the touch and the tiny, centered diamond seemed to reflect more light than was available.

"You're a Catholic, I see," Maria said.

Sharon's thoughts were elsewhere. "I'm sorry, did you say something?" she asked.

Maria smiled. "I was just admiring your cross. Certainly does sparkle."

Sharon looked at it again then let it fall to her chest. "Yes, it does, doesn't it. Lenny gave it to me a long time ago. He said it would protect me."

Maria smiled. "I'm afraid the Mathesons are quite lax in that area. I suppose I'd go to church if Jerry went. Oh well, no matter. Come inside, I'll show you your room."

The door opened then and onto the porch stepped Maria's mother, resplendent in dark blue, crisply pleated slacks, red, long sleeve blouse, blue scarf and flaming red hair compliments of Loreal. She had obviously spent a great deal of time on her makeup, but the lines in her face, severe beyond description, her reward for almost sixty years in the sun, refused to be hidden. When she smiled they multiplied in proportion to the size of that smile. Her eyes, however, were still clear and bright.

"It's lovely, just lovely," she said to Maria, referring to the house.

Maria, anticipating a gush of parental excitement that would only make Sharon uncomfortable, spoke up quickly. "Mom," she said, "this is Sharon. She's just been through a tremendous ordeal."

"Oh, I'm so sorry. What kind of ordeal, dear?" Loretta asked, addressing Sharon.

Maria pulled her mother aside. "Her husband was murdered."

"Murdered!"

"Mom, please!"

Loretta Simonson projected an immediate and profound sense of loss and commiseration. She wrapped her arm around Sharon and, ignoring her daughter, led her into the house, utterances of great sorrow running from her mouth in torrents. Sharon, who seemed oblivious to her, allowed it. Maria and Tad followed, while Maria thought of Jerry and the look of consternation that he would proudly display until her mother left.

Dinner that evening was, for Jerry, an eye-opening, thought-provoking, and at first, pleasureable experience. Sharon had opted to eat alone, in her room. Given to frequent and severe emotional outbursts, she hadn't wanted to ruin everyone's meal.

Jerry and Maria sat across from each other, as did Tad and Loretta. Loretta was on Jerry's left, Tad on his right. Maria had prepared a loin roast and potatoes au gratin, both favorites of her mother. The good china, a delicate flowered pattern, was set out in honor of the occasion—her mother's first visit.

Loretta's dinner conversation began simply enough. Although the house was divine, she said, there was something about it, something she couldn't quite put

101

her finger on.

"Maybe it's because it's so old," she continued. "It just doesn't project a lot of warmth, know what I mean? Maybe you need some vibrant colors, Maria. What do you think?"

Maria knew exactly what her mother meant. She didn't want to go so far as to say the house was actually cold, despite the weather outside; that was far too clichéd. But, in fact, there were times, and certain rooms—those in the north part of the house generally, that seemed to stay cool. And, of course, basements were always a fairly constant temperature, but the cellar door—and she had Jerry verify this—was actually cold to the touch. One of these days she would have to get a flashlight and go down there. One of these days.

Loretta took a sip of what Jerry said was a local Cabernet and said, "It does have atmosphere though, lots of atmosphere." She stabbed a piece of meat with her fork, "So, Jerry, speaking about atmosphere, what's your next book about?"

She leaned toward him and smiled, waiting for an answer. Jerry took mental notes, not on what he saw, but on what he wanted to see; makeup-encrusted facial lines, full, wide lips assaulted by layer after layer of dark purple lipstick, a ludicrous cloud of flaming red hair, long black hairs as thick as brush bristles on the tip of her bulbuous nose. His appetite took the brunt of this hate-exaggerated visage. He glanced at Maria and wondered if perhaps she hadn't been adopted. Her father was dead, but he had seen photographs. She certainly favored him, not this survivor from a Max Factor bombing.

"I like to keep those things a secret till I'm done," he said. "You understand."

Loretta stuffed the meat into her mouth and smiled a supercilious smile. "You don't know, do you?"

Jerry glanced at Maria then back at Loretta. "Yes, I know."

Loretta swallowed noisily, stabbed another piece of meat, stuck the fork in her mouth, began to chew. "Them why don you ell me?"

"Excuse me?" Jerry said.

Her question had fought through a thick wad of partially chewed meat.

Loretta swallowed, again noisily. As before, she hadn't chewed long enough. "I said, then why don't you tell me?"

"Call it . . . superstition."

"Yeah, right, superstition! Okay, I'll give you that. How much are you getting for it then?"

Jerry smiled patiently. "Enough."

Loretta returned his smile. "Four figures, five figures, what?"

"Mother," Maria interposed, "If Jerry wants to tell you, he'll tell you. If he doesn't, he won't. Okay?"

Suddenly Loretta let her fork rest on her plate as a look of utter sadness crossed her face.

"So awful," she said and looked around the table. A stony resolve replaced the sadness. "She should be with people!" she announced, referring to Sharon. "When your father, bless his poor soul, passed on, I surrounded myself with loved ones. She should do the same!"

"We're hardly loved ones," Jerry said quietly.

"We're all family in His eyes," Loretta argued, raising both her knife and voice for emphasis.

Jerry looked at her. Her eyes were slit with conviction. Arguments didn't last long around Loretta, not with Him to fall back on.

"Pass the salt, please," he said to Maria.

He took the salt, very much aware of his mother-in-law's piercing eyes. She had thrown out the bait and he hadn't taken it.

She looked at Maria. "They have a nice Catholic church here. I saw it when I drove through town."

"Mother, Jerry's not Catholic."

103

"Then what *is* he?"

She was good, Jerry had to admit, she was real good. Another time, another place, she had told them about a nice Lutheran church, and before that a nice Episcopal church. If anyone could piss him off, she could. And she usually did so by referring to their lack of religious preference, and of course no preference meant they were doomed, or worse. And she had always wondered about him and Harry, about what they wrote—that demented garbage that probably incited Christians to murder.

"Mother, please," Maria said.

Loretta gazed hard at Tad. "And you, young man . . ."

"For heaven sake, Mother!"

Jerry, remarkably calm, given the circumstances, said, "How's your painting coming along, Loretta?"

It was then when he saw movement in the doorway. He squinted and as he did, he saw a ghost of himself standing there, arms crossed, smiling, apparently amused by this little slice of Americana. The ghost passed his arm over the assembled, pointed at his own eyes then at Jerry, which obviously meant, "They can't see me, Jer, only you can see me."

"Are you trying to change the subject?" Loretta asked.

"What?"

"Are you trying to change the subject?"

"Guilty," Jerry answered.

She looked at him for a very long time, but acquiesce she would. She knew that. He always knew which note to hit.

She busied herself with her food, choosing to look at it instead of him. "I've done a few things," she said as she cut. "Mr. Boynton at the gallery on Winton Road said I have potential."

Jerry looked at her. Out of the corner of his eye he saw his ghost step into the dining room and take up a position behind his mother-in-law, its lips spread, its eyes mirthless.

104

"I guess you haven't had time to hang any of my gifts yet?" Loretta continued.

Jerry looked at his ghost. It was running a finger along its neck, its eyes opened wide, its tongue hanging to the side.

"No, not yet. We, uh, have to find the right place."

He wondered if the downstairs john had enough wall space. And if you were out of laxatives . . .

"I should think the living room would be perfect," Loretta offered.

Jerry's ghost reached around Loretta and wrapped its hand around the large carving knife on the side of the roast beef platter.

"No, don't . . ." Jerry yelled.

"Excuse me?" Loretta said.

The ghost picked up the knife, immediately rendering it equally transparent.

"Jerry!" Maria said, "what's wrong with you?"

Jerry wrapped his left hand around his still full glass of milk, his right around his spoon.

"What?" he said, wild-eyed.

The ghost ran the blade along his fingers, pretending to be cut, pulled them away quickly and sucked on each individually.

"I don't think it's too much for Mother to ask."

"What? Oh, yeah, right. No, I guess not."

Loretta grinned smugly, having won a battle, if not the war.

"Then the next time I visit . . ."

"Sure, why not?" Jerry said obligingly.

The ghost, having thoroughly tested the knife's lethal properties, raised it high above his head, in both hands.

Jerry smiled.

"You find that amusing?" Loretta asked.

The knife came down swiftly and at once separated Loretta's ghost from her, a quickly dying ghost, while the still very much alive Loretta remained seated, basking in her minor victory. Loretta's ghost fell limply to the floor at Jerry's feet, eyes round with surprise. Its sweat blended with pancake makeup and created a thick porridge mixture that Jerry found vastly interesting.

"Jerry," Maria asked, "What the hell are you looking at?"

Loretta looked at the floor then at Maria. "There's nothing there!" she said with a confused shrug.

Jerry smiled as the ghost knelt, grabbed Loretta's ghost by the hair, pulled her neck back and slit her throat slowly and efficiently. The blood that painted the floor was the same color as Loretta's lipstick and the same consistency as her makeup. Jerry, as excited as he was amused, didn't feel the glass break, didn't see milk splatter all over his mother-in-law. He only watched as his ghost stood, kicked Loretta's ghost squarely in the kidneys, then walked slowly out the door. Seconds later Loretta herself followed, very unladylike curses fouling the air.

"God, Jerry," Maria said, "why can't you two get along?"

The next sound Jerry heard was Loretta stomping back into the house followed by a request that their car be moved so that she might leave. Maria followed her out, pleading with her.

Jerry, smiling, sat at the table with Tad. His smile, however, dissipated quickly. There had been some dark humor in what he had seen, certainly, but when you took away the alter ego with the sight gags, what was left? His mother-in-law dead at his feet, her neck slit wide open, that's what. And that, regardless of how he felt about the woman, certainly lacked humor. And to derive such pleasure from it . . . He rose with a flourish and went outside, where he found Loretta and his wife. Loretta was in her Audi, the engine running.

Jerry stuck his head into the open driver's window.

106

"Look, I'm sorry," he said with all the sincerity he could summon. "I don't know what happened. I certainly didn't mean to splatter you like that, honest."

He heard only the first two words of Loretta's response; "I suppose . . ." before his attention was drawn to the passenger window. His ghost—alter ego—was there cleaning his fingernails with the blood-soaked carving knife.

Chapter Eleven

THAT NIGHT

Sharon lay on her back staring blindly at the dark ceiling, her thoughts inchoate. The room, situated to the right of the sitting area at the top of the stairs, and facing the cemetery, was spartan yet comfortable. She had a feather pillow and the bed was firm enough to keep her nagging back problems at bay. The double window that faced the cemetery was covered by both shades and heavy drapes. On this night, cool enough to complain about at this time of year, Sharon opted to keep the shades pulled and the drapes drawn, which left the room in almost total darkness. On a small nightstand to the left of the headboard sat a thick decorative candle carved into a likeness of Niagara Falls. It was, in total, as decent a place as any to spend the night, given the circumstances. Still, she felt as if she were a prisoner here. The room, though certainly larger than a jail cell, was so sparsely appointed it could have passed for one. But, she decided, the sight of Len's body had become indelibly etched onto the wall of her mind, making her feel like a prisoner to that experience. And in the dark, as she was now, her mind staged intricate and horrific dramas. She pulled the white, goose down comforter to her neck and laced her fingers together on top of it. The Mathesons were apparently sleeping, but every now and again she could hear someone—Jerry, she assumed—let loose with a quick, grating snore, as if he had forgotten to breathe. Each time she heard the sound, it called her back with a start from wherever her thoughts had temporarily taken her. Sleep was a lost cause. Even before she pulled down the covers she knew that. With sleep would come nightmares, nightmares about Lenny and his grostesquely carved-up remains, perhaps even about who might have killed him, her mind supplying everything pertinent, the details following a logical course. He—definitely he—was huge, probably hideously ugly and more than likely tattooed. He was also extremely stupid; intelligent people killed, sure, but not like that. African beasts didn't even kill like that. She could even imagine a look of intense satisfaction on his face while he did the deed, his eyes round with pleasure, a river of sweat falling over his face, huge drops of it dripping off his nose and onto his victim, bubbling drool gathering at the corners of his mouth and suggesting the look of a rabid dog. And during this mental journey, as the killer transformed from something remotely human into some crazed, rabid beast, she even went so far as to imagine his canines gleaming with spit and fresh blood.

Her chill deepened as she thought these things, as she understood the killer's pleasure and also felt Lenny's unbelievable pain. She could only hope that the end for Lenny had come quickly and with comparatively little pain.

Again she mentally rechecked the scene as she had discovered it. "Hmm," she mumbled as her mind supplied the scene in even more graphic detail. At the time, her mind numbed by the sheer horror of her discovery, she hadn't noticed it. But now she was able to look upon the scene with a certain degree of objectivity. *Maybe I should tell the sheriff,* she thought. *Maybe it would help in his investigation. Maybe even narrow down his list of suspects, if he has any. But,* her inner dialogue continued, *what was there when I found Lenny would surely be there later, there's no reason to think otherwise.* She couldn't help but think of the rabid dog that had replaced the "human" killer. Had those wounds been the reason she had conjured up that vision in the first place? Had those wounds in Lenny's neck been the catalyst? Guy Henry pushed into her thoughts again. Maybe she should talk with him, offer her services—she had, after all, been the first on the scene. Maybe there were things buried deep in her subconscious, things that a hypnotist could chisel into, things that could have changed between the time she found the body and the sheriff saw it . . .

The doorbell rang. She heard the door across the hall open, footsteps.

Now who the hell?

She sat up in bed and waited. A few minutes later she heard voices outside her door, then a soft knock. "Sharon? Sorry to disturb you."

Father Monroe?

"Sharon, if you're still awake . . . ?"

"Wait a minute."

She got up and slipped into her bathrobe.

"I know it's late," Father Monroe continued, leaving that thought unended. Those four words had about covered it.

She opened the door, smiled as best she could.

Father Monroe worked his black hat through his fingers. "I, uh, I was with a parishoner for a very long time. I only now heard about what happened. Sharon, if there's anything I can do . . ."

She had known Father Monroe for a very long time, and she liked him. He didn't breathe fire and brimstone like some clerics; in fact, he was maybe a little too soft-spoken. But he had always been there for her, even when her cat died. She stood aside and he came in.

"I said a prayer," he said.

"Me, too," Sharon answered.

He looked at the bed almost longingly, like someone who was very tired. "Sit down, please, sit down," Sharon offered.

With a thin smile of thanks, he did as asked. He looked a little pale, she thought. Almost sickly. "Are you okay?" she asked.

"Oh, yes, just a little tired."

There was a moment of silence that made her uncomfortable. It was broken when Father Monroe said, "Are you . . . comfortable here?"

"Yes, yes I am."

Father Monroe looked around the room like a man who had lost something. Then he looked again at Sharon. "You're sure?"

"Father? Is there something . . . ?"

"No, no, of course not. It's just . . . it's just that when I came in I felt . . . anxious."

Sharon shrugged it off. "Yeah, I did, too. But with everything that's happened."

"Of course, of course."

He looked at her then as if he wanted to say something, some qualifier for his reaction, but he didn't. Instead he seemed to force a smile as he gently dropped his hand onto hers. "I'm here for you," he said. "To see to your spiritual needs. And Mrs. Matheson was gracious enough to allow me into her home at this late hour to do just that."

"Yes, she is nice."

"Maria, I think she said."

"Yes, Maria."

She wanted to tell him that she was very tired, that she appreciated his offer, but for now sleep would be even better than fortifying her spirit. (If she could sleep.) But she didn't say that, she couldn't. But Father Monroe saw it in her eyes anyway. He got up. "But there'll be time for that when you've rested."

"Oh, no I . . ."

"Yes, I know, you wouldn't hear of it. Well, you

111

always were very thoughtful."

She didn't argue and Father Monroe left. She closed the door behind him and went back to bed.

Some time later she heard another knock, not quite as soft as Father Monroe's.

"Sharon?"

Jerry? she thought. Now what the hell does he want?

"Sharon?"

"Hold on."

She got up, put on the borrowed red terrycloth bathrobe and opened the door. The lightless hallway offered only a large, dark form, inches away, which again startled her. She put her hand to her chest and caught her breath. "Christ, Jerry! You scared me," she whispered.

"I did? I'm sorry," he whispered back.

She just looked at him for a moment, then, "Do you know what time it is?"

"I know it's late. Listen, can I come in? I'd sure hate to wake up the family."

She hesitated only briefly. "Why not," she answered. "I can't sleep anyway."

She stepped aside, let him step past, then closed the door behind her.

"Let me get the light," she said.

"No, no, that's okay. I won't be long. I just wanted to see if you were comfortable."

"Reasonably so, I guess."

"The bed's okay?"

"Yeah, it's okay."

"Good. Listen, Sharon, I just wanted to tell you how sorry I am, how sorry we all are. So many horrible things happen around us and we, well, we become jaded, don't we? I mean we see so much of it on the tube and at the movies that we become desensitized."

That was, for the most part, true, but regardless of how many uniquely gruesome deaths Hollywood could supply to the public, she would never become desensitized to what she had found just inside her front door.

112

"I want you to know that in me you have a soul mate," he continued. "Someone who recognizes your inner pain and commiserates."

He seemed so understanding, so gentle.

"When you think about it, what more could a human being ask for?"

He didn't give her a chance to respond. "There's a candle over here, let me light it."

Sharon watched as he pulled a wooden match from his pocket, struck it on the radiator and lit the decorative candle on the nightstand.

"Cozy, don't you think?" he said with a smile, as flickering candlelight communicated throughout the room.

He sat at the head of the bed, near the nightstand and said, "Come here, Sharon, sit down next to me."

She wondered if perhaps he hadn't gotten his hair cut this evening. She hadn't seen him since she arrived, so he could've gone out for a while.

"Please, let's talk," he continued.

Sharon sat down next to him willingly, very much appreciating the soothing effect he had on her, so unlike the conflicting emotions she felt as he changed her tire.

"Good, very good," he said. "Tell me something, Sharon. You ever give a thought to what my brother might be doing?"

"Your brother? You mean, Harry?"

No answer.

Sharon smiled inwardly—what a strange question under equally strange circumstances. "Well, I really don't know him very well. I only knew him from school, like you."

"Been a long time, has it?"

"A very long time. Look, if it's all the same to you . . ."

"He's done pretty well for himself."

"So I've heard."

"And you know what else? He takes a joke as well as anyone. Good jokes, bad jokes. Isn't that right, Sharon?"

113

"Well, I don't know, I mean, how would I know?"

"But sometimes jokes get out of hand. And that's too bad."

Sensing an anxiety inducing turn to the conversation, she forced a light response. "A joke's a joke." Her following smile was as forced as her response.

"Well you know, that's true. A joke's a joke. Very profound, Sharon, very impressive. Look, I want you to do something for me."

"I don't know, it's awfully late."

"Won't take but a minute."

He was inordinately persuasive.

"Well, okay, if I can."

He opened a drawer in the nightstand and withdrew a pen and a piece of note paper. It was then, muffled by the closed door, that she again heard the quick, grating snore she had earlier. She had assumed it to be Jerry, but obviously she had guessed wrong.

Her thought died as he pushed the pen and note paper toward her.

"I've written a short letter, very brief. I'd like you to read it."

It seemed a strange request, but still she took it from him.

It had been written in a flowing, feminine hand, which, somewhat alarmingly, was very similar to her own. She leaned toward the candle and read. In the flickering light the words seemed to be moving.

Dear Mr. and Mrs. Matheson, and, of course, Tad.

Words cannot describe my appreciation to all of you for the hospitality you have extended me, but I find that I must suffer this loss silently and alone. I elected to leave in the middle of the night because . . .

She stopped reading and looked at him.

"I want you to sign it," he said simply.

114

"I'm sorry, you want me to sign this? I don't understand."

He smiled again. "Well, Sharon, it's really not awfully important whether you understand or not. What's important is that you sign this letter."

"Jerry, look . . ."

He cocked his head confusedly. "Jerry?" he said.

Her skin began to tingle as if a thousand millipedes were scampering over her. At the same time she noticed her cross on the nightstand. It pulsed with light. She smiled nervously. "Is this some kind of bad practical joke or what, because if it is . . ."

He reached out and stroked her cheek with a huge, cold hand. "A joke? Why certainly not, Sharon. I don't play jokes. Jokes are for children."

"Look, you'd better leave. I know this is your house and everything, but . . ."

Suddenly the muscles tensed on his face, which also seemed to drain of blood until it assumed the chalky white dullness of old pottery. "Sign the letter, Sharon. Sign it or I'll rip your tongue out before you can scream."

The room suddenly stank miserably, like an old, wet dying dog. She felt the gorge rise in her throat. She fought it back. But she couldn't fight the tears, nor the quivering of her chin—outward manifestations of fear that seemed to amuse Harry.

He waited for a moment, then pointed at a line at the bottom, where her name was neatly printed. "Right there," he said. "Sign it there."

"Please, don't do this . . ."

"Impressive forgery, don't you think. We got a hold of one of your letters, by we I mean Christine and myself. Christine forged this letter. The wording is my own, but the beautiful hand is hers. Excellent work, don't you think?"

No answer.

"Sign it, Sharon. My patience grows thin. And I'm not very nice once I've lost my patience."

115

Bleakly, remotely, Sharon wondered if he could hear her heart pounding against her ribcage. And somewhat less remotely she wondered just how much longer it would.

Tad Matheson offered a smile to the dark room. He was dreaming, and unlike other dreams of late, this dream was pleasant. Tomorrow evening, his mother said, he and his dad and Mr. Norville would be going into town. They were having some kind of festival. His mother said it was an annual event. His dad said it would be a great chance to take in some local color. (Which would help him with his book, Tad thought.) A contented sound worked out of him as he envisioned himself on a Tilt-A-Whirl, if they had one: him and his dad, their faces all pushed back, their hair blowing wildly, holding onto that safety bar for dear life.

While riding in the dream-sponsored Tilt-A-Whirl, he felt a sudden and almost overpowering need to go to the bathroom.

Chapter Twelve

THE PAST

Harry Matheson cranked the page from his Underwood. His character, a tall, bright, beautiful woman named Amelia, had been written into a ditch at night. Her pursuers, murderers equipped with infrared scanners, were closing fast. He read the scene for atmosphere and tension; his trademark. When he was done he sighed a deep, somewhat exasperated sigh, then let the page flutter to the floor and took a long swallow from a Coors Light. The scene had all the tension and atmosphere of working tile scrub. Maybe he had written too damn many of these scenes; maybe he was all dried up. Or maybe he was only tired. Twenty-two pages since five that morning had left his neck stiff and his thoughts unfocused. Perhaps he was expecting too much from himself. He took another long pull on the beer, forgetting how he had grimaced just seconds earlier as the warm, golden fluid flooded into his mouth. He grimaced again. Two six packs today. Christ, maybe he was becoming an alcoholic to boot! He got up, his joints noisily rejoicing, and went into the kitchen for no other reason than to be somewhere other than his study.

Thumbtacked to a cork bulletin board to the right of the sink was an advertising flyer he had found under a wiper the day before at the supermarket. He took a hard-boiled egg from the refrigerator and peeled it while he read the flyer. Bizarre, unique, captivating, imaginative, and not for everyone. This collection of superlatives started the flyer and, as its author had hoped, had caught his attention before he could crumble and toss it. But it hadn't been only the string of superlatives that had made him read further; it was the location of this festival that had caught and kept his attention. Just forty minutes south along Route 5, the flyer continued. Tarot cards, experts on the afterlife and reincarnation who will mystify and fascinate you. Let us tell you of things you have only sensed, things that are more real than you ever thought possible. You *will* be astounded. And for the kiddies, monsters galore—werewolves, vampires, even aliens long since escaped from their Air Force captors in the New Mexican desert (yes, the Roswell aliens). At the bottom, in bold letters, were the words, ADMISSION FREE, JUST BRING YOUR IMAGINATION. JUNE 22 to JUNE 25th.

Harry tugged the flyer down and looked at it. The wrestling crowd would love this, he thought. He could imagine a bunch of them with National Enquirers folded into their back pockets, wandering through this supposedly preternatural festival, ohhs and ahhs rising from every corner as past lives were exposed and monsters in not very realistic costumes did their best to frighten the kiddies. ADMISSION FREE, JUST BRING YOUR IMAGINATION. Yeah, sure, imagination. His body suddenly tensed as the old, grievous injury came back to him. Bastards! he thought. Motherfucking bastards! He smashed the egg on the counter and went into the living room. It was June 21st. Tomorrow was the 15th anniversary of That Night.

THE PRESENT

Jerry Matheson poured a line of honey into his coffee and sat down at the kitchen table. At first he didn't see the note leaning against the salt and pepper shakers; when he did, his heart raced. Maria was upstairs, as was Tad. One of them was running water into the sink. He put on his glasses and picked up the note.

Dear Mr. and Mrs. Matheson, and, of course, Tad.
 Words cannot describe my appreciation to all of you for the hospitality you have extended me, but I find that I must suffer this loss silently and alone. I elected to leave in the middle of the night because I didn't want to disturb you. Someday I hope I'll be able to return your kindness. Please, pray for Lenny and me.

Your new and good friend,
Sharon Griffin

Jerry got up and looked out the window. He had driven her car here the night before and parked it behind his own. It was gone. And so, obviously, was she.

Maria came into the room, startling him.

"I knocked on Sharon's door," she said, "but she didn't answer. Guess she didn't get to sleep till late."

"She left," Jerry said almost casually.

Confusion mapped Maria's face. "She what?"

"She left. She wrote that note there on the table and left."

Maria snatched up the note and read it quickly. "Oh, hell, first mother and now this!"

Jerry only sipped his coffee, which, Maria thought, was equally odd. He should have been just as surprised as she. "You didn't say something to her, did you?" she asked.

Jerry turned on her. "Say something to her? What the hell are you talking about?"

"C'mon, Jerry! You obviously didn't want her here. Her or Mother!"

Jerry turned his back to her again. "That's not true," he said, his tone too light, too conversational.

119

Maria, wondering if she should try to contact her, to straighten things out, didn't respond. Jerry, obviously, had said or done something. And Sharon, the poor, poor woman, was too much of a lady . . .

"Mrs. Griffin's gone," Tad announced from the doorway.

Maria and Jerry looked at each other, then at their son. "But how did you know that?" Maria asked.

"I saw her leave, with you, Dad. Last night."

THE PAST

Why the hell am I doing this? Harry thought. Because I need to exorcise an old demon? That seemed logical. But if that were true, he'd have to see it through to the end. He'd have to go up to that house and say to the owner, "Look, when I was a kid, something horrible happened to me, and it happened here. What I'd like to do is this . . ." Right, Harry thought. That'll go over great! But although that plan had viability, he would have to test the water first. He couldn't simply confront his demon, he'd have to circle its lair for a while, then, and if he could summon the courage . . .

The headlights punched through the darkness as the car pressed southward, toward Naples Falls. Harry drove slowly; he was in deer country now. During the day you could see tens of them gathering near the edges of surrounding forests. His eyes flicked from right to left as he attempted to see a headlight-panicked deer before it darted in front of him. He had planned to leave earlier, but his character, Amelia, still wouldn't reveal herself and then he had lost track of time, which was about normal when he became engrossed in his work. As he rounded a sweeping curve, he passed a handwritten sign that said, NAPLES FALLS FESTIVAL—STRAIGHT AHEAD, 2 MILES.

The first thing he saw, once he passed The House and the town cemetery that flanked it, which more or less acted as the town's northern edge, was a banner slung over the road.

NAPLES FALLS WELCOMES YOU
TO IT'S ANNUAL TOWN FESTIVAL
Alcoholic beverages not allowed.

The careless punctuation made Harry smile, and as the banner flapped noisily in a rising wind, he smiled again as the word "not," between "beverages" and "allowed," folded out of sight. Make up your minds, he thought. Humor, for Harry, had always been a good port in a storm.

Just as he remembered, tents of varying shapes and sizes, illuminated by long rows of hundred-watt bulbs strung along tall, wooden poles, lined the main drag. The night sky, clear and starlit, was just an oily blackness beyond the confusion of lights.

He drove slowly, less than five miles an hour, but not out of choice; traffic, inexplicably, was very heavy. Finding a place to park was not going to be easy.

There was a definite carnival atmosphere here. The smell of festival foods was almost cloying in the humid summer air, and balloons of all colors were in buoyant abundance, each a floating advertisement for THE NAPLES FALLS FESTIVAL.

He passed tents of all sizes that did, indeed, offer everything from palm reading to zodiac charting, but every now and then he caught flashes of bright color. A closer look revealed that between tents, and sometimes behind, merchants were selling paintings that depicted vile and painful death, everything from drowning to beheading to impaling, all done by creatures hideous beyond belief. A few paintings looked very much like those he remembered seeing so many years ago. Their

121

horrifically explicit subject matter had been enough to render them unforgettable.

He watched the milling crowd, not one person in particular, just a forest of legs and arms and bobbing balloons. His attention, however, was drawn to a small boy who was tightly clutching his mother's hand and who had stopped to stare at him. Seconds later his mother turned and, instead of scolding him, simply stared along with him. And that, Harry thought, was mildly disconcerting.

He opted to smile and wave casually. No response.

"Any parking places up there?" he yelled above the din, which, he knew, was a pretty lame question. Strangely enough, he felt better after he had spoken to them. But now both mother and son had fixed a tight, hard, unblinking gaze upon him. And others, suddenly, were doing the same: an old man in blue overalls and straw hat, a middle-aged man in black walking shorts, black socks and a madras shirt, two twin girls holding hands. Harry smiled at each of them separately then collectively, but still they only stared, or at least, seemed to be. But why? he wondered. Someone write something on the car? My hair turn blue? It was then when he remembered where he was; in a moving car. He looked back at the road just as his bumper touched the bumper of a Dodge Daytona ahead of him. The driver peered into his rearview mirror and saluted him highway style. Harry smiled apologetically and the incident died as both men realized they were going too slow to cause any damage.

He turned his attention back to the woman and the others, but by now each, it seemed, had turned their attention to other matters entirely, their faces no longer displaying the coldness—the unreserved hatred—each had displayed just seconds earlier. Had he imagined the incident? There was that possibility. But why? He looked around him again, at the crowd, the tents, the paintings;

especially the paintings. Why? he thought. Power of suggestion? Or maybe the looming presence of old demons.

THE PRESENT

"That can't be, son," Jerry said. "The last I saw of Sharon, Mrs. Griffin, was when I told her goodnight, right after I tucked you in."

Tad was perplexed. Last night, as he left the bathroom after having been rudely awakened by a full bladder, he had seen Sharon Griffin walking down the stairs followed by a man he thought was his father. But now, he realized, that wasn't possible. His dad wouldn't lie about a thing like that.

"Oh," he said simply.

"You must have been dreaming," Jerry said.

That, Tad allowed, made sense, although he *had* come to know the difference between dreams and reality. But maybe when you got older you dreamed differently. He thought about that. As he saw Mrs. Griffin leave with a person who he thought was his dad, he only shrugged and went back to bed. He hadn't felt uncomfortable or scared, like in a nightmare, so if he had been dreaming a new type of dream, it was okay.

"Yeah, Dad," he said, "that must be it. But she is gone, right?"

"That's right. She left this note." Jerry picked it up and handed it to his son, who read it without speaking.

Without thinking about what he was saying, Tad said, "You didn't say nothin' to her, did you, Dad?"

"What is this, a conspiracy?" Jerry said, his tone suggesting humor, not the anger Maria expected.

Tad realized instantly that he had spoken out of turn. "Sorry, Dad," he quietly added. "You just looked like you didn't like her or something."

123

"Son, what's to like or dislike? I barely know her."

"But you talked about high school with her."

"Okay, so I knew her in high school, but only as someone to say hello to in the halls. You know people like that, don't you, son?"

"I guess."

By now Maria had come to the conclusion that Jerry hadn't wanted Sharon Griffin here at all. Normally he would have exploded at his son's quickly blurted question, but he had responded almost defensively.

"Look," Jerry said, "let's have some breakfast. I've got a very important chapter to work on today, but later we'll all go into town and see what this Naples Falls Festival is all about, okay?"

The festival—Tad had all but forgotten about it, what with his new friend Sharon just leaving like that.

"Remember now, son," Jerry continued. "I don't think they have any rides. It's not that kind of festival."

"What kind of festival is it then, Dad?"

Jerry had been a camp counselor during the summer of 1970, the one year the Mathesons had lived in Naples Falls. Beyond what Walker Norville had told them, he knew nothing.

"Well, I guess we'll all find out, won't we?" he said.

THE PAST—JUNE 22ND

By the time Harry got to the other side of the festival, he realized he wouldn't find a parking place within a mile. But he did remember a few spots on the other side of the cemetery.

He turned around, a maneuver that once again raised a few highway salutes, fell in line and, a few minutes later, passed the cemetery again. There were NO PARKING signs on the road in front of the cemetery, but he did manage to find a spot further on, where the stars were visible and the nearby hills rose like black ocean swells against a dark purple sky—where the festival was but a weak flush of light, a campfire in a beast infested forest.

On his way to the festival, he passed a few people heading back to their cars. He barely noticed them, his thoughts filled with the past and the house that was drawing ever closer.

As he approached the northern end of the cemetery he finally did see the house, only barely visible. And it was also then, precisely then, that he sensed a fine thread of apprehension. No, he thought, not apprehension. Anxiety. Anxiety was a much more accurate word. Fear might even suffice. He had felt it before, back then. Even blindfolded. He wondered if he should skirt the demon's lair, test the water, as he had planned, or suck it in and just do it. He drew in a deep breath. He was here, as was his courage. Later, after he'd walked around the festival, it might not be. If he didn't do it now . . . well, if he didn't do it now he might be forever relegated to the horror story, the telling and retelling of That Night in a myriad of versions. That Night exorcised would leave him a choice, the choice of the real novelist. Then he could finally write what he really wanted to write, not something dictated by one night of agonizing terror.

Given this final motivation, Harry started up the driveway toward the house. As he did, his anxiety expanded and became full blown, gut-wrenching fear, much as he expected.

There were no lights on inside the house but on the porch, dully lit by a low-wattage bulb that bathed the area in a muddy yellow glow, he saw the top of a person's head. A closer inspection revealed the head to be very small, the hair long yet thin. The head moved slowly back and forth, as if the person were seated in a rocking chair. His first thought, which, in a normal person would have prompted a wave of pity, was of a cancerous child balding from chemotherapy. Although surprised to discover that someone lived here, he was also mildly relieved.

He stepped closer and as he did, he heard, "Festivolly,

125

Festivolly. Welcome to festivolly!"

The words smacked onto his ears like tin being pulled over a bed of rusty nails and stopped him just as surely as if the earth had suddenly yawned open before him.

It was then when the person seated in the rocker stood and stepped closer to the screen. Harry's heart thumped once, twice, three times. Looking down at him was a very short old woman, her features only barely visible in the soft, muddy yellow glow. But even in that meager light Harry saw that her features were grotesquely huge, almost comical, as if she had stepped behind a huge magnifying glass. All Harry could see of her was her upper torso, backlit yellow, her stubby arms splayed to the side. She did, however, appear to be smiling.

"Hello," Harry said.

A small, cackling chuckle filled the air. Harry backed up slightly.

"I'm sorry if I disturbed you," Harry added. "I don't know why I came up here . . . No, that's wrong. I do know why I came up here."

When she spoke it seemed that her lips did not move, a condition Harry attributed to the scarcity of light, "People don't usually come up here at night," she said. "They are afraid. They always leave when I "welcome" them. They don't know what makes them afraid. That's why they are afraid."

Harry was fascinated. "Do you know what makes them afraid?"

Again that thick, cackling chuckle. "You would not believe me if I told you."

Harry felt challenged. He regained the step he had lost earlier. And this was too close, too wild a shot in the dark . . . "If I come up there, on the porch, will you tell me?"

This time she laughed, a laugh that was old and coarse, the sound of rats scurrying along the floor of a cave. Harry winced at it. The laughing stopped.

"You are brave," she said. "Why is that?"

"Let's just say I'm familiar with the fear this house has to offer."

A pause, then, "familiarity with fears does not necessarily make one less afraid. Surely the opposite is true."

Harry silently agreed, but he was also puzzled. He had made reference to foreknowledge of this house and she had shown no interest whatsoever.

"Are you going to tell me?" Harry asked.

"What makes them afraid?"

"Yes."

"I think not."

Harry hadn't expected that answer. "I'll pay you," he said.

"If I tell you, you will know and that is not good. Things could happen that you may not want to happen. Things that could have happened to you before and did not."

"Then you know what happened to me?"

The woman regarded him for what seemed an eternity before she said, "Yes. I was told."

"Told? By who? By those bastards . . ."

"No. Not by them."

"But they were the only ones . . ."

"No. That is not true."

That night flashed through Harry's mind. There were others, yes, but certainly they were only part of the joke, certainly they couldn't have been anything but. He had a wild, impatient thought. What if the joke had somehow extended itself; what if they saw him—the boy, his mother . . . the others. What if they knew and they came back—tonight—expecting him to be here, at the very same house where it had happened.

Harry smiled a confident smile. "You're a plant, right? Those motherfucking bastards arranged this, didn't they? They put the flyer on my windshield . . . They fucking knew!"

She was unfazed. "Come up," she said. "Come up and

127

hear of things you may not want to know. Come up and talk to Greta. Come up Mr. Writer. Let us talk of revenge."

That word seemed huge to Harry. It had always—always—been close at hand, especially when he thought of That Night; and now it was being spoken collaboratively. But how—and why—would she want to help him gain revenge? Again he suspected a conspiracy.

"Sure, come up and talk about revenge. Right. And have it happen all over again? What do you think I am, a fool?"

"Three of them are still here, Mr. Writer. In this town."

Harry was struck by the extent of her knowledge. But then, co-conspirators had to know each other.

"And you're gonna tell me how I can get my revenge, right? Well, I'll tell you, revenge has some appeal, sure, but I came here to rid myself of that night, to prepare myself for a better future."

She laughed. "You are afraid after all," she said. "Just like any tourist who happens to wander into this yard, you are afraid. I mistook you to be something you are not. You can go now."

Still chuckling, she settled back into her rocker.

Harry, confused and afraid, but most of all, concerned about his overwhelming need for revenge, walked up the driveway and stepped onto the porch.

Chapter Thirteen

Guy Henry pulled into the driveway and shut off the engine. It was well past dinnertime, but if he got this chore done he could call it quits for the day. By then he would have questioned each of the five new arrivals, those who had moved into town over the last six months or so.

He had saved the Matheson's for last because she, Mrs. Matheson, Maria, he remembered, had done Sharon an act of kindness; certainly not the actions of someone culpable in a murder case. He hadn't as yet met her husband, but if he were somehow involved—if he was, in fact, an evil person given to murderous inclination—that evil, Guy thought, might be reflected in those with whom he lived. He saw no evil reflected in Tad and Maria Matheson, just the opposite.

The other four families new to town had all been sufficiently mortified at the events. He had chosen not to inform them of the ghastly details, murder itself was enough. Only one, the Bowman's, who had moved into a farmhouse on the outskirts of town, inquired about suspects. There were none, of course, it was still too early in the investigation, but given time he would bring the perpetrator to justice, of that he was sure, despite the fact that the case was being officially handled by the state police—more precisely, a large, tall, and overbearing cop named Amans. That was a fact he would mention only if asked, and he hadn't been asked yet. Sure, Amans had been respectful and he had applied all the proper professional courtesies, telling him something about how his input would be greatly appreciated, but that the state police were better prepared, and staffed, to handle an investigation of this magnitude. But Guy Henry knew when he'd been put in his place and he didn't at all like it. His "input" would be the solving of these heinous crimes. Never can put too much meat in a stew, he thought. He smiled at his witticism and walked up the stone pathway to the front steps. As he did, he recalled that, until about five years ago, this house had been empty for years. And until now he had only seen it from the road. He stepped onto the porch and experienced a variety of physical reactions that, if felt by a prospective buyer, might explain just why it had remained empty for so long. Before he could ring the doorbell he felt his throat constrict. At the same time his skin became cool and dry. Finally, he felt his testicles shrivel like slowly collapsing balloons. He forced another smile and thought, Christ, even the welcome wagon would avoid this place. Like Harry Matheson, Guy Henry also found some comfort in humor.

He rang the doorbell. As he waited, his gaze drifted toward town, toward the odd collection of tents that marked the festival. He had made his very first contribution to the festival this year: a clay rendering of a gargoyle, the best work he had ever done. He had worked on it with a sense of purpose that had not marked any of his previous work. Thinking about it now, however, he wondered mightily about the subject matter and the fact that the work had been actually inspired, as if modeled by hands far more talented than his own. Well now, that's pretty crazy, he thought. He swiped a line of sudden sweat from his forehead and then nervously ran the brim of his hat through his fingers. The door opened.

"Hello, sheriff," Maria said. She had half expected him.

"Mrs. Matheson, I, uh. I'm touching bases . . . is your husband home?"

Maria regarded him with growing suspicion. Why would he want to speak with Jerry? "Yes, he is, but . . . ?"

"Routine," Guy said, sensing her momentary discomfort. It was the first time he had used the word "routine" and it made him feel somewhat more like a cop and not a small town's babysitter.

Maria pushed open the screen. "Come on in. Look, maybe you should know, Sharon's not here. She left."

Guy Henry was nonplussed. "Where'd she go?"

"Home, I guess. I mean back to Rochester."

"Why would she do that?"

"She left a note. Would you like to see it?"

"Yes, yes I would."

Guy Henry stepped past her into the living room. Across the road, through the picture window, he saw Walker Norville.

While Maria was gone, Jerry entered the living room. He looked at the sheriff for a moment and said, "You're here about Mrs. Griffin, aren't you."

"Well, no, not originally . . ."

"Then why are you here?" Jerry asked.

"To see you, Mr. Matheson. First things first though. Your wife tells me Sharon, that is, Mrs. Griffin, left last night."

Beyond the sheriff, and through the picture window, Jerry noticed Walker Norville strolling up the driveway. "Well, yes, she did, but I guess I can't blame her," he said, almost as an aside, eyes averted.

"Oh?"

Jerry looked at the sheriff, realizing that perhaps he had spoken too quickly. He smiled too broadly. "Let me explain."

"I'd appreciate that."

Intentionally, Guy Henry had assumed an official air. Jerry had precipitated it, not by his demeanor but simply by insinuation; something had happened here that would make a guest uncomfortable, uncomfortable enough to make them leave in the middle of the night.

Maria came into the living room, the note in her hand. Guy Henry took it from her. When he was done reading he scratched a spread of poison ivy on his arm, contracted while hunting, and looked at Jerry. "You were going to explain why you thought she left."

Jerry looked at Maria, she at him, and cleared his throat. "My mother-in-law was here yesterday. We, uh, we had a misunderstanding for which I take full blame. I think it made Mrs. Griffin uncomfortable."

"What kind of 'misunderstanding'? I mean you'd really have to get into it . . ."

"Look, sheriff, it was nothing. We just don't get along, that's all. Never have and probably never will."

"And you think Mrs. Griffin left because you don't get along with your mother-in-law?" His question was more a cementing of fact than a question, although Jerry did detect a humorous intonation.

"Yes, I do."

Guy Henry, who, in the course of his preparatory studies for the job, had read a few books on body language, applied that knowledge now. He looked closely at Jerry Matheson, blatantly so, and read this: *He's lying. Plain as a cheese pizza, he's lying.* It was in Jerry's eyes that he detected this falsehood, those filmy windows to the soul. Jerry Matheson's eyes were shifty, definitely shifty. They avoided his just as surely as if he were looking at blinding twin suns. Guy even had the urge to snap his fingers and say, "Over here, pal, over here." But he didn't. That would only alert him. No, there was something going on here and he wasn't going to find out what without subtlety.

The doorbell rang, once, not twice, and out of the corner of his eye, Guy Henry saw Tad Matheson answer

132

the side door. Seconds later Walker Norville stepped into the kitchen, then, seeing Guy in the living room, came in and nodded to him. They had known each other for a long while, but only casually. And his daughter's missing person's case was still active.

"Mr. Norville," Guy said.

"Sheriff."

The sheriff turned his attention to Maria. "Look, can I keep this note?"

"I don't see why not. Do you think it's important?"

"I don't know, but we have had two murders in Naples Falls in a very short period of time. And now this."

"What do you mean, 'now this?'" Jerry said.

Jerry, Guy noticed, looked straight and hard at him. That, Guy thought, was just as incriminating as avoidance.

"This strange behavior on the part of Mrs. Griffin."

Jerry couldn't help but smile. "Strange behavior, she wants to be alone—is that so strange? I mean her husband's been brutally murdered . . . !"

"I'm sorry, Mr. Matheson," Guy said, "but has someone talked to you about Len Griffin's murder? I only ask because you did use the word brutal, and not all murders are brutal."

Jerry glanced at Maria, then back at Guy Henry. "Sheriff, murder is brutal, regardless, I mean the taking of a live . . . any life, human or otherwise . . . !"

Guy Henry wouldn't let him finish. "You're right. I'm sorry."

"No need to apologize."

"Appreciated. Now where were we. Oh yes. Mrs. Griffin's strange behavior . . ."

"In your opinion."

"That's right, sir, in my opinion."

"Why don't you just call her?" Jerry asked.

"Thank you, Mr. Matheson, but I know how to do my job."

"Speaking of which, two murders seem like something

133

the state police might look into, not a town sheriff."

Guy wondered when he'd get around to that. "The state police are investigating, but this is my town and they have asked for my assistance."

Jerry gave in slightly. "Of course. I didn't mean to imply anything."

"I understand. If I were you I'd guess I'd want to know what was being done and if my family was in any danger."

"Are they?"

"Sir?"

"In any danger."

"Not if you keep your doors locked and your alert level raised a few notches."

Jerry was mildly impressed by his response. At least he hadn't lied. At least he hadn't wildly underestimated his intelligence by suggesting that everything was under control.

"Will you keep us informed?" Jerry asked.

"Of course. And will you keep your doors locked?"

"Count on it."

On the way to his patrol car, Guy Henry thought: *Informed? I'll do better than that, pal. Much better.*

Jerry watched the patrol car pull away and silently asked that he be saved from small-minded small town sheriffs.

Some minutes later, while jet contrails scarred the deep red western sky, the Mathesons and Walker Norville left the house. The top quarter of the sun was just now nestling into the horizon. When it did, the festival would begin.

AT THE FESTIVAL

Maria held Tad's right hand, Jerry his left. As they strolled around the festival, Maria gripped her son's hand like someone moving through a crowd of thieves with an exposed wad of twenties.

134

"Mom! You're hurting me!" Tad said. She apologized and loosened her grip, but not for very long.

Most aptly put, the atmosphere was disarmingly bizarre, the landscape dotted by at least a hundred tents, all white or gray or gray-white, depending on age, some ornamented by balloons, some by Chinese lanterns, a few displaying flags of unknown origin. These tents lined the street and even spilled onto the flowing green lawns of the dark, long-since vacated high school. Old people sat in lawn chairs and Adirondack chairs and collected fares at a few, but most people simply displayed a sign and a spread of flapped-back canvas like a bat's wing. Scores of tourists and locals had worn undulating paths into the grass. The greatest degree of wear marked the most popular spots.

There were games of chance, but even these suggested something macabre, like Naples Falls' version of flip the frog onto a lily pad—the frog had been replaced by a bloodied corpse and the lily pad had become a miniature casket. People crushed three deep to play.

Some people were in costume: werewolves, Franken-stein, green-skinned aliens. Norman Bates grinned madly; a young couple costumed as caped, red-eyed vampires strode by (although their malevolence seemed questionable as they turned to reveal that sodas—not necks—were the objects of their desire).

"Gets worse every year," Walker confided. "Whole town gets into it now it seems. Everyone's done something, some artsy-fartsy little thing." He nodded toward a collection of statuary on a large wood table with folding legs. To a piece, the statuary depicted something that was either dead, could easily cause death or something that spent time in both worlds: a large, leering, horned devil filled that last need. On the surface, it all seemed to be good, clean fun, but there were small pockets of "artsy-fartsy" items that went a little further than that. After Walker took Tad for a hot dog and Jerry wandered off, Maria found just such an

135

item—a clay rendering that depicted a man standing over a woman. At first glance the piece seemed innocuous enough, but when she picked it up and turned it sideways she saw that not only was the man engaged in an act of rape, but that rape—committed with a hideously long and thick penis—was being accomplished through the woman's stomach. That alone caused a wave of nausea to wash over her, but when she further realized that the woman was smiling, she dropped the piece instantly. The man's head broke off as it hit plywood flooring and immediately an old, leatherfaced woman pushed herself out of her folding lawn chair and walked slowly over. "That'll be twelve fifty, deary," she said. "You break it, you bought it."

Maria fumbled open her purse and fished around in her wallet until she found two fives and two ones. She pushed the money out in front of her and left as soon as the old woman snapped it up. The woman, seemingly unperturbed about the fact that Maria was fifty cents short, pocketed the money and reclaimed her chair.

Within seconds the broken piece was scooped up by a wide-eyed, tow-haired boy of about twelve. Winks were exchanged before the boy ran off to some private place to further appraise his prize.

Maria found her son at a hot dog stand just down from the Silver Spoon, safe haven, she thought, from festival wierdness. It wasn't. Ketchup was dispensed from anatomically correct heart-shaped plastic containers. A squeeze of the container created a sound that very nicely mimicked a heartbeat.

"Least the hot dog's good," Tad said, chomping down.

They sat at a picnic table and watched the pre-halloween-type crowd parade by.

Milt Langtree, self-described agent and treasurer for a group of artists whose paintings were being displayed behind a Tarot card tent, had seen it before. Now he

136

began to wonder about wild horses, whether even they could pull this guy away.

Earlier, before the man had become so engrossed in the painting, they had struck up a conversation about how nicely detailed and strangely hypnotic these paintings were, a fact that manifested itself in the way that the man slowly, yet surely, had become drawn to one painting in particular. A conversation that ended as Milt said, "Strange stuff, but these tourists snap it right up, yes sir, they reach down deep . . ." The painting depicted a Norman Rockwell type family gathered around the dinner table. Surrounding them was a host of hideous, multi-colored, long-toothed pellucid demons, who obviously wished to partake of their own feast. The painting often caused the reaction Milt was now witnessing, a reaction that often preceded descriptions like "vile" or "extremely perverse," or even, "makes me wanta throw up." But Milt was not a mind reader. Milt did not see the painting's participants change to become Jerry's family; Tad, Maria, Loretta. Milt did not see the assembled demons disappear only to be replaced by Jerry himself, a huge, cloaking version of himself. Milt did not see necks being torn open by powerfully muscled hands, vital organs being cast randomly about the nicely decorated dining room, or arms and legs being ripped from torsos and then thrown into a sickening, oozing pile. Milt did not see these things. Milt only saw the smile on the man's face, which did give him the shudders and which was, of itself, strange enough.

Chapter Fourteen

THE PAST

For the longest time the old woman simply rocked, neither fast nor slow, just a steady, rhythmic, mesmerizing motion. During that time, Harry studied her. She could, Harry thought, either be very old or middle-aged. But for some reason, he guessed that daylight might reveal a woman close to eighty, maybe even older. Her age was difficult to determine because of the soft, yellow light, around which flew a dozen or so appropriately tiny insects; the larger the wattage, the larger the insect.

Harry stood near the door, hands in pockets. Every now and again he glanced toward the cemetery to his front and watched as the wind soughed through the dark branches of the huge, centered tree, causing those branches to wave gently, like some giant prehistoric bird. Above that tree he saw a few of the more brilliant stars, those capable of competing with the lights of the festival. And through the branches of the tree he also saw a rising quarter moon, but only snatches of it as branches swayed unpredictably in obedience to the vagaries of the wind.

When the old woman finally spoke, her voice was distant, as if Harry were hearing it from semiconsciousness. Then he realized that although she spoke in what sounded like German, he could understand every word.

"We will be traveling soon."

"We?" Harry said.

"Yes. We. My immortals. Vampires, if you wish."

She hesitated then, allowing Harry time to either digest what she had said, or respond to it, or both.

Harry did neither. He felt suddenly silly, like a schoolboy who's accepted a double dare. He had come up here at the beck and call of exorcism, that and the mystical quality of the setting, the supernatural patina that had, despite his previous experience, very easily captured his imagination. But now, after this little woman made casual reference to beings that, to any sane person, were only myth and conjecture, Harry felt somewhat used, even violated. Like he had been That Night.

"Bullshit!" he said.

She could only smile, very much as if she had expected such a response.

"Where do you keep these vampires? Over there?" Harry said and gestured loosely toward the cemetery.

Again she spoke, and again her first few words started as German and then were magically transformed into English. Harry looked at her closely, as closely as possible given the soft lighting. Could it be possible that her lips, as had been earlier intimated, were *not* moving when she spoke?

"I keep them no where. I cannot keep them. They are beings of mist and fog, beings that exist yet do not exist, beings that live outside the world of reality, that are not confined to laws of physics. You have seen them, Mr. Writer. Long ago."

Harry's muscles became rigid as she made reference to That Night and to the beings that, even now, Harry thought had been simply co-conspirators, albeit very convincing co-conspirators.

She slowly nodded. "Yes, they are real. They exist and

139

have existed for countless thousands of years. But there are some, like mine, who need . . . guidance. Oh, do not misinterpret what I have said, they are still immensely capable of inducing any human to their will, but they are comfortable being guided."

Harry's interest was, by now, piqued. If nothing else, this old woman was entertaining.

"I guess I find that difficult to comprehend. What you describe, a mindless army of vampires, almost zombielike beings, is certainly not what one envisions when one hears the word "vampire." I've always imagined vampires to be all-powerful, the evil end-all."

She inclined her head slightly, a bemused look on her face. "Imagination, Mr. Writer, I should think that you would have that in great abundance." She seemed immensely happy to be in control of this conversation, as Harry reluctantly admitted to himself she was.

Almost flippantly, Harry said, "Then what you're saying is, that because of their vast number, some have to be followers and some have to be leaders. Right?"

"Exactly."

"Then what are yours? Charlie Mansons or boy scouts?"

A tone of amusement and disbelief had again snuck into Harry's voice. But still, she was unfazed.

"Unfortunately, boy scouts."

"Alas, so many followers, so few true leaders," Harry said almost mockingly.

Again she inclined her head toward him. "What are you, Mr. Writer? Follower or leader? And there is the question of your revenge."

She had lingered on the word "revenge," thereby expanding its significance. But this was still only a well disguised joke, a huge and admittedly frightening practical joke. He was no closer to revenge than he was to the nearest star. And would he even take revenge if it were offered? He looked at the woman, at her sinister smile, at her huge, gruesome features. He thought of an

140

enormous squatting toad and took mental notes of it all, so that he could later transfer what he saw to paper.

"They're in there somewhere, aren't they? All of them, Lenny and Tom and Sharon, all of them, having one great time at my expense."

"Go in, find out."

Harry couldn't help himself. He laughed out loud, partly because he still found humor in this situation and partly to allay a strange, festering fear.

She rose and opened the door to the living room. "It takes but a moment and lasts an eternity," she said.

And although she had spoken softly, Harry heard each word clearly, even through his own raucous laughter.

His laughter abated slowly, but it did abate. He looked into her huge eyes, eyes that were overly bright, overly reflective. He felt his blood course through him, icy cold and ready to violate its constricting veins and arteries. His heart strained against his ribcage like a caged animal, and he lost his spit, all because he was now ascribing some potential for truth to the old woman's claims.

He looked into the dark living room, and a numbness shot through him. Was he staring into his own tomb? A snarling deja vu crawled through him, even though he hadn't seen this part of the house That Night. It was also then when he detected movement in the doorway to the living room, just to his right. His skin tingled and he briefly saw a tall, thin person step out of sight into a pitch-black room.

Harry stared into that room, positive that the person he had briefly seen now stood in there, watching him.

"They're waiting," said the old woman. "They're waiting for a leader. For you, Mr. Writer. Go in, follow them to your reward, to your revenge. If you are not afraid."

But he *was* afraid, as afraid as he could ever remember being, a fear that matched the fear he had known That Night, for now he was reliving that night, despite the fact that now he was unbound, free to do as he pleased.

"Follow them, Mr. Writer," she said, whispering now. "They are inside, just inside. Waiting."

Her voice had a metronomic, hypnotic quality. Harry looked into that dark side room, toward the person—the thing—that was there and was not there, and he envisioned a powerful and just revenge, a revenge that he had not allowed himself the luxury to even dream about. He felt great, overwhelming pleasure at this vision, at the viewing of their pain.

The old woman chuckled as if she were privy to that vision.

Harry turned to her, smiled. "I'm going to go in there, old woman. I'm going to rid myself of an old demon and I'm going to quiet that damnable laugh of yours at the same time."

And so it was that Harry still clung to his disbelief, a disbelief that even now was quickly weakening. He stepped inside and the old woman shut the door softly behind him.

Although he was here in the same house where he had been tormented fifteen years earlier, Harry felt his anxiety subside. He had expected a putrid stench, something to parallel his experiences with the old woman. But there was no stench. And he had also expected to see someone—something—standing in the room to the right. He saw no one. He stepped closer to the door that led out of the long, wide living room and stifled an urge to strike a match or turn on a light. He was going to do this right. He had endured That Night in relative darkness, he would endure this one the same way.

He stepped into the room to the right of the living room and ran his hand along the wall to his right, finding an empty bookcase. He squinted. The whole room was one large bookcase. To his left was the dining room, beyond it, the kitchen. He stepped toward the dining room. But there was something else happening now. With each step he noticed that the smell of the house had changed, almost subliminally, as if he were drawing steadily closer to something decaying yet confined, aching to be unconfined. He stopped. Nothing in decay ached for anything. And anything in the process of decay was certainly not alive. Perhaps the woman had left something out overnight, something that would spoil. That sane solution, that complemented his own sense of logic, served him well. He stepped into the dining room. From here, and through the large bay window, he could see the side yard. In the darkness he thought he saw a deer, at least the bright, reflective eyes; his conclusion was based on the height of the eyes. It was then, looking into the eyes of a nocturnal something which may or may not have been a deer, that Harry remembered That Night in magnificent, jarring detail.

Kidnapped. Harry Matheson thought about that word—which also heightened the fear that gnawed at his belly. Undeniably, he, Harry Matheson, barely eighteen, tall and lanky, his face thin enough to render normal-size features large, had been kidnapped. He leaned against a slick, lichen-encrusted wall and flexed his muscles in a futile attempt to loosen the ropes that bound his hands and feet. He looked toward the cellar door. Torches burned on either side, the flames easily a foot tall. He surveyed his prison. He was in a corner directly in line with the wooden stairs. The basement itself was huge, forty by eighty, he guessed. Ten torches—he counted them, had been placed every ten feet or so on the walls of the basement, more than enough light to detail each ceiling dangled web and whether or not its owner was home. How the torches were affixed, he couldn't tell. There were no windows, and standing up straight too quickly wouldn't be wise—the ceiling was about five feet from the earthen floor.

His captors had taken him by surprise near the school and then forced him into the back of a van. Then, and before he could even scream, they had gagged and blindfolded him. He remembered the gag covering his nose as well as his mouth, making him wonder if they weren't going to kill him. But even then he couldn't help but wonder why. What had he done to them? But if they were going to kill him, why had they blindfolded him? Within seconds he heard one of them say, "Christ, be careful—you wanta kill him?" His eyes grew large as he tried to suck air through the gag, his lungs beginning to ache. "What are you talking about," another one said.

"The gag, asshole, you got the gag around his nose, too!"

"Shit!" came a quick response.

Instantly, the gag was pulled down from his nose, initiating a tremendous gasp for air, which also drew a chuckle from one of them, one of the girls.

"Albert Fucking Einstein, we got us Albert Fucking Einstein," said a boy, the driver, Harry thought.

Laughter. The sensation of speed.

"You're just jealous, Tommy." A girl whispered. "You're lucky if you pull a C+ in gym."

More laughter.

Tommy. He catalogued the name.

"Keep it cool, Sharon. You want him to hear us? No names!"

The same girl, even softer now. "Then why'd you say my name, asshole?"

No answer.

Another girl: "I think he's kinda cute."

Another boy: "You would."

The same girl: "His brother's cuter, though."

Tommy. Loudly: "Yeah, asshole. Why can't you be like your brother? Least he don't beat everyone over the head with how fucking smart he is. Christ, how the hell can twins be so goddamned different? Maybe you better take lessons from your brother."

The same girl: "His brother's got nice buns, too. I love to watch him run up and down the basketball court. Makes me tingly all over!"

Tommy: "Yeah? Well I'll tell you, I bet I can make you tingle even more!"

144

About a minute later he heard crowd banter, a low rumble comprised of shuffling feet and conversation. The annual Naples Falls Festival was under way. Later he would wonder if the festival hadn't been their inspiration.

So it wasn't their intention to kill him. They only wanted to scare him. But what about the fact that his hands were still tied and that, even worse, they had poured gasoline over him? He stank of it, gallons of it, he assumed.

Why would they do that if they didn't intend to harm him? No, they wanted him to stay here, that was why they'd put those torches all over the place. He dared not move. One false step—which would be easy enough on the uneven dirt floor, and with his feet bound, and he'd burst into flame, a human sacrifice. He wondered how long it would take for the gasoline on him to evaporate and decided that even if it took all night, he probably shouldn't trust the fact that he was merely dry. He would still be a tinder box. No, what he would have to do was simply wait them out. If this was the extent of their little joke, he could handle it. He wasn't irrationally afraid of spiders or anything else that made a home in places like this. Snakes, of course, were another matter entirely, but snakes didn't customarily house themselves in basements. No sun.

After he had thoroughly appraised his basement prison and was about to test the strength of the ropes that bound him, his kidnappers began their tormenting. Above him he heard wails of agony, shrill and discordant, and thumps followed by dragging sounds that were apparently supposed to remind him of a body being dragged along the floor. Occasionally one of the girls would yell, "Help me! Help me, Oh, God, they're everywhere, Oh, God!" and similar pleas while the thumping and bumps and dragging continued. He thought of Marley's ghost and at the same time pictured his tormentors up there with a cassette tape, sniggering and having one whale of a time. It was an image that made him smile. They really weren't very good at this, not at all. In his spare time he wrote this kind of thing. Just thinking about his short stories rose more goose flesh than the idiocy they were employing. He settled back and wailed right along with them. But the louder he wailed, the louder they responded, as if to say, "Dammit! We'll see who scares who!" It was, Harry decided, a childish attempt at best. Eventually he closed his eyes, tired from his ordeal, as well as bored, and dozed off.

When he awoke he discovered that, with the exception of the torch to the right of the door, all the torches had burned out. Light was restricted to about one quarter of the basement, leaving Harry and the remaining seventy-five percent of the basement in total darkness. The air was considerably clammier now, too, much more so than before. The torches, he decided, had kept the place dry, free of moisture, and now that they were out . . . He sniffed at his shirt, then, with his hands still behind his back, rolled the fabric on the back of his shirt between his fingers. It was slightly damp, but not soaked, as it had been. It had dried, even down here in this oppressive gloom. He wondered about the time and, because he was hungry, guessed that it was early morning. He had, he thought, slept through it all. He tried to move his hands. The ropes weren't as tight as they had been, but they were tight enough. Still, with a concerted effort he might be able to free himself. He strained against his bonds for the next five minutes, but his struggles were not rewarded. His sweat, in combination with the thick dust he had raised trying to get loose, lay on him like old oil. He stopped, rested, tried again, but again the ropes held firm.

As he was about to continue his struggle, he thought he detected movement in the farthest reaches of the cellar, an area that had been previously lit by torchlight. He smiled again. While he slept his captors had snuck down here and extinguished the torches. This, apparently, was a last gasp effort to frighten him.

They stepped closer, but still they—all four of them—were only shadowy and inconsistent dreamscapes, bent because of the low ceiling. He strained at his bonds again, and was surprised when they finally loosened. His sweat had aided him, causing the ropes to stretch ever so slightly. They drew closer still and Harry said, "Scary, you call that scary? Shit! That's about as scary as the tooth fairy!"

No response.

Harry felt the rope let go. He pulled his hands free and thought briefly about how he might be able to scare them; but there was no way, not really. A hasty retreat would be his best course of action. From the safety of his room he could puzzle through his revenge.

"Didn't work, fellas," he said. "It just didn't work." Then he untied his feet and got up. He taunted them as he painstakingly brushed himself off, then walked slowly toward the stairs, shying away from the one remaining torch.

The door, oddly enough, was locked. He inspected it. Locked from the outside. Obviously one of them, one of the girls, had locked them all in. He turned. They hadn't yet reached the bottom of the stairs, but he could hear them shuffling across the earthen floor. He stepped down a few steps and bent at the waist. They were about thirty feet away now, tightly grouped. He decided to take a chance with the torch; he should be dry enough by now. He rolled his shirtsleeve to his bicep, withdrew the remaining torch from its perch, and shoved it toward them, careful to keep it at arm's length. As light fell upon them, they stopped and raised their arms in what Harry thought was mock terror. They had, he silently admitted, done a decent job with their disguises. They did very much resemble slavering, bloodthirsty vampires, right down to the odor, which was even more pungent in this dank environment. He took a step toward them. He thought he knew them, or at least recognized their

147

voices, but now he wasn't so sure. Or perhaps they had simply done a very convincing job with their disguises. Sure, that had to be it. Still, even their size had altered. And only one of them was a woman, a dark-haired, ethnic-looking woman who seemed to be the boldest of the four. She even took a step in his direction, mouth agape, hands raised to reveal lethally pointed nails, her manic, protuberating eyes fixed upon him.

"Okay," Harry said, "I got a few goose bumps. You can skip the rest. You got me."

He heard it again, the wailing and moaning he had heard earlier, before he dozed off. But if they were still in the house, above him, making those ridiculous noises . . . His pulse quickened dramatically, and with knowledge of the truth, he felt a vertiginous swoon. The torch did lazy circles in front of him just before he fell, hitting his head and dropping the still lit torch beside him. He felt consciousness start to drift away. He groped for it. At the same time he saw the creatures step closer, ever closer. Slowly, consciousness returned. But by now they were almost upon him, their chalk-white faces pulled back in snarls, revealing their fangs, their smell alone enough to induce vomiting. His hand beat the floor for the torch, coming up empty, but he dared not look away, dared not. Above him the song of his tormentors continued, but he only remotely heard them because they—the creatures—were almost on him now.

He screamed, he had no choice, and at the same time, he vaguely felt his bladder let go. A rivulet of warm urine tracked down his thigh and he screamed louder still, provoked by both fear and outrage. They seemed oblivious to his screams, even excited by them. And now they were bending to him, closer and closer—but why? Were they going to eat him, for God sake? Were they going to tear him apart and eat him a piece at a time?

Their mouths were yawned wide, their animal-like snarls fouling the air.

Escape, somehow he had to escape. But how, where?

All he had left now was instinct, and instinct told him to scamper backwards in a furious crabwalk. But he had forgotten about the torch, and what was worse, he had forgotten about his gasoline-soaked clothing.

His clothing ignited instantly, as soon as the flame touched his shirt, pulling a wretched, agonized scream from him that spoke loudly of his impending death. His eyes were round with terror as the flames rose around him, and through those eyes he saw the creatures back quickly away, again shielding themselves from the flames, curious looks of blended fear and anger on their chalky white faces.

"Help me, help me!" he screamed, rolling at the same time as he tried to smother the flames. "Oh, God, oh, God. I'm going to die! Please, please, help me! Help me!"

The door, he thought, I've got to get to the door. He pushed himself up, but in his panicky state he forgot about the low ceiling. The back of his head smashed into a cross member; bright light strobed before his eyes. He grabbed at the wound, then fell heavily. Seconds later, he lost consciousness.

He woke up in a hospital bed. And when he woke up he screamed, remembering his fear and pain. A pretty young nurse ran into the room and tried to comfort him.

"It's okay," she said. "You're not going to die, you're going to be fine."

Her voice was soothing. He looked at her. Was she an angel?

She smiled and said. "It's okay, really, it's okay. There will be some scars, but not many. You were very lucky."

After she left, he couldn't help but remember how he had soiled himself in the cellar, how he had almost died, how only his quick thinking had saved him from a terrible death. And he also thought about those who had let it all happen to him, those who would someday suffer as he had.

The nurse also told him that he owed his life to someone named Sharon Olmstead, a classmate, that she had rescued him by frantically rolling him in the dirt. That's impossible, he thought, she was one of them, one of the bastards who almost got me killed! No, she didn't save me, I saved myself. I did it all by myself.

That phrase echoed through his thoughts now as he walked into the kitchen and stared at the cracked open cellar door. Was it true, were they down there? And were they surrounding him as well, in the other rooms, hiding somehow, in ways he couldn't even imagine?

He stepped toward the door and remembered what the old woman had said. *It takes just a moment and lasts an eternity.* But that was if they actually did exist, which wasn't very likely, despite his memories, which were probably all blown out of proportion. Sure, over the years, as he thought more and more about That Night, he had, more than likely, added more and more horror, much more than had actually befallen him. He had been vulnerable, very much so. Hell, the beings he saw were probably nothing more than other classmates, people he hadn't seen before, part of that clique. It had been dark, very dark, the torches had all gone out, all but one. He had almost died.

I'm rationalizing, he thought then. I'm trying to make that night something less than it was because . . . because I'm frightened? If I am, it's with damn good reason! What if it is true, what if that old woman was telling the truth all along?

He inhaled deeply, let it out. Then I really can claim my revenge. And I can take my time doing it, too. No rush, just something appropriate, planned out.

Shit! C'mon, Harry, get it together. It's impossible, it's all still only a joke for Chrissake!

Then why don't you go down? Why don't you open that door and go down into that cellar?

Why don't you just shut the hell up? You're the sneaky little bastard that got me in here in the first goddamned place!

No answer.

Reason, thank God, finally the voice of reason. It's simple now. I'll just open the door, go on down, have a look around, and leave. What could be simpler?

Harry had always been a sane man, certainly, but a sane man given to flights of fancy, to a wandering and far-flung imagination. His good sense told him the old woman's lips did, in fact, move. His good sense told him that vampires did not live in the basement of this house, or of any house for that matter. And his good sense told him that as soon as he got this over, the better. But it was his imagination that ruled, an imagination that offered a wonderful revenge, even immortality. An imagination that actually did consider what the old woman had said. *It only takes a moment but lasts an eternity*. He could withstand a second of pain, regardless of the severity, to live for an eternity. And although these alternatives were not pondered consciously, they were definitely considered and as he opened the door and stepped down, he actually wished it were all true.

The damp coolness was cavelike. And *their* presence was cloying. They didn't give off a "vampire" odor, nor did they scream piercing, silvery screams. In fact, they were silent. But still, their presence was undeniable. Like moon shadows. Gradually, Harry worked his way down the stairs. The darkness was complete, velvety, but he remembered this cellar. It was clean of debris, anything on which he might hurt himself. At least it had been back then. All he'd have to do was make sure he stayed bent and then walk to the other side and walk back. A double dare. Simplicity itself.

He started for the back wall, his hands pushed out in front of him. Within a few feet he unconsciously raised up and felt his head brush against a beam, reminding him of how he had knocked himself out so many years ago. He bent further, in exaggeration, and continued.

He could smell them now. They were here, he just

151

knew it. But still they hadn't showed.

He pressed on.

About halfway he felt something brush against his arm, something wispy and light. A moth perhaps. His flesh turned cold. Shuddering, he stopped. Waited.

After what seemed like an eternity he whispered, "Do it, dammit! Just do it!"

Something brushed his leg, much larger than a moth. He yelped like a hurt puppy and heard a high-pitched laugh, a woman's laugh, but far off, on the other side of the basement.

Fear suddenly overwhelmed him. He couldn't do it, he just couldn't. He needed light, anything, a candle, a match. A match, yes, he had a box of matches. He fumbled in his jeans pocket, felt something cold and dry brush against his cheek. His sense of defilement was complete. His muscles tightened and his head thrashed from side to side to keep the thing away. Quickly, he pulled out the box of matches, opened it, spilling most of them, and clumsily took one out and struck it.

The smell of sulfur preceded a momentary blindness as the flame crackled and rose. For a few agonizing seconds he could see nothing except the top of his own shaking hand. He squinted, pushed the match away from him, felt something brush against the back of his neck.

Pain. Unlike any he had ever felt. A deep, piercing pain that seemed to reach into his marrow to burrow like some hibernating animal. Lightheaded now, he pressed the wound. Blood trickled between his fingers.

More laughter.

He dropped the match, but it remained lit. And by that light, he saw them, three of them, shadowy and nondescript, in front of him. There was the woman, ten or so feet away, the same woman, the dark one. She was laughing. The other two were on her right. But there were four. Where was the fourth? He turned. The fourth was behind him, grinning: A young, handsome man with long, dark hair and dark eyes. Blood—his blood—

152

dripped from his fangs.

"Please," Harry pleaded, "don't kill me! I want to be one of you. Please!"

The woman laughed, as did the young handsome man.

"No, you don't understand," Harry continued. "I can lead you, I can. Really!"

The young, handsome man stopped laughing and said, "You believed her? That was stupid, very stupid. We follow only one leader. Her."

From the bottom of the stairs the old woman watched as her charges siphoned Harry of his blood and then silently retreated.

Chapter Fifteen

THE PRESENT

David Warner loosened his silk tie and quietly studied what was left of his drink, a very dry martini. He turned the glass slowly and watched as liquid lapped at the sides, then, in what to a casual onlooker might have appeared to be an act of finality, tilted his thick neck back and threw down the remainder. Having grown accustomed to the burn, David barely flinched. He simply slapped the glass down and pointed at it as the waiter walked by. The waiter, a tall, slender, dark-haired man, stopped briefly and acknowledged him with an almost imperceptible nod.

In the muted light of Aladdin's, a series of red, blue, green and white lights trained upon the assembled through frosted ceiling glass, David looked ten years younger. His receding hairline was not as noticeable, nor were the veins that tracked his round face, a malady directly attributable to the number of very dry martinis he had consumed over the last ten years. But even this light could not disguise dull, shadowy eyes, eyes that had once betrayed a quick, fertile mind, but were now almost the eyes of a man given over to a terminal disease. At one time, eons ago, he had been an athlete, and even now, upon very close inspection, a hint of that lifestyle remained. He could still take an arm down, at least most anyone present, and he even occasionally played racquetball with a junior partner at the law firm where he had worked for the last twenty years. But David drank for one reason and one reason only—his inability to stop time. Middle age was a monkey on his shoulder and with each drink that monkey grew more defined, more a reality than an escape from reality.

Aladdin's was crowded this evening, regular customers for the most part, people David recognized either by name or face and, almost to a man, dressed as he was—suit and tie, or sportscoat and tie.

David was dressed in complementing shades of gray, his suit bought on sale, off the rack, at a local discount store. Like three others, it had been bought for use during jury trials, when he had to somehow give a jury the impression that he was just like them, that money was tight. He couldn't do that decked out in an eight hundred dollar suit. He wanted their sympathy and trust and he wanted them to listen to him while he talked. He didn't want them envious because he spent as much on his suits as they did on their mortgage.

He glanced around, his attention drawn to a man he hadn't seen before. He was a tall and well-built man with angular features and a granite jaw, and he stood alone at the end of the long bar nursing a very simple looking drink. And he was the only person here that wasn't wearing a necktie. He was dressed plainly in tan, pleated and cuffed slacks, a white, long sleeve, button-down shirt and peach-colored sweater. Every so often someone would try to engage him in conversation, but those conversations, David saw, didn't last very long. He had been watching this tall, handsome stranger out of the corner of his eye, not sure whether he had been noticed or not. If he had, then the man certainly hadn't given any indication, and David was adept at watching people without their noticing.

It had been David's intention to somehow get the man's attention, but an acquaintance, a man he had met

155

here a couple of weeks earlier, smiled and sat down across from him. He was a middle-aged man with perfectly coiffed, thinning blond hair, small, economical features, and piercing blue eyes. His name was Adam, and he worked for a major accounting firm. He wore a lavender colored tie, an off-white suit and a pale blue silk shirt. David had explored the possibility of a relationship with him but ultimately decided against it. Parsimonious clerks weren't his style. Still, he was civil. As he spoke, he couldn't help but notice the tall, handsome stranger glance furtively in his direction.

"Adam, good to see you. How are things?"

"The usual, sleep, eat, screw a little, work as hard as necessary to keep the bill collectors at bay." He took a sip of his drink, something with a lime floating. As he did, depression took up tenancy on his face. He put the drink down, smiled boyishly. "Actually, David, things could be better."

"Oh? Sorry to hear that."

"One of our accounts folded."

"And nobody saw it coming?"

"Maybe, I don't know. Someone might have gotten their hands dirty. It happens. Rumor has it that layoffs are imminent. By this time next week I could be out of a job."

"That's too bad, but I shouldn't think . . ."

Adam smiled less boyishly, more a smile of acceptance. "One never knows, David. Sure, I've been there a long time, but one never knows."

There was an uncomfortable lull in the conversation then that prompted both men to smile mechanically. David certainly didn't want to share this man's problems. It might be a different story if they were lovers, but they barely knew each other. Maybe by sharing this bit of bad news he hoped to gain his trust, his friendship. He noticed the man at the bar again. And this time their eyes met. He looked back at Adam. He didn't want to be rude, but in truth, Adam had been rude.

"Look, Adam, it is good to see you, and I am sorry that things aren't going well, really I am . . ."

Adam smiled knowingly. He had expected a brushoff, but still, he had to try. He rose, glanced toward the bar, wished David good luck and disappeared into the crowd.

During that time, David temporarily lost sight of the man at the bar. He turned ever so slowly, sipping his drink at the same time, intending to invite him over, when and if their eyes again met. The man was gone, no where to be seen. Disappointment rushed through him— first Adam and now this. He thought about leaving. He looked at his watch, almost ten. He was due in court at nine tomorrow, an early evening might be wise.

"Oh, well," he said as he got up, "such is life."

As he picked up his umbrella, he heard, "Not leaving, are you?"

The man, the same man who had been standing alone at the bar, stood a few feet away. David smiled up at him and at the same time realized that he wasn't as good looking as he had thought. His features had an almost Neanderthal quality. But he did project an awareness, an intelligence, that, for David, offset his middle-of-the-road looks. He was taller than he had appeared as well, and larger. But from a distance, David knew, size could be illusionary.

The man held out a large hand. David put down his umbrella and shook it, noticing both the coolness and the awesome, restrained strength. His hand was wrapped as he might wrap a child's hand.

"No," David said, "well, yes. I guess I was leaving."

"That's too bad," the man said, smiling.

"Well, I suppose. It's just that I've got an early case . . . Oh, what the hell. David, David Warner. Please, won't you join me?"

"Thought you'd never ask."

"And you are . . . ?"

"Harry."

"Just Harry?"

"Last names can be burdensome at times."

"So true."

Harry and David sat down across from each other and it was immediately apparent to David that the man's presence, oddly enough, was both unnerving and relaxing. Looking at him coaxed visions that, until now, had lain dormant for many years. He remembered when he was rock hard, the envy of his classmates both on and off the playing field. Perhaps, he thought, it was this man's body, lean yet thickly muscled, that inspired those visions.

"You remind me of someone," Harry said, leaning forward.

"I trust that's favorable."

"In some ways yes, in some ways no."

"An old friend?"

Harry leaned even closer. "When I was in high school, there was this guy, well, every school's got one. Anyway, he got some kind of perverse kick out of showing everyone up. He aced all the tests, he always wrote the best term papers, real nervy kind of guy."

David's visions were drawing sharper focus.

"Funny you should mention that," he said.

"Oh?"

"Yes, I was just thinking . . ."

"Don't tell me, you had one of those, too?"

David smiled a small smile, looked at Harry more closely and said, "Yes. You, uh, you said, Harry?"

"That's right. Harry."

"Funny, you remind me of someone, too. Do we know each other?"

Harry ignored the question. He leaned back and seemed to think a moment. "You know, David, sometimes, and this is weird, I look in the mirror and you know what I see?"

"What?"

"Nothing. Absolutely nothing."

David was surprised by his admission. "You shouldn't

158

have such a low opinion of yourself, Harry. You're quite . . . formidable."

"Formidable? Interesting choice of words, very interesting. Keenly accurate, as well. But when I said I see nothing when I look in the mirror, I didn't mean it as a scathing self-analysis."

David leaned back as the waiter placed another martini in front of him. He picked it up, sipped, put it down. "But certainly that's the only way you could mean it, Harry."

Harry leaned forward again, then slid closer to David and put an arm around him.

"No, really. Look," he said conspiratorially.

Harry reached into his shirt pocket and took out a small hand held mirror. Then he placed it in front of them, about a foot or so away. It reflected only David's very surprised face.

Harry put the mirror back in his pocket.

"That's quite a trick, Harry. I'll bet you're a lot of fun at parties."

Suddenly Harry pulled out a wooden match and struck it on his cheek, so quickly that David barely noticed. The flame danced before his eyes briefly before settling into a steady, even glow. Beyond it, David saw Harry's face, starkly white, just the hint of a smile on his lips.

"Naples Falls," David said vacantly. "Oh, God, you're him!"

Harry's smile broadened.

"Welcome," Harry whispered and leaned ever closer.

From the bar, Adam watched, disheartened, and while he watched he thought, Christ, least they could do is take their act outside! Animals! He turned away and called the bartender over.

AT THE FESTIVAL

Milt Langtree was awfully concerned. Nobody had ever stared at that painting for this long a time. Maybe it was time to check into it. With hands in pockets, which, he thought, might project calmness, he walked up to the man and tapped him on the shoulder.

No response.

He tapped again, harder this time.

Nothing.

He grabbed the man's shoulder and whirled him around. "Look, pal, what gives?"

Milt quickly backed away, hands out in front of him defensively. "Sorry, didn't mean nothin'. You go on, do what you gotta do."

Jerry stepped toward him, his face dripping sweat, his breathing heavy, his eyes wild and unblinking, homicidal.

"Christ Jesus," Milt mumbled. "Fucking festival!"

Behind the man he saw a woman with an old man and a boy. Then he heard the woman say, "Jerry!"

Jerry stopped.

"Jerry, what the hell's wrong with you?"

Jerry turned.

At the same time, Milt Langtree lost his balance and promptly put his elbow through one of his clients' paintings.

TWENTY-NINE HOURS LATER, JUST BEFORE DAWN

Beatrice Warner picked up an old photograph of her son, David, and silently remarked that at one time, he was, indeed, a very handsome man. But time, as well as a lifestyle she had long ago accepted, had taken a toll. She had often wished that her son had been like the majority, the heterosexual majority. But God did work in mysterious ways.

The fact that her son had chosen to come here and spend the night was extremely odd, but she was glad he had. She could mother him now—he did look wretched.

Maybe she could even convince him to spend more than the day with her. That would be nice.

She was a short woman who, at one time, had been described as Rubenesque, a term she didn't consider to be entirely unflattering. But now, close to seventy, Rubenesque did not apply. She was a portly older woman who, if she wasn't careful, could easily become a fat older woman. But she was careful. She wanted to live at least another twenty years, longer, if that life was vital, if she was still able to at least carry on a decent conversation without drifting. She didn't want to end up a burden to a son who had too many burdens to bear already.

She put the photograph back on the nightstand and looked at him. He slept so peacefully. She had covered him seconds earlier; there was a chill in the air. His breathing, she thought, was inordinately shallow, but that only meant that he was sleeping deeply, the best kind of sleep. And obviously sleep had done him a world of good. The color had already come back into his cheeks, almost matching the rose-colored bedspread in this, his old room.

She always woke early, ever since her husband had passed on. But this morning, she had arisen even earlier than normal. She'd had a rather perplexing dream about David. In the dream he had been actually hostile toward her, or at least his demeanor had suggested hostility. That, of course, was ridiculous. He had never so much as raised his voice to her, let alone hurt her. Her therapist would have a good time with that one, if she told him, which she didn't think she would do. Her relationship with her son was the only stability in her life. If that was undermined . . .

Movement. In the hallway, just beyond the half open door.

Beatrice froze. "Who's there?" she whispered.

Robberies were a common occurrence in this part of the city, and most of those robberies took place in the early morning hours, like now.

She saw a shadow on the hall floor, huge and unmoving, cast from the hallway light. She stifled a scream and backed up toward the bed. "David," she whispered. "Wake up, David. There's someone in the hallway. Oh, God, David, please, please wake up!"

Without looking, she reached back and shook him. Still he slept. The shadow moved, ever so slightly. She heard her son mumble something, felt him stir. She dared a glance. His eyes were opening. She looked toward the door. The shadow had moved further into it.

"David, please, wake up!"

She heard the bed squeak, but she dared not let her eyes stray from the doorway.

More mumbles.

It was then when her fears were realized. Harry Matheson stepped into the doorway and grinned at her.

Beatrice Warner screamed and pushed herself backwards, into her son.

"What do you want? Oh, please, don't kill me! I'm just an old woman. Please!"

It was as she sought the comfort of her son's closeness when her nightmare came true. Turning to him she saw a face that did and did not belong to her beloved David, a face that was hollow and lifeless, yet still strangely glowing and so full of vile hatred. And now his mouth gaped wide, wide enough to reveal the dull white fangs. A sound came out of him, a vicious, keening sound. It was enough to cause her failing heart to burst. She fell dead onto the floor, easy prey for David, who fell onto her and drank from her ravenously, totally unaware that Harry Matheson, his master, whom he had terrorized so many years ago, was watching.

"That's four," Harry said.

Behind him Christine only stared.

That set a shadow on the hall floor, huge and murmuring, cast from the hallway light. She stifled a scream and backed up toward the bed. "David," she whispered. "Wake up, David. There's someone in the hallway. Oh, God, David, please, please wake up."

Chapter Sixteen

THE NEAR PAST

One last glance into the mirror revealed, once again, that she was a pretty woman, maybe not ravishingly beautiful, but pretty enough to turn both male and female heads. Then why did men avoid her? Well, that wasn't quite true. Men didn't avoid her, they did, in fact, seek her out. But never had a relationship lasted more than a month. And that was perplexing. She often wondered if it didn't have something to do with the fact that she refused to stoop to their level, that she wouldn't compromise her position on political, philisophical or religious issues. Probably. But a real man, someone confident in his masculinity, without raging insecurities that needed constant nurturing, would understand. She had yet to meet that man. She wondered, at the age of forty, if she ever would.

She looked around the apartment that she had shared with a fellow teacher for the last ten years, at the few things she had accumulated over that time, things that would remain behind: a love seat, a pair of antique mahogany chairs, an original oil painting by a local artist. She had taken a loss on each item, but because this move represented a new start, packing bits of the past would be self-defeating. But was she making a mistake by going back to Naples Falls, where they had real winter, not this California version? Where life crawled and dreams died? Without a full time teaching position she was certainly taking a gigantic risk, although the school board in Naples Falls did tell her that the waiting list was short, that in about a year she would be offered a full time teaching position, that until then she could substitute teach. That was good enough for her. She had grown to dislike California and its people, most of whom had crossed its borders dreamy-eyed, only to see those dreams shattered beyond repair. It was a land of want and plenty, with no in-between. At least in Naples Falls there was an in-between. Besides, with her mother dead, her father needed her. He was still vital, alive, but at his age, you could never tell. She loved him immensely. She would feel just awful if one day she got a phone call saying he was dead, that if someone had been there, he might not be dead. Yes, this was the right thing to do, the only thing to do. She closed the door behind her, confident in her future and looking forward to going home.

It was around suppertime when her plane touched down, the sky awash with fish-scale clouds, portents of bad weather.

Her father was waiting for her. After he had put her bags in the trunk of the car, he informed her that he had made something special to honor this momentous occasion.

"You didn't have to go to all that trouble, Pop," she said as she slid into the passenger seat.

"Trouble? No, no trouble. My little girl has come home. There is no trouble too big."

"Pop. Your little girl?"

He leaned over and kissed her on the cheek. "Yes, my little girl, my big girl. You may not be a little girl any longer, but . . ."

"Yes, Pop, I know. I'll always be your little girl."

He smiled at her lovingly. "Took the words right out of

164

my mouth. Next time you do that, leave the teeth."

She laughed. He had always been able to make her laugh. Very few men had ever been able to do that.

They arrived about forty-five minutes later. She got out of the car and looked across the road, toward the house by the cemetery. Long shadows angled off of it, either hiding its windows or enhancing them. It was late winter now, that fickle time of year that could be numbingly cold or shirt sleeve warm. Today was shirtsleeve warm, even though the sun was low on the horizon. In a couple of hours, however, it would again be bitingly cold.

"Still deserted, huh?" she said.

"What's that?" Walker asked.

"The house across the street."

"Well, I'll tell you, Chrissy, it ain't deserted no more." He had her bags, all three of them. The strain of their combined weight showed on his face.

"Let me take one of those, Pop," she said.

He gave her the smallest and they walked together toward the house.

"You mean somebody actually moved in over there?" she asked.

"Oh, sure. Some years back, too. I don't see him much. Hardly at all. Night owl, he is. Writer, according to Charley."

"Charley?"

She opened the door.

"You know, Charley Merriweather? Delivers the mail. Says that fella gets lots of mail from some New York City publisher."

"A writer. Well, isn't that interesting."

"Thought it would be, you bein' an English teacher. Anyway, every now and again there's another car in the driveway, but I don't think he ever drives his. Keeps it in the garage on the side there."

"You mean just one person lives in that great big house?"

"Near's I can tell."

"Well, don't you think that's kind of strange?"

"A mite."

"And you haven't met him yet?"

"Nope."

"Gee, Pop, what kind of neighbor are you? We'll have to remedy that right away."

Walker was in her bedroom by then. Wondering just how many brick dresses she had packed, he flopped her bags onto the bed. She had a point, he hadn't been much of a neighbor. He had gone over there only twice, years ago, and during the daytime. But the man hadn't bothered to answer the door. And his car had been in the garage, too. The second time, a couple of weeks after that, the man still refused to answer the door.

As he came back into the living room, he found Christine staring out the window. "You wanta introduce yourself you'll probably have to do it at night," he said.

Christine still stared. "He's probably just one of those writers who sleeps during the day and writes at night," she said. "I had a professor like that in college, at least before he became a professor."

"Could be," Walker answered, moderately interested.

She turned away from the window. "Now about that surprise."

He smiled. "Liver smothered with onions. How's that sound?"

Her face squinched up as if a particularly aromatic skunk had wandered past. "Yucch!" she said. "I think you've just excited my gag reflex, Pop."

Walker laughed and pulled a huge tenderloin from the refrigerator.

Two nights later she decided to visit their only neighbor. She asked her father if he wanted to go along but he said his bursitis was acting up and that he would have to decline her invitation. She knew he was lying, that he only wanted to give her some time alone with a man who obviously fascinated her, but still, she appreciated the gesture, even though her intentions were, at least initially, strictly neighborly.

But, she thought as she crossed the road, if he wants to look at a few of my poems . . .

She carried a chocolate cake in a grocery bag. Misty rain gathered on the bag, and she was glad she had wrapped it. As she stepped onto the porch, she wondered if he even liked cake, and if he did, if he liked chocolate cake. She scolded herself for thinking that way. A gentleman would graciously accept her gift, regardless of flavor.

She rang the doorbell and silently remarked that her uneasiness had been spawned by the ridiculous home-grown mythology inspired by this house. And now a writer lived here, a horror writer, again according to Charley Merriweather, who had only yesterday delivered a box of books.

The door opened and Christine instantly forgot what she had planned to say, something not very original about, "Here, neighbor, hope you like chocolate." The sight of him left her speechless. Although he wasn't a handsome man in the classical sense, he had a presence that overwhelmed her. Not only was he tall and large, his skin was absolutely flawless, not a pimple, not a freckle. Like animated porcelain. When she did finally speak she had the feeling that she was speaking to a large, heavily muscled ceramic puppet.

"So, you . . . you're a writer?"

He seemed not to hear. "Can I help you?" he asked with polite indifference.

His voice had the quality of far-off thunder.

"Look, I'm not some crank, really, I'm not. It's just that . . . well, I live across the road with my dad and . . . here."

She shoved the cake out in front of her, angry with herself for being so sophomoric.

She decided that she would go quickly, as soon as the amenities were over. He took the bag from her and looked

167

inside. Then he smiled, which brightened his face immensely.

"Chocolate. My favorite. You shouldn't have."

The tension she had felt, as if her body were twice its normal weight, slowly fell away.

"Chocolate's always a good choice," she answered, returning his smile.

"Always. Well, unless you're fifteen and out of Clearasil."

She laughed quietly, a laugh he had pulled out of her. It felt good. She stopped laughing and they just looked at each other then, both smiling.

Finally Christine said, "Welcome to Naples Falls."

"Thank you, but, well, I think it is I who should be welcoming you, Miss, uh . . ."

"Christine Walker."

"Harry Matheson. Please, come in, won't you? Would you like some?" he asked, lifting the corner of the bag slightly.

"Only if you'll have some, too."

"Well, I'd love to, but I had some dental work done today and I really can't. I promise that as soon as I can I'll eat the whole thing."

"Scout's honor?"

"Scout's honor."

He smiled at her, broadly and openly. And it was then when she had a fleeting vision of the two of them making wildly passionate love. The image startled her. She blinked her eyes and it was gone. She smiled inwardly and thought, my God, Chris, you just met him!

Harry cut her a piece of cake, apologized because all he had to drink was tap water, and sat down at the dining room table across from her. While she ate she had the same vision three more times and each time the vision was more distinct, more unsettling. She even wondered if she were blushing. By the time she left she felt like a child who's had their first trip to an amusement park; adrenalin-filled yet frightened enough to wonder about

168

ever coming back again.

In bed that night she tried to analyze her experiences. She was forty, reasonably passionate, certainly not frigid. And it had been two years since she had been with a man. What she had envisioned had been perfectly natural. Chances were, he had envisioned the very same thing. At least she could hope. She even felt a measure of pride. He wasn't movie star material, no one to go instantly ga ga over. She had obviously been drawn to his intellect, his creative nature, his . . . She smiled. Sure, Chrissy, his intellect and creativity. You're just horny and you know it!

She went to sleep then and dreamed. When she awoke she felt as refreshed as she had ever felt. She couldn't quite remember what she had dreamed, but she guessed it had had something to do with him.

She went to school cheerfully, wondering if he had yet sampled her cake, a double entendre that, although not observed consciously, still made her blush.

It was during class, during a debate over Salinger, when it happened. Carla Stevenson, well-read, intelligent, and on the debating team, was driving home a point when the boy beside her, who did very much resemble Harry Matheson, winked at her, and obscenely flicked his tongue in and out. All she could do was look at him, frozen by the absurdity of the moment and by such blatant disregard for the teacher-student relationship.

Finally she said, "Richard, I'd like to see you after class."

His expression reflected great surprise. "Me?" he said, pointing at himself.

"Yes, you!"

"But why? What'd I do?"

"You know why! We'll discuss it later."

Of course, later interrogations met with the same degree of surprise. He hadn't winked at her, he hadn't. He would never; his father was a minister, he was an A student with dreams of Princeton. Why would he

169

jeopardize that? Why?

He was very convincing and Christine finally told him she would forget the incident but that she never wanted it to happen again.

Vacantly Richard said, "Sure, whatever you say," and left just shaking his head.

THAT NIGHT

She awoke suddenly at about three in the morning. Something feathery had brushed the inside of her thigh. And when she woke, she had an ever so fleeting glimpse of a dark silhouette in bed with her, on all fours . . . as if . . . but no, that was absurd. And impossible. The windows were closed and locked, as was the front door. She was simply rehashing a pubescent fantasy. What more could it be? She had met someone who very easily aroused those thoughts, someone she would, she admitted, share her bed with. And she *had* been in the midst of a somewhat lurid dream. She got up and parted the curtains.

Although she couldn't be sure—his house was totally dark—she thought she saw a dark figure standing in the living room window.

The next day, a day off, she wondered if perhaps she hadn't imagined him standing there just as she had imagined him between her thighs. When she thought these things her emotions became tangled. There was confusion, even anger, but there was also very real interest. He had neither said nor done anything to insinuate any kind of erotic relationship, and yet such a relationship ruled her thoughts, both waking and sleeping. And she also knew that suppressing those thoughts was unnatural, even unhealthy.

After a week more of even more lurid dreams she felt the best thing to do was to confront him, perhaps engage him in lengthy conversation, thereby drawing out the real Harry Matheson, not that person who was simply physically overwhelming. Then she would be better able to analyze her strange desires. God, she thought, that all sounds like something from a Harlequin romance. And although circumstances did smack of pulp fiction, she realized she would have to do something. And moreover, she realized she wanted to do something.

She went over at night, respectful of his routine, a routine she had guessed and he had confirmed during their first and only visit. Yes, he did sleep during the day, usually, except when he had dental appointments, etc, and yes, he usually did write at night. Because he wrote horror, and because horror was dark and shadow-strewn, he felt it best to wait until darkness to relate the details of his imagination. "Well, that makes sense," she had said.

He didn't answer the door. She rang the buzzer repeatedly and yet, he didn't answer. And there was a low wattage light on in the kitchen. To the west lightning suddenly flashed. Seconds later she heard the thunder. It, the storm, would arrive shortly. Bad weather ordinarily tracked west to east. She rang the doorbell again. He could be working. He could be wearing earphones, listening to music, unable to hear the bell. That made sense. With that logic firmly entrenched, she tried the door. It was open. She went inside.

"Harry?" she said moderately loud.

Another bolt of lightning, strong enough to briefly bathe the sparsely appointed living room in a ghostly white light.

No one answered.

She went into the kitchen. A night light had been plugged into a wall socket to the right of the sink. The kitchen, just as it had been the other time she was here, was spotless.

The storm surged ever closer. The first raindrops pelted onto the windows like tiny stones. She left the kitchen, went to the stairway and gazed up at the dark landing. Again lightning flashed, basking the landing in

171

another brief, fluorescent glow. "Harry? Mr. Matheson?" she called.

She didn't hear a typewriter, although with the rain now hammering down . . . But if the door were closed . . .

She started up the stairs. Once she reached the landing, she stopped and looked out the picture window toward the cemetery. Lightning strobed the night, recreating daylight in stuttering bursts. Tombstones shone, then disappeared, shone, then disappeared. How atmospheric, she thought. Simply perfect for a writer, I would think.

Each door was closed up here, but under the door of the bedroom toward the front, she saw a flush of weak light actively competing with the lightning. She walked over to the door and knocked lightly. Then she put her ear to it. "Mr. Matheson? It's Christine Walker. Are you in there?" She spoke loudly as the storm raged around her.

Again she heard nothing. She tried the door. It was open. She pushed on it and went inside.

The room was empty, save for a single linenless bed beneath a bare window. The flush of weak light had, again, come from a night light, this time beneath the bed.

She was beginning to feel somewhat foolish, almost like a cat burglar. She started to leave, but stopped. Fleetingly, as if only thought and not seen, she had detected a form on the bed, the simple mattress on a simple single bed, sans headboard and linen. She smiled ever so feebly. How odd, she thought. What could have . . . Again she saw the form, not as fleetingly now, recreated and given life by the lightning, there then gone, there then gone. Intrigued, she stepped closer. It was her. She gasped, covered her mouth. She was prone and naked, writhing, her gyrations only exaggerated by the hundreds of lightning strikes. And she was transparent. Oh, God, she thought miserably. What's happened to me? Is this my reward for two weeks of . . . sexual tension!

172

Then the lightning revealed another figure, this one in the corner beyond the head of the bed. She stepped backwards. It was Harry Matheson, as naked and as transparent as the image on the bed. She was mesmerized. Her bedded, lightning flickering image beckoned to him and he stepped toward her. She could see her chest heave. And Harry was ever so willing, ever so ready. His penis, huge and erect, reminded her of the statuary she had seen briefly at the festival, statuary that her father always quickly pulled her away from. Harry drew closer to her image, there on the bed, and when he finally stood over her, she reached out her arms to him. Christine could only watch and as she watched, she found herself mimicking what she saw. She felt her pelvis thrust, she felt her chest heave and her pulse quicken. She was being pleasured by invisible hands, and her pleasure was magnificent and draining. But she also felt dirtied because of it, even though that fact did not lessen her pleasure, did not cause her pelvis to thrust any less boldly or her sweat to flow any less slowly.

Finally she had an orgasm, a natural blending of pain and pleasure. It was a nightmare fall and then an awakening, a quick journey into unconsciousness, a knowledge of death and then, immediately, life. It was everything she had hoped it would be. And it was over far too quickly.

But afterwards, immediately afterwards, she felt even more dirtied. Even the afterglow of orgasm failed to diminish her revulsion. She turned, intending to go.

The doorway was blocked.

She looked at him. He was as naked now as his image, but this time he was not transparent. This time his porcelain skin, that shone like moon-dappled stone in the pulses of lightning, was real. Again she was speechless.

"Immorality is all of that, and more," Harry said. "Let me take you there."

She backed away, her memory ripe with revulsion and pleasure.

But curiously, Harry backed out of the doorway, away from her, beckoning to her, much as her bedded image had beckoned his image.

"It takes but a moment and lasts an eternity," he said, his words echoing throughout the house, even dominating the storm.

She followed, despite herself.

She followed him down the stairs and then into the kitchen, as if pulled by an invisible tether. He reached behind him, still beckoning, and pulled open the cellar door. A surge of cool air blew into the room, but she didn't feel it. By now she was his and only his, transfixed by the twin orbs of bright light that were his eyes. He glided down the cellar stairs and she followed. He moved to the north corner, her way no longer lit by the storm, but by his presence. And she watched as he reached down and pulled open the trap door that led into his tunnels.

Chapter Seventeen

THE PRESENT

Guy Henry slammed the receiver into its cradle and then ran his fingers through his thinning hair. A garbled, almost growl-like noise escaped him; he was too upset to speak. When he finally could all he could come up with was, "Thanks, pal! Thanks a whole goddamn bunch!"

Was this what they thought of him and his office? Not to mention the people of Naples Falls, whom he protected, who had elected him. Treating him like this was just as much a slap in their faces as in his. And how could he protect them if Amans and his bunch didn't keep him properly informed? How? He couldn't, he just couldn't. One by one everyone in town would be killed and one by one their bodies would disappear, just like Thomas Jefferson Smith, just like Lenny Griffin. Then the tabloids would get the news and there'd be four inch high letters about the whole goddamned town that just up and disappeared. Well maybe when he caught the killer he wouldn't tell them. How would they like that? If their time was too damn precious to keep him properly informed, then by God his time was just as goddamned precious. Sure, he was supposed to remain detached, clinical, his attention focused on the best way to solve the case at hand. He knew all that. But dammit, he was only human. If they could keep him in the dark, he could damn sure return the favor. And he knew who the killer was, too. Well, maybe he didn't have a set of prints taken from a chocolate bar or an eyewitness who had perfect vision and an unblemished past, but he did have his suspicions. Did they? Had they even spoken with Jerry Matheson? Had they studied the man? Had they looked deep into those eyes, deep enough to see the glowing, glaring truth? Probably not. They didn't have his cunning, his guile, his sense of purpose. They didn't have a town to protect!

"Things really have been hectic, sheriff, you understand," Amans had said. "I realize we should have informed your office right away, but, well, what can I say. I take full responsibility for the oversight."

Oversight, hell! He picked up the receiver and again slammed it into its cradle. Truth was, they wanted to keep him in the dark for as long as they could. The fewer people who knew that both Tom Smith and Lenny Griffin had disappeared, the better. Well, that was okay. He could understand the need for secrecy. He didn't want to panic the citizenry. But that didn't mean he couldn't do his part. No, sir!

Outside, shadows had gotten as long as they would get. The sun was setting. There were intimations of a warm and dry evening.

Chapter Eighteen

Probing, Maria shoved her broom under Jerry's computer desk, then swept it from side to side. Dust balls gathered on it like magnets. She pulled them off, squeezed them into a tight ball, and dropped the ball into a Hefty trash bag. Jerry was upstairs, in the attic. For what purpose she didn't know. She glanced at the small stack of bond paper, the sum total of today's work, neatly collected in an out box on the side of his desk. Did she dare? She glanced toward the stairs, listened, just to make sure Jerry wasn't coming down, then, with the broom cradled in the crook of her arm, picked up the pages. She thumbed through them, front to back. Ten pages in all, about twenty-five hundred words. A healthy number, a good day's work, she thought. She had snuck glances in the past, but not since the move. She felt a strange anxiety this time. They had, after all, moved here for the inspiration, to the "Cadillac of inspirational settings" as Jerry had put it. If this work wasn't noticeably better . . . She read objectively, as she always did, and after the first few paragraphs she discovered that she couldn't stop. Her eyes were drawn to the words like a moth to a flame. Within five or so minutes she had read the entire ten pages. She was breathless. It was easily the best work he had ever done. The flow, the word choice, the obvious inspiration—it was absolutely magnificent work. And still only a first draft. A pride swelled within her, a different kind of pride, the kind reserved for a newborn, which was appropriate. She always knew he had ability, but she had never dreamed . . . Well, now she could dream. Now, she could allow herself that luxury. She wanted to run to him, to tell him how much she loved this new work, that he had been right about the move all along. But she didn't. She couldn't. Only on invitation was anyone, even her, allowed to read his material. Especially first draft, "the raw, bare bones stuff waiting to be fattened," as he had called them. She would have to wait until he said, "Hon, if you've got some time would you mind looking at a few scenes?" But could she control herself until then? Could she keep from blurting a litany of platitudes once she saw him? Well, for the sake of their relationship, she would have to. She didn't want to draw any more anger out of him—he had displayed enough anger the last few days—and if he knew she had read his work without asking, his anger would certainly be aroused.

Smiling unknowingly, she took her dust broom and hefty bag upstairs, happy despite everything—the murders, Sharon Griffin leaving in the middle of the night, her mother huffing off. Her dear, driven husband had leaped some gigantic literary hurdle. He was going to be famous. She was immensely happy for him.

The twelve boxes Jerry had planned to store the night Lenny Griffin's vision intruded upon him lay neatly stacked against the north wall. A few spiders had already begun their homes around the edges,

"I knew you weren't going to finish the job, so I did," Maria had informed him with irritating matter-of-factness. With a measure of disdain he slanted his head femininely to the side and slowly lipsynched her words.

The boxes were stacked three high and four wide. The stack was tilted slightly because some boxes weren't quite as full as others, nor as heavy. Each was marked, but that would do him no good whatsoever. Maria, ever efficient, had devised a numbering system, or, more precisely, she had borrowed a system devised by her mother. Another of Loretta's contributions to mankind, he thought sarcastically. Each box was marked with numbers ranging from one to twelve. Each number corresponded with a list she had made, a list detailing that particular box's contents. The numbers, written in a perfect, calligraphic hand, each about six inches tall, stared back at him. According to Maria, typed lists were much easier to read than scrawled upon boxes. But Maria's care in numbering the boxes had been for naught. She had lost the corresponding sheet of paper, the key. Or it had been tossed during the move. The system—Loretta's system—had failed miserably. Now he'd have to root through each box to find what he was looking for: *The Clarion,* his old Naples Falls High School yearbook.

The search had been prompted by a jarring of his memory, brought on by his last "vision"—the death of the man in the bar. He had known him, just as he had known the others, Len and Thomas and Sharon. And she was also a victim. Even though he hadn't yet witnessed her death, he would very soon, that was a given. Moreover, he also remembered that each was a member of the same clique. They ate lunch together, they went to ballgames together. They did everything together, even got married, as was the case with Sharon and Len. But there was one other person, and if his theory was correct, she—that much he remembered, his memory embracing delicate features and shoulder length hair—would also become a victim. And although he couldn't remember her name, he would remember her face, if it stared back at him from *The Clarion.*

His search started on the top right, box number four. Eight was beneath it, twelve beneath eight. Maria, in an effort to be as efficient as possible, had stored the boxes left to right, in descending numerical order. Jerry silently cursed her system as he pulled the tape off the box and flapped it open, revealing an array of knickknacks wrapped in tissue paper. Why hadn't she simply written the contents on the outside, like normal people did, for Chrissake? Why? Because of Loretta, that was why. His anger shifted focus from Maria to Loretta. Then, because it was simply more satisfying, he silently cursed both women.

Within five minutes, boxes and their contents had been strewn about the otherwise bare and humid attic as if some confined storm had taken place. Maria, if she were to walk in right now, would be livid. Jerry didn't really care. With only three boxes left he was beginning to wonder if she had stored the yearbook at all. She could have tossed it along with his decades old trophies, won for almost every sport imaginable, from baseball to ping pong, trophies whose only purpose, it seemed, had been to gather dust, as had his athletic ability. Why he had even bothered to save the yearbook was an even bigger mystery than where it was. The year his family spent here had been a disaster, at least for Harry, whose state of mind had always been important to him. And something—even today he didn't know what—had happened to Harry that year. He had been hospitalized because of it, scarred, miserable, defensive. And it had happened here, in this house, the very house Harry had "sold" him, the house Harry himself had inhabited. He had asked Harry about that night a number of times, but each time Harry had flatly refused to discuss it. Maybe, Jerry thought, when he gets back from Hollywood. Maybe then. And he really did want to discuss that night with him now, much more so than he ever had. His "visions," repulsive yet also strangely pleasureable and inspiring, were somehow, someway, linked to Harry. He had nothing on which to base this suspicion, only intuition. But that intuition was strengthened by the most powerful of relationships, that of identical twins, the mystical arrangement that confounded scientists and by now had become the subject of many a university study. How did one explain the fact that twins, separated at birth, married women with the same names, gave their children the same names, took the same types of jobs and even had the same hobbies? Very much as if one was simply the flip side, the mirror image of the other. Jerry wouldn't even have begun a literary career if Harry hadn't been so fabulously successful. Jerry—unlike Harry, who was a staunch atheist—believed that any supreme being—God—would be democratic enough to insure that each half of a split zygote received like amounts of talent, and in the same areas. If Harry had been a bricklayer, then, in fact, Jerry would have been a bricklayer. If Harry had been a pimp, Jerry would have been one, too. It was a philosophy that obviously gave Harry the lion's share of whatever leadership ability had been granted them; but, for Jerry, that was acceptable. It was also a philosophy that he had shared with no one, not even Maria.

But even with intervening intuition, the fact remained that Harry was in Hollywood, so he had said, which would make any connection to recent events impossible . . .

A thudding knock on the floor beneath him. A piercing yell for help. Maria. Christ, Maria! Jerry dropped Box Number Five, then ran down the stairs and into the bedroom. Maria was in the corner to the right of the door, a sheepish look on her face. She pointed at the bed and smiled. "I just . . . reacted," she said. "I know I shouldn't have, but I did. You know how I feel about spiders." She smiled again, apologetically.

On the bed, a full grown wolf spider spotlighted by a nightstand lamp, walked with majestic aplomb toward the brass headboard. Jerry, whose eyes had fixed upon the sought after yearbook the instant Maria banged on the ceiling with the broom—that was still clutched tightly in her white-knuckled hand—raised *The Clarion* high over his head, hesitated for just a split second, and brought it down onto the spider with a crisp *thwack*. Death was instantaneous. Although he wasn't an arachnophobic like Maria, wolf spiders were another matter entirely. He gave them a wide berth.

"Thanks," Maria gasped, still smiling sheepishly. "What's that?" she continued.

He looked at the yearbook, first one side then the other, then at Maria, and smiled, somewhat amazed. "The Clarion. My high school yearbook . . . from here."

"God, I thought I threw that thing away with your awful trophies," Maria said. She no longer held the broom in a death grip.

Jerry smiled. "Well, I'm glad you didn't."

"What in the world do you want with that?"

Jerry shrugged. "Memories. You know, little nostalgia, little down-home flavor for the book."

"Oh, yeah, the book." She wondered if he saw the childlike glee on her face. "Listen, honey, about that . . ."

"Yes?"

She smiled. "Nothing. Really, nothing."

"You haven't . . ."

"No, no, of course not. I know how you feel about that."

"Good. I mean it's pretty decent, surprisingly so, actually. But, well, it'd be like you cooking a meal. You wouldn't want me sampling it until you had added all the proper ingredients? Right?"

Even while he spoke, Jerry realized he shouldn't have. But it never dawned on him that he had said what he had just to be argumentative, simply as a provocation.

"Jerry," Maria said, "I hate it when you try to be macho. You're really not very good at it. Me eat—you cook. Me smack chest with fists! Hunt wild buffalo! C'mon, honey!"

Jerry threw up his arms. "Christ," he said, "I was just

182

trying to make a point, no need to get so goddamned defensive!"

His reaction, almost explosively hostile, somewhat startled her. She jumped back a half step as soon as he had started his brief tirade.

She gathered herself and took a step toward him. "Look, honey, I'm sorry." She reached out her hand, touched him on the elbow. "You okay?"

"Fine!"

Cautiously, she said, "Well, you don't sound fine."

"Skip it. Let's just skip it."

"Sure."

"Fine!"

Maria inhaled, let it out. "Not to change the subject, but didn't you tell me you hated the year you spent here?"

Jerry just looked at her for a second, as if trying to decide whether to let her off the hook or not. Finally, he said, "That was many years ago, Maria. Times change, people change. And I only hated it because Harry did. I was always telling him to cool it, you know, try to be like everyone else, but you know Harry."

Must I explain everything? Christ!

She remembered his strange behavior at the festival. How could she forget? Did he want that yearbook to search for characters, or for some other purpose? She knew about Sharon. They had attended high school together. And she also knew that Lenny Griffin had been Sharon's husband. But what did *he* know? Was there something he wasn't telling her—or the police? And in the dustiest, most remote corner of her mind, another thought began to blossom, a thought wrapped by a thick, almost impenetrable cocoon of trust and love and the certainty that Jerry would never involve himself in anything even remotely criminal. And that thought was this: had her beloved husband been somehow involved with the death of Lenny Griffin and the disappearance of

183

Sharon Griffin? Clearly he hadn't wanted Sharon here. Her or Loretta. But still, these thoughts were only cocoons of suspicion, not even close to being consciously realized.

"Well," she said, "thanks for . . . you know."

She looked at the bed, shuddered. The spider's flattened body lay just inches from her pillow. Looking at it Jerry was reminded of the drug-induced charges of the NVA, whose bodies always wound up in a tangle of concertina wire, or blown halfway back to Hanoi by a claymore mine, or cut in half by a flurry of machine-gun bullets. That's all they were, just spiders with semi-automatic weapons and camouflage on their faces. Maria didn't see the NVA, she hadn't spent a year in Nam. She could only imagine awakening to a closeup of that hideous, eight-legged body as it clambered onto her chin and then worked its way toward her mouth and nose. That alone made her grimace.

"I'll get rid of that," Jerry said.

"Thanks. And if you could, just have a look around. Where there's one . . ."

"I know. Kill one, a hundred come to the wake."

"Let's hope not."

"Yeah, we haven't been to the market yet. How would we feed them?"

She smiled. That was more like it, she thought. The old Jerry, a joke for any situation. But still she wanted to touch every base as far as the spider was concerned. "That thing carries its young around on its back, you know."

"How'd you know that?"

"I read."

"Oh."

"Think I'll vacuum the bed."

"Good idea. I'll check the rest of the house. They're, uh, they're not poisonous, you know."

"Depends on your definition. They're certainly poison

184

to me. One look and whammo, my heart does a quick freeze!'' The flash of a nervous smile appeared on her face.

Her fear was deeply entrenched. As a kid, living near a woods, she and a group of friends had spent the night on the porch. During the night she'd dreamt that she was being tickled, from the top of her head to the tip of her toes. Upon awakening, however, she and her friends discovered hundreds of small spiders scampering over them. Ever since then her arachnophobia had flourished. And here, it would only strengthen. The fact that she had even consented to this move was a tribute to both their marriage and his literary potential. She knew about the spiders, she'd seen enough of them during their visits with Harry. But Harry, ever the eccentric, only laughed at her fears. He even had names for his spiders, a practice that Maria thought bordered on lunacy. But Jerry respected her fears, enough so to do as she had asked and search the house. In the process he found five more, one of which did, in fact, have her young riding sidesaddle. Each met the same fate as the one that had found its way into the bedroom. The last, the mother, he found near the cellar door, scampering furiously in that direction as if word was out that a giant with an old yearbook was after anything with eight legs. After he killed it, he stood there and simply looked at the door. In his thoughts he imagined Maria down there, a hundred of these huge wolf spiders crawling over her, screams of agony coming out of her fast enough and loud enough to swell her throat shut. He still had *The Clarion* in his hand. He held it under the overhead light and flicked away the remnants of his last kill.

Thumbing through the yearbook some ten minutes later, Jerry suddenly felt his pulse quicken. Staring back at him was Ann Cook; chess club, chemistry club, national honor society member. Beneath her picture was this quote: "Live every moment, love every day—cuz

185

before you know it your precious time slips away." At that he had to smile. How appropriate, he thought. A minute passed, then two. Sweat fell onto the page, onto her picture. Then a low, guttural sound came out of him. Inside of him a competition was being waged; she was an innocent, a possible victim, someone who drastically needed his help. No, she was better off dead, better off as fodder for one of his death scenes. This give and take, of course, was an ancient one, the stuff of which volumes were written, stuff Jerry himself wrote. Which was why he was better equipped to handle it. The evil inside of him was strong, almost overpowering, nurtured by being witness to no fewer than three murders, his view as detailed and as clear as if he had been there in person. But that evil was still weaker than its combatant. With a great, sustained effort, his pulse slowly weakened. His inner dialogue continued, but reason and sanity found stronger voice.

He wondered if she was as pretty now as she had been then. Her hair was long and dark, her features small, pleasant, inviting. Her eyes sparkled with life.

He tore out the page, folded it neatly and put it into his billfold. Then he went into the kitchen and looked in the phonebook for her name. There were no Ann Cooks, just a series of A Cooks with middle initials. But his finger, as if guided over a ouiji board, stopped abruptly on an A E Cook who lived on Linton Avenue. It was her. He was positive. It was her. He knew it with the instinct of a hungry baby near its mother's nipple or a lemming near a cliff. He looked at his watch. Almost ten. He picked up the phone, dialed the number, waited.

After three rings he heard air being exhaled then, "Hello?"

It *was* her.

"Hello!" she said again. Her voice was husky, sexy. Like Demi Moore's, Jerry thought.

"Hi."

"Yes?"

"You don't know me. Well, you did once. My name is . . ." He hesitated. Should he actually tell her his name? What if she thought he was a lunatic or something. She'd call the cops then there'd be a real stink. "Gary. Gary Larsen. We went to high school together."

"We did?"

"Sure, in Naples Falls."

"Gary Larsen, you said?"

"That's right."

"Well, I don't remember you, Gary, but that doesn't mean very much. What do you want?"

"This is rather difficult."

"Look, this isn't an obscene phone call is it, cause if it is?"

"No, no, it's not. I, that is, there's a possibility that you could be in danger."

Silence, save for the crackle of a bad connection.

"Did you hear me, Miss Cook?"

"From who?"

"Well, I don't know, all I know is that some of your friends, people you hung out with in high school, have been killed, and . . ."

"Look, I know all about Tommy and Len. What do you really want?"

"Just what I said. I think you're in danger and I'd like to help."

Without realizing it, his intonation had snuck higher.

"What makes you think I'm in danger, anyway?"

"I'd rather not talk about it over the phone."

"That's the only place I *will* talk about it."

"Look, just give me ten minutes . . ."

He had a thought. He flipped open *The Clarion* again and turned to the seniors.

"Hello? Are you still there?" Ann Cook said.

"Yeah, hold on. Just a sec."

187

"Christ!" she said under her breath.

He found it, the picture of David Warner. Sure, his hair was fuller, his face was leaner, but it was the same man he had "seen" killed at the bar, what he thought might have been a gay bar.

"David Warner," Jerry said. "Did you know a David Warner?"

"Yes. Why?" Her tone was cautious now.

"I think . . . he could be dead. I'm not sure about that, but he could be."

Silence, long and deafening.

"Miss Cook?"

Then, gently, he lost the connection.

Chapter Nineteen

To Tad, unlike most children, sleep was a very good friend, someone standing in a huge ballfield beckoning to him to come and play for a while. But when he heard his dad stomping around the attic, swearing every now and again because he couldn't find what he was looking for, his friend took his ball and went home. Then his mom screamed like a banshee, propelling him from his bed as if he had lain down with a crowd of snakes, not entirely sure why he was running toward the source, only knowing that he didn't want to be alone, not then. But even as he turned the door knob, he stopped. She had, she said, seen a spider. A silly old spider. Everything was okay. Well, maybe not for her, she was deathly afraid of spiders, but at least no one was being murdered. He left the door open and listened to his parents. Their discussions started peaceably enough, deteriorated abruptly, then returned again to normal. He hated it when they fought, which wasn't often but certainly seemed so lately. For a long while after, he heard his dad in all areas of the house, ordered by his mom to kill any spider he could find. The gunshotlike sounds, issued as death sentences were carried out, startled him with their ferocity.

Still on his back, he wiped away a pool of sweat that

had gathered in the hollow of his thin neck, then turned his head to the left and looked out the window. The graveyard, phosphorescent in a wash of moonlight, was tranquil, even soothing, and he was proud of the fact that with each passing day he had grown, if not comfortable, then at least more accustomed to its proximity.

Beside him Prince mewled lowly, also unable to sleep. Tad reached over and scratched his head, a gesture that raised a slight groaning sound of pleasure from the dog.

At the same time, Tad's stomach growled, loud enough for Prince to hear. The dog raised his head, cocked it questioningly, and pointed his ears. "That's me," Tad whispered to him. "Your stomach would growl too if you had what we had for supper. Yucch!" Dessert, however, had been a different matter entirely. The family had shared a pint of Ben and Jerry's New York Super Fudge Chunk, which usually depleted the whole supply. But it *had* been on sale, and when things were on sale, his mom usually bought double. They only sold Ben and Jerry's in pints, which Tad found interesting. Good things, apparently, only came in small packages. Heck, he'd rather have a scoop of Ben and Jerry's then a whole gallon of any other kind.

Eventually he envisioned a pint of New York Super Fudge Chunk adrift before his very eyes. It was a vision he could not resist. He threw the sheet off of him, put on his slippers and padded into the hall. Interested, but exhausted from a day of chasing anything on four legs, Prince only watched.

Tad searched for light under his parent's door. There was none. They were asleep, or at least headed in that direction. He took the stairs as noiselessly as possible, went into the night-light-lit kitchen, and crossed to the refrigerator. His slippers rubbed across the linoleum like sandpaper. A harsh stream of white light that illuminated an area up to and including the closed cellar door, escaped as he opened the door.

He scanned quickly, alert for the telltale bloodred container. Nothing. Sensing the worst, he moved aside a bag of frozen corn, then some shoestring potatoes. Someone, his dad probably, had done a good job of hiding that second pint—he shoved aside a box of fish fillets— but not good enough. There it was, his prize. New York Super Fudge Chunk—a little slice of kid heaven. He took the container out of the freezer, pulled open the silverware drawer, took out too large a spoon, and sat down at the kitchen table.

After a few very large mouthfuls he heard a noise, but the house, like all old houses, made lots of noise.

Sharon dabbed away a tear and looked down the long, narrow, almost perfectly cylindrical earthen tunnel. Webs of varying sizes and shapes, like shattered glass, blocked her way. The thought of crawling down that tunnel, of combating the architects of those webs, was repugnant, but she had no choice. It was either that or die. She looked up into Harry's eyes. Small flames danced there, reflected from a long wooden match held in his hand. Hell in miniature. She searched the corners of her mind. It had been so hard to think lately. What had he said? "Bring me the boy and you can live." Was that it? Was that what he had said? "Because you were the only one who showed me a kindness, I will give you this chance." Yes, that was it. Or something like that. She couldn't be sure. She was so confused. So frightened and confused. The match went out, leaving them in a cloying, velvety darkness, but only until Harry struck another match with his thumbnail. He smiled at her—not a menacing or maniacal smile, but a friendly, almost cherubic smile. It made her feel strangely at ease. It lifted the giant weight that she had carried here, to the yawning mouth of this spider-infested tunnel. Suddenly he wrapped her head in his huge hands, drew her up to his

191

height and kissed her. Blood, her blood, oozed down the side of her chin. And even though part of her conjured up that vile, unspeakable thing that lurks beyond the deepest cave, that smells of old death and flutters ominously at the door of our most vivid nightmares, she still felt greater pleasure than she had ever known. He pushed her softly away, ran his finger through the blood on her chin, sucked it off and then gestured toward the tunnel. She climbed into it willingly, gratefully. And although stones the size of dimes bit into her forearms, for the first twenty or so feet she didn't notice. Nor did she notice the spiders that scurried over her, frightened and enraged as their homes were torn from their foundations. That one kiss had almost drained her of conscious awareness, leaving her with only the memory of it, that and the unspoken promise of even greater joys.

A short while later, while Harry stood at the opposite end and lit her way, she arrived at the trap door. Here she could stand. She wiped her hands on her robe, the robe she had taken with her into the tunnels, really having no choice. How I must look! she thought suddenly as the memory of his kiss faded. If he sees me like this . . . if anyone sees me like this. She looked down the forty foot length of the tunnel, at Harry, seeing only his black outline and the dim yellow light cast from his shoulder-height held match. "I look awful," she said. Harry didn't answer. "I can't let him see me like this. What will I say?"

While she waited for his answer, the match went out. At the same time the trap door opened and Sharon heard a woman say with a strange flippant detachment, "Tell him you're hurt. Tell him anything." Then, less flippantly, "Lure him, Sharon. Don't sit down with him and talk about his day—lure him! That's what Harry wants, you know. He wants to know that you are his, totally. Lure him. Do you understand?"

Sharon looked into the opening. "Who . . . ?" she began.

"Do you understand?" The woman repeated.

"Yes, I understand." Sharon said evenly, torn once more between fear and obedience.

A hand came down. Sharon took it and was effortlessly lifted into the cellar. As soon as she was, the trap door slammed down like a tire striking pavement. Again she was in total darkness.

"Straight ahead," the woman said from behind her. Sharon turned.

"Now it's behind you, deary," the woman said tiredly.

She turned again and now that her eyes had adjusted, she saw a faint, thin shaft of horizontal light under the cellar door. She felt cold hands upon her back, then a light push. She stopped, half-turned, mumbled something unintelligible, and continued, her hands out in front of her. She heard laughter, low and derisive, followed by a warning, "Remember, Sharon, death is not an exclusive club." Then even more laughter.

When she reached the top of the stairs, she turned the knob and pushed the door open a few inches, just far enough to see into the kitchen. There was someone seated at the kitchen table, facing away from her, eating. She looked back into the cellar, then back into the kitchen, and whispered, "Tad?"

The spoon stopped within inches of Tad's propped open mouth. A dullness loitered before his eyes, a dullness that temporarily left his eyes useless, a dullness not caused merely by the sound of his name, but by the disembodied quality of the woman's voice. Had he thought it and not heard it? Could he think of something spontaneously enough and crisply enough to make it sound as if someone had actually spoken to him?

His thoughts were interrupted.

"Tad!" the voice said again, sharply this time.

The voice had a direction now, less a disembodied quality.

He turned in his chair. The cellar door was open about six inches.

"Tad. I'm here, Tad. In the doorway!" said the voice.

He squinted, started to stand, thought better of it, sat back down. "Mrs. Griffin?" he whispered. "But how . . . ?"

"Yes, it's me. Please, come over here. I need your help! I'm, . . . hurt."

He saw a dark hand gesture to him from the doorway, then disappear. At the same time the spoonful of New York Super Fudge Chunk ice cream slipped silently onto the table. Almost a half minute later he asked, "But why don't you just come into the kitchen? I don't understand!"

"No, I can't. Really, I can't," she whispered back.

He searched for pain in her voice. There was none. But if she was hurt . . .

Suspicion coated with rising fear crept into his voice. "What's wrong with you?" he asked.

Footsteps, above him. "Then, "Tad? Is that you, Tad? What are you doing up?"

Jesus—his dad, at the top of the stairs! What to do, what to do? He felt a surge of excitement. "Yeah, it's me, Dad, it's me. God, Dad, you'll never guess . . ." he said.

"No!" Sharon demanded from the gloom. That single, whispered word echoed through the kitchen.

Silence.

"Guess what, son?"

"Don't tell him I'm here," Sharon said.

He squinted toward the slightly gapped door. God, he wished he could see her! "Why not?" he asked.

"Son?"

"Please, Tad! Trust me!" she whispered.

"Listen, I'm coming down there . . ."

Tad turned his head toward the dining room, half

194

expecting his dad to appear in the doorway at any moment. Five seconds passed, then ten.

"Please, Tad!" Sharon repeated.

Finally he said, "It's nothing, Dad, really. I, uh, I found the other pint of ice cream, is all."

Another lingering silence.

"I'll be up in a little while. I was just hungry."

After a few seconds he heard, "Five minutes, son. That's it, just five minutes. And, Christ, don't eat all the goddamn ice cream!"

"Sure, Dad. Five minutes. Gotcha."

Tad listened while his dad went back into his bedroom and closed the door. Then he whispered, "How'd you get down there—and why don't you want my dad to know?"

"I just don't."

"But why? That's stupid!"

"Please, Tad!"

There was total and utter silence then, only the noise of his thoughts. "What, what happened to you, anyway?" he asked.

"I'm hurt. I need you to come over here and help me."

He spoke quickly, impatiently. "Where are you hurt?"

Silence.

"Sharon?"

"I, I hurt my ankle."

Her voice was strangely mechanical, still lacking the edge pain would lend it. Maybe, he thought, he should tell his dad. If she was telling the truth—and why shouldn't she be . . . ?

"Please, Tad. I need your help."

By now Tad had grown ever more cautious. Why would she want him to come into the cellar this late at night? And with no light, how could he see to help. Why didn't he just come in and sit down? Something was wrong, terribly wrong.

"Maybe I better get my dad," he said.

"No, Tad, don't! If you must know, I came down here

195

to hide. Lenny's killer is after me. He wants to kill me just like he killed him. Please, you've got to help me. Please, help me!"

"How?"

"Come down here. I'll show you where I'm hiding. You can bring me food. Please."

"But why can't you come in here?"

"Tad. Dammit, Tad! It's your dad! Your dad killed Lenny! Now he wants to kill me!"

"My Dad? But he wouldn't, he couldn't!"

"Yes, your dad! Right after your grandmother left he came up and admitted it to me! He said . . . he said he wanted to get rid of his terrible burden. Please, you've got to help me!"

Again a dark arm came through the doorway, gesturing, beckoning. But his dad a killer! That was ridiculous. She was lying. She had to be. His dad would never . . .

He really had no choice. Obviously Mrs. Griffin was not right. She needed help, more than he could give. "I'm gonna go upstairs and get my sweater," he said. "It's cold down there, I should have a sweater. Mom said."

Sharon heard movement behind her, close behind her. She turned. Then she heard, "You failed, Sharon. Too bad!"

In an instant she felt an amazingly tight and focused pain, a pain that, as if borne on a vibrating steel cable, found its way to her heart. A loud gasp issued from her, her eyes rolled back into their sockets, her body quivered violently. Then she breathed a series of quick, tortured breaths. Her last.

Tad stood, and as he did, he heard; "You're going to tell your dad, aren't you? You're going upstairs to tell

196

your dad I'm here. All you're doing is signing my death warrant, that's all. You know that, don't you?"

Confused, Tad stopped. That wasn't Sharon's voice.

Suddenly he heard strange, accusing laughter followed by, "You are, aren't you! Don't lie to me, you little shit!"

His blood turned to ice. It wasn't her!

Something moved in the doorway. Frozen by fear, he could only watch from his chair.

The floor creaked under a sudden weight. And now, as the doorway opened just a little further, he was able to make out a woman's outline. Then, he saw her. A woman he had never seen before. She was smiling, slowly working her way beyond the doorway and into the kitchen.

Even in the dim light, her face was remarkably white, making her full red lips seem cartoonish. Her hair was tangled and matted, and the cool, damp air escaping through the open cellar door grew more nauseatingly foul with each closing step. As her smile corrupted into a grin, Tad burst right past her into the dining room, where he barked his shin against a chair before he ran up the stairs, taking two at a time.

Two steps from the top he stopped. His dad was there, looking down. Tad turned and pointed, expecting to see her just behind him, at the bottom of the stairs. "Dad? God, Dad, there's a woman in the kitchen! There's a woman in the kitchen!" he yelled.

But to Jerry his son was only a bothersome insect, buzzing through a still vivid and horrific vision, his words no more than blood pounding in his ears.

Tad looked into his father's eyes. Light reflected off of them like moonlight off flat stones. Behind Jerry, Tad watched as his mother drew ever closer, her face harshly reflecting the anguish of confusion and fear.

Jerry had witnessed Sharon Griffin's death. He had seen her fear contorted face, but from an odd angle, from the side. Then it appeared that she had been pulled away

197

from the light, from the doorway. Seconds later, and fading, he had seen a woman reaching toward that door. Then there was only darkness.

Later, Jerry took a flashlight and a poker from the fireplace into the basement. He searched long and hard for Sharon Griffin and the other woman his son said was down there, the woman he had also briefly seen. His family waited at the top of the stairs while he searched, his light revealing only a colony of wolf spiders and a few quick silverfish. He had half-expected to stumble onto Sharon Griffin's body, but the basement was surprisingly bare. He found absolutely nothing. Only the traces of a highly unpleasant odor.

Chapter Twenty

Maria propped herself onto her elbow and studied her sleeping husband. He was on his side, facing away from her. Maybe sleep was a release for him, a hiding place, she thought. But then, maybe he wasn't sleeping, maybe he was only pretending to sleep, hoping to minimize the severity of their situation. And as far as she was concerned, the situation had definitely gotten out of hand. Tad had been extremely persuasive, very believable. Frighteningly so. Jerry rolled onto his back and now Maria could see his face. His eyeballs were moving back and forth beneath his lids as if he were watching a table tennis match on fast forward. REM sleep. He moaned a little and she had the urge to wake him up, but she didn't. He needed his sleep, regardless of what he dreamt. They all needed their sleep for that matter. But as she thought about it, she wondered if she really wanted to close her eyes and block out the night; especially this night. And what about Tad? Would he be able to sleep now, given what he had seen, real or imagined? She got up quietly and crossed to her son's half-open door. He lay on his side, one arm sprawled over the bed, his hand resting on Prince's back. Dog and master appeared to be sleeping. She was glad for that. She smiled. Just like your dad, huh, kid? Just sleep your cares away.

Without warning she suddenly felt huge rashes of

gooseflesh raise on her naked arms. She rubbed them and glanced up and down the hallway. Satisfied that she was alone, she looked back at her son. She was afraid for him, for all of them, maybe that was why . . . But suddenly she realized what had really caused her chill, for she saw it again. For one brief and very frightening moment, she had imagined her dear son in his coffin, one arm sprawled over the side as if his last living act had been to grope for his beloved pet. Seeing this, tears swelled in the corners of her eyes. She raised her hand to wipe them away, but did not. There was no one to see, not now, not here. She could cry if she wanted. She could release her long-repressed concern for her child. What's going on in this house? she thought as fat tears worked slowly down her cheeks. In this town? And what price are we going to have to pay for Jerry's success? She had known when they had embarked on this "great adventure," as Jerry had referred to it, that there would be dangers, but she hadn't considered those dangers to be anything but financial. Still sleeping, Tad scratched his nose. Perhaps a dream butterfly had landed on it. Maria snuffled and silently remarked that more than anything in the world she wanted to leave this house. She wanted to go into her son's room, scoop him up into her arms and just leave. But what she wanted, she knew so very well, was not what her husband wanted.

From the other room, she heard Jerry moan again, louder this time. She blew a kiss to her sleeping son and went back to bed.

Chapter Twenty-One

During the remainder of a night that was largely sleepless save for twenty minutes including the brief period when his mother stood in the doorway, Tad had mentally reviewed each word he and Mrs. Griffin had said to each other—a conversation he would have preferred to forget. And it was because of that conversation and other recent events that the house had begun to close in on him, as if he had somehow grown ten times his normal size. During the night it had become a dream house, with long, narrow passageways that stretched to infinity and ceilings that scraped the edge of space, a vantage point from which he saw himself shivering in a tight, dark corner, waiting just waiting, but for what, he didn't know. It was the not knowing that gnawed at him. Now he wanted to get away, to forget, if only for a few, nerve-quieting hours.

The night before had been summarily dropped as a topic of conversation, that much became abundantly clear as he sat down for breakfast and said, "You sure there was nothin' down there, Dad?"

His dad didn't respond, at least not verbally. He only stared, his eyes like glinting steel. Maria poured him a cup of coffee, which at least dulled the shine of his stare, and said, "If your father said there was nothing down there, Tad, then there's nothing down there. Okay?"

He just stared at her for a moment, to see if she really believed that. Then, unable to determine whether she did or did not, he said, "Yeah, okay, Mom."

But the fact remained that he had spoken with someone who had sounded very much like Sharon Griffin and he had seen another woman come into the kitchen, a middle-aged woman who, Tad found time to admit during the night, was very pretty, despite her tangled, matted hair and blanched skin. They, Sharon and the other woman, hadn't been "figments of his abundant imagination," as his mother had said. He knew imagination when he saw it and he hadn't seen it last night.

Rising, he chugged his orange juice, tapped his leg, said, "C'mon, boy," and left, Prince following.

He stopped abruptly as Maria called after him, "Where are you going, Tad?"

For the first time in his young life Tad became agitated with her. He was a kid, just a little kid. And it was summer. How did he know where he was going? Down to the swimmin' hole, maybe, if they had one in this town, or over across the tracks to look for old Indian warheads. How did he know? Kids didn't have places to go, not until they became adults. Gees! Why were parents so stupid sometimes?

"I don't know, just around," he answered, trying, but failing, to disguise his impatience.

"You got Prince's leash?"

"Aw, Mom!"

"Tad, you know the trouble that dog gets into. Put him on his leash!"

Further angered, Tad went back into the house, took Prince's leather leash from a hook by the door, and left. After he had reached the end of the driveway and was out of sight, he emancipated his dog, in complete disregard of his mother's wishes.

In the depths of thought, mechanically putting one foot in front of the other, Tad lost track of the distance he had traveled. Again his thoughts had centered on Sharon Griffin and the other woman, especially the other woman. She had projected a homicidal quality that Tad would never forget.

Above, a huge dark cloud trimmed in gold hid a broiling sun and bathed the town in that shadowless cast peculiar to approaching storms. It was a little after ten in the morning. By eleven it would be raining.

Tad stopped, his brain temporarily numbed. He had walked quite a ways, further than his mother would probably allow, to the edge of the festival. The leash in his hand came into focus in his perpheral vision.

Prince! God, where's Prince? he wondered somewhat frantically.

Absorbed by his thoughts, he had forgotten about his dog. He looked left, toward the road. A blue pickup truck trailing blue-gray smoke roared past, kicking up stones and a cloud of dirt from the shoulder. After choking down a lungful of dust, he waved the cloud away and looked to his right. And sighed. Prince, thankfully, was squatting beside him, his head cocked, his huge eyes probing. Tad stroked his head, mumbled something about how his dog *did not* get into trouble, then surveyed what lay before him.

The festival, at night, had made him feel like a tightly wound toy, broken in that position, thereby having no release. It had not been an uncomfortable feeling, not really, just odd. A different feeling than he had ever felt. He had been subdued by his surroundings, tethered by them. A prisoner to them. His sense of awe and wonder had been unparalleled. But it was daytime now. Whatever made him feel that way should be gone, in hiding or something, waiting for the sun to go down. And, for the most part, it was. But staring out at this slumbering festival, he felt something else, something sinister, threatening. Analyzing it, he could only equate it to the sinking emptiness he felt as his father climbed the stairs to discipline him after he had done something terribly wrong. But he had never done anything quite this wrong. Never.

There were only a few poeple milling about. Some wandered into and out of tents, some got into cars parked along the side and drove off and still others stood and simply talked. No one seemed to notice him. All of the tents were drawn tight, closed for business until later that evening. To his left, across the road, he saw the high school and the tents pitched on its lawns. He envisioned a blot of measleslike circles on the ground beneath, where the grass had died. It seemed strange that a school would allow that to happen. Another black cloud drifted by, prompting Tad to gaze skyward. The air was teeming. Thunderstorm weather, he thought. He'd heard his dad talk about the weather often enough, usually to himself when he was only sitting at his word processor, instead of writing.

It occurred to him then that he had, indeed, walked quite a distance. And he was thirsty from that walk. Dirty little balls of spit rolled inside his mouth, a gift from the truck that had roared past. Down the road, just beyond a street light and on the right hand side, he saw a large vertical spoon suspended by horizontal posts: the Silver Spoon Restaurant. He shoved his hands into his jeans pockets; a thumbtack pecked at his finger as he fisted the contents. An inspection revealed a golf tee, the aforementioned thumbtack, and sixty-three cents in the form of two quarters, a dime and three pennies. Enough, he thought, to buy a Coke.

He paired Prince and his leash and, a minute or so later, pushed open the door to the Silver Spoon. He had been here before with his mother. They had occupied a booth where they had scanned the wall full of snapshots given to Al Sanders, the owner (only part-owner now) by high school kids who had long since grown up and left Naples Falls. Al displayed the snapshots proudly. How many people, Al often wondered, could boast that many friends, anyway? A whole goddamn lifetime of friends.

Two things became immediately apparent to Tad as he entered: an odor, coppery, sharp and nauseating (the smell of something dead but only loosely covered); and Al Sanders, a beefy, bulldog faced man dressed in a stained, short-sleeved blue shirt. Tad remembered a much gentler face, but, he thought, maybe the smell—much stronger now than it had been during his other visit—must have something to do with that look. Al glared at Tad from behind the vacant lunch counter very much like a teacher who's had to repeat himself.

A deep, exasperated breath was his prologue, then, "You read, boy?"

Tad looked left then right, but saw nothing except a SEAT YOURSELF sign right in front of him.

Al pointed rigidly and said, "There, in the window. See it?"

Tad turned. The sign, to the right and beneath the arched restaurant logo, said simply, NO PETS!

Tad studied the sign for a moment, his brain supplying the closest answer it could. Letters were turned, but still, they *were* in the right order. "Step on what?" he asked finally.

Al's dark-circled eyes slit quizzically. Then he grinned menacingly. "You tryin' to poke fun at me, boy?" he asked. "The sign says No Pets and what you got on that leash is a pet! Least ways it sure looks like one from here. Christ, we got enough smell round here without caterin' to animals!"

Prince squirmed backwards as he attempted to hide behind his master. Tad, feeling a trifle foolish for his interpretation, said simply, "Oh."

Al Sanders only mumbled something incoherent.

"But I just want a Coke, mister," Tad continued, half pleading. "Then me and Prince will leave. I'm real thirsty. And Prince might get hit by a car if I let him go . . ."

"Look, the sign says No Pets and that's what it means!"

"Oh, let him stay until he gets his Coke," came a low, friendly, female voice. The woman was seated at a table parallel to Al Sanders. She was hidden from view by the SEAT YOURSELF sign. Tad stepped to his left. She was a fat, dark-haired woman with a crop of small, dark blotches on her large-featured face. A cigarette with a long looping ash like a malignancy dangled between her nicotine-stained fingers. She raised the cigarette to her lips, careful not to upset the ash, took a puff, blew the smoke out her nostrils in a natural exhalation, and smiled. At the same time, the ash fluttered onto the table. Al looked at her, but the woman, who now owned controlling interest in The Silver Spoon and saw no reason to turn away cash money, brooked back any further protest by simply raising her hand.

Grudgingly, Al wiped his hands on his apron and said, "Coke's seventy-five cents. You got that much, boy?"

Tad walked to the counter, held out his hand and with unabashed optimism said, "I got sixty-three cents."

Al looked at the contents of Tad's small hand, then at Tad. He didn't smile, but his face softened like a spent rubberband, largely suppressing Mr. Hyde and revealing Dr. Jekkyl. "Oh what the hell," he said, "you can owe me."

"Thanks." Tad cheerfully replied.

He took the glass to the same booth he and his mother had shared and sucked up a refreshing mouthful of Coke.

Out of the corner of his eye he watched as a man came in, sat down at the counter, then got up again like he was going to leave. But Al, who could easily imagine a CLOSED DUE TO BANKRUPTCY sign going up very shortly, was too quick for him. With a flourish, he laid down eating utensils and a napkin and offered the man anything he wanted at what he called "Off season prices," prompting the man, a tourist who very well might have mistaken the odor for local color, to sit back down and order a ham and cheese on rye.

When the Coke was about half finished—not very long

206

after he had sat down—Tad felt his attention drawn to the snapshot cluttered wall just to his left, above the flaking, peach-colored plastic trim. His mind was processing what it had seen the night before and what it had only glimpsed days earlier. Tad's eyes scanned the photos. He felt a slight chill. He stood up, on the hard, plastic seat of the booth. Al, seeing this, promptly ordered him down. Tad didn't hear. Al repeated himself and started toward Tad who was now running his finger over the crowd of smiling faces, each describing the generation from which it came, either by hairstyle or clothing or both. By now Al was parallel to him, yelling. Shirley, the woman who had befriended Tad for the sake of a meager profit, had also started in Tad's direction. But by now, as they closed on him, Tad had found what he had been unconsciously looking for. He snapped the photo down and stared at it, his eyes like two great o's. Suddenly it was ripped out of his hand.

"Knew I shouldn't a let you in here," Al said. "Knew I shoulda kicked you and that mangy dog out first thing!"

Tad reached for the picture, much to Al's surprise, who stuffed it safely into his shirt pocket.

"Maybe you better drink up that Coke and go," Shirley advised.

"But you don't understand . . . that picture. I know her. I saw that lady before," Tad explained.

Al smiled, shook his head.

"What, she your mother or something?"

"Please, mister, I won't take it. I just want to see it. Please!"

The woman shrugged. "Let him see it," she said to Al.

"Dammit, these are mine. I've had these pictures for years and years, Shirley!"

"Relax, Al, all the kid wants to do is look at it."

"Christ," Al muttered as he took the snapshot from his pocket.

He looked at it for a moment and announced, "I'll hold it, you look."

Tad stared at the picture. She was younger, years younger, but it was her. The woman he had seen last night, it really was her.

"What's it say on the other side?" he said in a burst of inspiration.

Al took a deep breath and turned the photo over. "For Al, Love Chrissy Norville. That's all it says. Satisfied?"

Then he stuffed the picture back into his breast pocket.

The smell of fresh summer air, perfumed lightly by the fragrance of cinnamon rolls wafting from the bakery two doors down, was a welcome respite from the lingering death smell inside the Silver Spoon, but Tad hardly noticed. With Prince in tow, he ran through town and further, toward Walker Norville's house.

Chapter Twenty-Two

Ann Cook, in the corridors of thought, poured too much water onto her African violet then cursed because she had.

The call from Gary Larsen—if that really was his name—telling her that David was dead, and that she herself was in danger, had unnerved her to the point of distraction. She tried to busy herself with mundane things, but that, she finally decided after she had almost drowned her African violet, was the wrong thing to do.

As yet she hadn't heard anything about David, either on radio or television, but that really didn't mean very much. His body could have been dumped somewhere, left to the devices of wild animals and insects, a mental picture she left undescribed. And a call to his office, taken by his secretary, revealed that he wasn't in and wasn't going to be. He had called in sick. That, of itself, had further aroused her suspicions. There was a coincidence evolving here that stretched credibility and bred this notion: David might have been kidnapped and the kidnapper could have forced him to make that call. In fact, a murderer could have made that call to postpone discovery of the crime. Her suspicions were strengthened when she further learned that David was, coincidentally, not at home. She had called.

Her home was a small and spotlessly maintained

colonial. Small and spotless also described the way she tried to live her life, in diametrical opposition to the behavior that had ruled her formative years. The change had taken place for a number of reasons, but one loomed as large as any—Harry Matheson could have been killed that night. He had, in fact, been extremely lucky to get away with just a few scars. And it had been her fault as much as anyone's. She had gone along just for the thrill. And had he been killed, had he died a death as painful as any she could possibly imagine, she would never have forgiven herself. "No harm, no foul," was the way David Warner had put it then. But there had been harm, physically and emotionally. Harry had suffered tremendously. Now Len and Tom were dead. Sharon was missing. She had called her, too, but all she got was a quickly blurted message on the answering machine. Now this nonperson Gary Larsen tells her that David is dead and that she could be next. No wonder her paranoia was like that of a blind mouse in a lion's den. She found it impossible to keep her thoughts from focusing on that night, twenty years earlier, when Harry Matheson had almost been killed.

"Christ, be careful! You wanta kill him?" she said to Lenny.

"What are you talking about?"

"The gag, you asshole, you got the gag around his nose, too!"

"Shit!"

She felt her heart flutter as Lenny pulled the gag down.

"Albert Fucking Einstein, we got us Albert Fucking Einstein," Tommy said disdainfully, slightly averting his eyes from the road and narrowly missing a festival goer as she ran blindly across the road.

"You sure that house is safe?" she asked.

"Sure. No problem," Lenny said.

"The torches aren't going to burn the place down or

210

anything, are they?"

"No way. We put 'em halfway."

"Smooth as a baby's butt," Tommy said.

And, in fact, everything had progressed smoothly, at least until Sharon, suspecting something had gone wrong—his screams were too real, too filled with pain—pulled open the cellar door and found poor Harry Matheson rolling on the floor, ablaze, attempting to keep himself from becoming a human torch. It was a turn of events no one had contemplated, that vacated the house with all the dispatch of a ticking bomb (which, in effect, it was). And nobody had ever been the wiser. Or so she thought. Now she wasn't so sure. The fact that everyone involved was either dead, missing or half-mad with fear was a huge convincer otherwise.

She picked up her watering can and went into her small, stockade-fence-enclosed back yard, which was bordered by a detached one-car garage. Annuals and perennials of all colors and sizes encircled her like the canvas of a mad artist.

Out front a car pulled into a curbside parking space. The driver killed the engine. Ann, replaying that night once more, didn't hear. It was almost eleven A.M. and it was raining.

"And you say you told your parents what you saw?" Walker Norville said. Still trying to return a semblance of normalcy to his actions, he poured Tad a glass of lemonade. At the same time rain began to pelt against the windows like armies of suicidal insects.

"My dad even went down into the cellar to look," Tad said. "But he didn't find nothin'. Nothin' at all! My mom just told me I imagined it all. You know how moms are."

Rain waved onto the road now, driven by winds that were compressed and strengthened by the surrounding hills. Summer had belched. Heidi and King pushed themselves deep into the corners of their homes.

211

Walker sat down with Tad, his fingers laced together. He had an urge to call Guy Henry, to relate Tad's story. And he would have had he not known Guy as well as he did, at least by reputation. Guy Henry, because there were other forces at work here, because the crime now had the sheen of something other than a normal kidnapping or a missing persons, probably wouldn't know what to do with this new "clue." The sheriff, although highly capable with speeding tickets and drunken husbands intent on violently teaching their wives a lesson, probably wouldn't take this very seriously. The road paved by this new clue more than likely ended right there at the Silver Spoon Restaurant. Any checking to be done would have to be done by him.

"There's probably a real good explanation for all this," he said to Tad, unsure of what that explanation could possibly be but feeling a vague duty to at least mention the possibility.

"What about Mrs. Griffin? She talked to me, Mr. Norville. She said she was hurt, that she had hurt her ankle," Tad argued.

Still Walker groped, still he denied. "But you know, when you think about it, she sounds like she was a little confused. Could be that she was in your cellar and when you went upstairs, she left. Could be also that she went crazy cause of the way her husband died and she'd been hiding in the cellar all along. Husband gets killed, like to made her snap. Made her go crazy. And crazy people, well, they'll do most anything."

Because of his age and accompanying wisdom, Walker could have said about anything, but nothing he could say could refute the fact that the woman Tad saw entering the kitchen was the same woman whose photograph had been pinned to the wall in The Silver Spoon. The same woman now staring back at him from the tens of photographs displayed throughout this house.

Walker went to the window and looked out, in thought. Normally rain was soothing, cloistering. Now it

212

was savage and mindless.

Recently, he had remanded the word "vampire" to a remote corner of his mind, yet not so remote as to be irretrievable. Since Christine's disappearance he had read what he could on the subject of vampires. The books were still stacked neatly on his kitchen table, where he did most of his reading. Of course, there had been a reason for his sudden interest.

Christine's behavior during the week before her disappearance had been abnormal, at least to Walker. A totally analytical stranger would have termed it frighteningly bizarre. She rose at nightfall, almost precisely when the sun set, loitering only briefly before leaving until almost sunrise. Where she went, she told him, was none of his business. She was a big girl now and she could "damn well do what she pleased with her time." And she hadn't gone to work either. Each of the three days she was supposed to have worked, she called in sick, spending the entire day in her room with the drapes tightly drawn. The room, Walker saw only once, was as dark as the bottom of a well, and as musty. But she had indeed looked less than her normal self. Her skin had blanched sharply, and her eyes were forever bloodshot. Her hair was like wild, dry cornsilk. And she had always fussed over her hair, even as a little girl. She didn't eat either, which Walker found most odd. Not once did she even snack. She did, she said, "Eat at night." And being ill, she hadn't had much of an appetite anyway. She had snapped at him a number of times as well, which was very unlike her. He had, on the day of her disappearance, called Dr. Simmons just to see if he could drop by to have a look at her. She'd lost control when she found out. She threw things around—anything she could find, she swore at him viciously, using cuss words that he hadn't heard since boot camp, and then even a few more he had never heard, words that had a vaguely ethnic quality. Finally, she had

213

gone back into her room and locked the door. Two hours later, she was gone for good, before Dr. Simmons could see her.

In the course of his reading he learned that vampires were not really alive, that, guided by the devil's dark hand, they were only capable of mimicking life. Originally he had planned his research to put his mind at ease, to find some benchmark that would discount forever his insane and completely illogical thinking. But he found no such antidote, no cure-all for her behavior. Quite the contrary. Her behavior, as he had witnessed it, was detailed in each of the books he had taken out of the library. She could have been a case study. To Walker, however, that still proved little. His blind faith in her innate goodness was as rigid as that of ancient man who saw only a flat horizon, who was incapable of a larger, more truth-revealing vision. Plainly, and even during that week before her disappearance, she had been a living, breathing being. And the only proof offered to the contrary was behavior consistent with what he considered to be fictional accounts. But now this boy, this innocent had effectively weakened his arguments, had effortlessly given rise to real doubt.

Staring out through the rain, his mind's eye suddenly supplied him with what to a father was the most vile of images; his remarkably caring and giving daughter stalking and then ravishing a victim simply to satisfy her blood lust. The image was real enough to serve as an effective counter balance to his flat horizon philosophy, and it invoked from him this unspoken yet solemn vow: if his daughter had somehow, someway, become a vampire, then he would do what he could to release her from that eternal hell. Whatever the books advised. No matter how painful, for her or him.

"And my dad . . ."

"What?" Walker asked, as Tad intruded upon his most private thoughts.

"My dad. He's been acting kinda funny lately."

214

"What do you mean, funny?"

"Maybe it's because he's writing a book."

"Tad, please, you're not making yourself very clear."

"He's . . . mean. He was mean to my grandma and Mrs. Griffin and even Mom last night."

"And he's not usually?"

"No, well, sometimes, but not like he has been lately."

Tad got up and stood beside Walker. He had a photo of Christine in his hand. They both looked across the road at Tad's house. Any detail was obscured by the sheeting rain. *Something is definitely going on over there,* Walker thought, setting his face rigidly. *Is Christine somehow involved? And what about Jerry and Maria and Tad? Are they safe over there?* He had serious doubts. Jerry, at least according to Tad, was acting strangely. Why? But there was really nothing he could do, other than attempt to talk with Jerry Matheson, to tell him that the person his son claimed to have seen bore a marked resemblance to Christine. More than anything, Walker Norville wanted to cross that road and go into that house, perhaps even undertake a detailed inspection of the cellar. True, Christine could have left with Sharon Griffin, if, in fact, Sharon Griffin had been there at all, and true, Tad could have seen someone else entirely, just a remarkable— admittedly far-fetched—coincidence, but he thought not.

Walker put his hand on Tad's shoulder.

"You gonna go talk to my dad with me, Mr. Norville?" Tad asked.

Walker smiled at him, a smile Tad quickly recognized as forced, and answered, "You betcha."

Chapter Twenty-Three

Jerry's hands curled tightly on the wheel. The rain had decreased to a gentle, mesmerizing tapping. The sky was reduced to weak, straggling, gray-shaded clouds. Ann Cook's high school picture lay on the seat beside him. He picked it up and coarsely rubbed it with his thumb as if he were rubbing an insect off his windshield. He didn't notice his rapid respiration or the droplets of slick sweat gathering on his forehead. He put the picture back down on the seat. When he did, it seemed to change. He looked more closely at it, as if through a microscope. Yes, he was sure of it. It had changed. There was fear in her eyes now, and her silly, plastic smile had become a deep, sorrowful frown. A tear trickled down her cheek. Or was it a raindrop reflected off the windshield? Irrespective of the reason, Jerry found this all vastly amusing. Sudden movement, an old man on a bike, diverted his attention, and after the old man had pedaled slowly and shakily by, Jerry became fascinated by the clonelike colonials on either side of the street. In the lawn of the house to the right of Ann Cook's he saw an oversized maple tree, large enough to almost completely hide the house from view. Looking at it, he imagined Ann Cook dangling from one of its large branches, her neck twisted like wound licorice, her skin a midwinter blue, her sluglike tongue huge and bloated and lolled off to the side. But it was her

216

eyes bulging with fear, as eyes sometimes do if fear is strong enough, that drew the bulk of his attention. He imagined them ballooning to the size of oranges and bursting in a wash of body fluids and three-dimensional manifestions of injested fear. Tiny demons swam merrily in the pool, hissing and spitting and swearing a blue streak while Ann only dangled, her empty sockets like cigar burns on a blue tablecloth. Seeing all this, he asked himself, can I frighten her that much? Can I make her eyes bulge?

Careful.

Sure he could. Child's play!

Careful!

He could go even further than that, he could . . .

Rain, it's the rain . . . slow down, Jer. Bring it back. Get a hold, dammit, get a hold!

With a great sustained effort he was able to bring his respiration and state of mind back to normal. He picked up the picture and put it back into his wallet. With a final look at the house to reassure himself that he was doing the right thing, the moral thing, he got out of the car, walked up the sidewalk to Ann Cook's front door and rang the bell.

Maria pushed the curtain aside. Across the road, waiting for a line of cars to pass, she saw her son and neighbor. They were holding hands. Tad was carrying something that from here looked like a picture in a gold frame. She dropped the curtain and went out the front door to greet them. Seeing her now, Walker smiled and waved. She waved back and thought, *What a funny smile. So forced, so wooden.* Then, and for no apparent reason, other than Walker Norville's wooden smile, she thought, *Oh, God, something's wrong. Something's terribly wrong!*

As if such an action could somehow produce a louder

217

noise, Jerry punched the nipple of the doorbell with his knuckle, which peeled back the skin on that knuckle enough to reveal a flowering redness. He waited. Punched the bell again. She was home, her car, her blue Tempo, sat in the driveway off to the side, not three feet from the closed garage door.

"Dammit, will you just answer the fucking door!" he said under his breath. "I just want to talk. Dammit!"

He punched the bell again.

"Just fucking talk! What's wrong with that? C'mon. Answer the fucking door!"

Yet another punch. Now his knuckle bled openly.

"Fuck it!" he said as he clamped his hand around the doorknob.

Maria could only stare at the picture as she remembered the description her son had given her the night before—he had, by now, told her the entire story, from the beginning, including the odor that had almost knocked him off his feet at the Silver Spoon. They were in the kitchen, seated at the table. She gave Walker Norville a questioning look then looked at her son. Then she looked at the closed cellar door.

"Maybe we should check, huh, Mom?" Tad said.

She turned sharply. "What?" she said.

"Maybe Dad was . . . wrong. Maybe . . ."

A firm resolve affixed itself to her face. She had once imagined her son lost in the surrounding woods, at the blind mercy of a killer blizzard. Allowing him to venture into that basement would amount to the same thing. "No!" she said with an implacability that was frightening. "You must never, ever, go down into that basement. Do you understand me, young man? Is that very clear?"

"But, Mom . . ."

"Not another word, Tad! The best thing to do here, I think, and I hope you concur with me on this, Mr.

218

Norville , is to call the sheriff. Certainly he'll be able to see . . ."

"No. I can't say's I agree," Walker interrupted. "I know Guy Henry. The word of a child—one with a grand imagination at that, whose dad writes horror books, well, Guy Henry would probably laugh inside real hard. Oh, on the outside he'd look official and say sure, he'd check into it, but on the inside he'd just laugh. Count on it."

She looked at him with only slight surprise. Thus far the law had gotten nowhere, but this shaky bit of evidence seemed to offer a glimmer of hope. Apparently he wanted to handle things personally, and that was understandable. She would probably react the same way if the situation were reversed, if Tad were the one missing. But when everything was stacked and counted, when all ulterior motives were registered, what was left was the possibility that she, Maria Matheson, was very possibly the only completely sane person involved. Certainly Jerry had, for some reason, been acting awfully weird of late. And Tad, well, Walker Norville had struck the nail firmly on the head. Tad was his father's son. His imagination was remarkably vivid. The fact that he had described a woman who resembled the woman in the photograph could be attributed to many things. She was pretty, yes, but not uniquely so. Many women would answer her description. And perhaps he had seen photographs of her before at Walker's house, although she didn't think he had ever been inside until today. Perhaps Walker had described her to him. Yes, that seemed more logical. All this weighed, she made a choice. She got up, went to the phone and dialed the operator.

"Sheriff's office, please," she said.

Walker only watched, poised between action and logic.

"It's for the best," she said, covering the mouthpiece as she waited for someone to pick up the phone.

"Sheriff's office," a woman said flatly.

"Yes, is the sheriff in, please?"

219

"Well, no, as a matter of fact, he's not. Who is this, please?"

"When do you expect him?"

"Well, that's hard to say. Listen, ma'am, I need your name, for the record."

"Christ . . . Maria Matheson."

"Oh, yes, Mrs. Matheson, I know where you live . . ."

"Please, when do you expect him?"

Satisfied that Maria was a local and not attached to any state-operated office also engaged in the now much-discussed case, she spoke more freely, both in tone and word. "All he said to me was that he was going out and that he didn't really know when he'd be back, but that if he was lucky enough, he'd bring back a prize buck."

"A prize buck? But it's not even hunting season."

"Just his words, Mrs. Matheson."

"Well have him call me as soon as he comes in. Can you do that? It's very important."

She gave her number, hung up and said, "Guess we wait. Jerry should be back soon, anyway. At least I hope so."

It was like looking down a square tunnel. From the front door, Jerry could see all the way into the backyard, past the dining room on the left and the living room on the right. Ann Cook was there, facing away from him. There was a watering can in her hand. "Christ," he mumbled, "you deaf or what?"

He started toward her, mentally formulating what he should say, some excuse for just walking in. But he left those explanations unspoken. The closer he drew to her, the tighter his muscles became, like those of a predatory cat. And by the time he had reached the back door, only ten or so feet away from her, his hands had curled into talons. He could easily imagine her frail neck wrapped by those hands. And he could just as easily imagine the tremendous surprise on her face as he strangled the life

220

out of her, as her eyes bulged and bulged and bulged. But then, and without warning, he experienced an even more pleasing vision. Almost tasted it. In this vision, he traversed the distance between them in stunning silence, clasped her shoulders and then slowly pressed his teeth into the soft flesh at the base of her neck, puncturing the skin with ease and feeling his fangs dip deep into the river of a pulsating artery. She moaned, and her head rolled back in reaction to her uncontrollable pleasure as a thick, rich blood flooded into his eager mouth, as his head bobbed slowly up and down in rhythm with her heartbeat. Finally he stopped, stepped backwards and let her collapse almost majestically to the floor. Simple death, at that moment—knives, suffocation, drowning— seemed pitiful in comparison. And he knew exactly what he must do, what he had really always wanted to do. He stepped forward, fully intending to realize his vision. But Ann Cook, at least for now, had a friend, a foe of the demon that had surfaced. And although this foe had been substantially weakened, it still knew a few tricks. Without knowing it, Jerry said, "I told you, dammit! I called and told you. But no, you wouldn't believe me, you wouldn't . . ."

She wheeled. And her eyes did bulge. Then she screamed.

It was a scream that successfully surprised his demon, enough to suppress it, at least long enough for sanity to rise to an equal footing. She screamed again, and put a hand defensively out in front of her, backing away with the clumsy, stumbling gait of someone who knew that death was near. But finally and after he had successfully suppressed his demon, he ran to her, grabbed her by the shoulders and shook her gently. "Calm down, just calm down," he ordered, trying to keep his tone both authoritative and friendly. "I'm not going to hurt you!"

She shook away from him and backed up further, her eyes still wild with fear. "You're him!" she muttered, breathless.

"Who?"

"Him! Harry Matheson!"

"Harry? What's Harry . . . No, no I'm not, really. I'm his twin brother, Jerry. I'm not going to hurt you. I'm the one that called you. Remember? I used the name Gary Larsen."

She was braced against the stockade fence now. Like melted crayons, flowers lay crushed beneath her feet. The fear on her face made room for confusion. "But why . . . why would you do that?"

"I . . . well I thought you might think I was a nut or something."

It took a while, but finally a sardonic smile passed over her face. Then she announced. "This is all too weird. I don't know who you are, all I know is that you scared the shit out of me and that I want you to leave. Now. Do you understand? I want you to leave."

"I'm only trying to help. You've got to believe me. Someone may want to kill you. Look, if I wanted to kill you . . ."

Her eyes blazed. "Just leave!" she said. "Or I'll call the police. I may anyway. You broke into my house."

"No, I didn't." He gestured loosely. "The door was open. I rang the bell a number of times, but you didn't answer, so I just came in."

"The bell doesn't work. Now will you just leave? Please!"

Reluctantly, Jerry did as asked. But he didn't go home. He went to his car and just sat. Something was going to happen to her, that was a given. Maybe if he watched the house, he could prevent it. By nightfall, however, he had succumbed to a bone weariness that he had never known.

Chapter Twenty-Four

By nine-thirty Jerry's destination was on everybody's mind. He hadn't given Maria a clue. He had simply left the house. That had been hours ago, although it seemed much longer. Maria and Tad both decided that Walker should stay until he returned.

They stayed in the living room, although Walker had to stifle an almost overwhelming urge to go into the basement, with or without company. They sat within a few feet of each other and watched television and talked and sipped hot chocolate. Once, when his anxiety was like water risen to his neck, Walker talked about the past, about his life with Harriet and Christine when life was simpler and much happier. But as reality crept into his monologue, as worry and truth clashed, he stopped talking and smiled and took a sip of his hot chocolate, leaving his story unfinished. Then they watched the Rosanne Barr show. But despite the fact that more than a few laughable lines had been spoken, nobody laughed. Laughter was an unearned and somewhat exotic luxury. There would be time for laughter later on, when the world began turning in the right direction again. If it ever did.

They were poised like statues in front of that television, their thoughts hurried and uncertain, a collage of past and future events, their faces as filled with unspoken thoughts as that of a psychiatrist. They felt as if they were balanced on the sharp edge of a razor blade, where even the slightest movement could be fatal. But there was security in doing nothing, in simply waiting for something more to happen, if only because they didn't know what to do. Their only tether to the outside world was the call Maria had left at Guy Henry's office. But Guy Henry, like Jerry, it seemed, also refused to join and complete their circle. And no one, least of all Tad, had any plans to leave the room. Breaking away from the group, was unthinkable.

Tad had drunk far too much hot chocolate, so much that his legs were shaking. Finally, unable to hold it any longer, he looked at Walker Norville and then at his mom. "I gotta go," he said almost apologetically.

Maria looked at Walker, he at her. Then she looked back at Tad and smiled. "Use the powder room down here, okay?" She spoke nonchalantly, as if the upstairs john needed cleaning.

"Yeah, I was going to," Tad replied.

She combed the hair off his forehead with her fingers and gave him another smile. "Don't linger," she added. She knew instantly that she had misspoken. Tad didn't linger. He was businesslike in the john. Don't linger, she realized, was just a euphemism for, "If you stay in there too long, something's going to get you."

"I just don't want you to miss the show," she added.

"Sure, Mom."

"You want me to go with you?" Walker asked.

"No, that's okay," Tad said. He was past that.

"You're sure? I'd feel better . . ."

Prince wandered over and nudged his master.

"I'll take Prince," Tad said. "Okay?"

Walker rubbed the dog's head. "Okay," he said.

Maria watched her son get up slowly then shamble off, disappearing into the gloom beyond the living room. Prince trailed at a leisurely pace, his tail slung low.

Seconds later she heard a noise. She stared into the

dark study. Her mind fumbled with that noise. First it was nothing, then something, then nothing, then something again. Finally, she settled on nothing. None of their homes had ever been broken into, anyway. If she got up now and went into the bathroom to see if her son was okay she would just be admitting that possibility. She didn't want to do that. But as the minutes passed, as Tad did, in fact, linger, she found that she was forced to rethink her logic. Finally she got up, gave Walker a frightened, expectant look then went to the bathroom and knocked on the door.

No one answered.

Jerry awoke with a start. He sat up straight. "Jesus," he said as he scrubbed his face with his hands. A couple with their arms around each other walked by on the sidewalk to his right. They glanced at him, then continued on at a quicker pace. Up and down the quiet street, mercury vapor lamps spotlit patches of sidewalk and road to a dark infinity. The houses on either side were darkened hulks, with just the occasional bright trim color revealing a particular shade. The sky was a misty black, stars outshone by the not so gentle veil of light cast from the streetlamps. Night had arrived like a cat burglar, only deepening his troubled sleep. He flicked on the overhead, squinted at his watch. Almost ten now. He looked at Ann Cook's house. The sameness with other colonials on the street was even more astounding at night, when colors faded, leaving only varying shades of gray. For a very brief moment he even wondered if this *was* her house. But he couldn't remember moving the car—it had to be. Maybe he should try to talk with her again. His wits were about him now. He smiled. His *demon* was slumbering. Now he would be rational, coherent. She might even listen.

But even as he thought that he discounted it. Again he saw a vision—she was standing right in front of him, facing him. His pulse quickened and his skin greased with sudden sweat. "Go away!" he said impatiently, as if he had witnessed nothing more than a mosquito entering the car. "Leave me alone, please, just leave me the hell alone!"

But then he realized that what he was seeing was not the reincarnation of his own personal demon. His sleep-dulled brain had delayed the right response. Ann Cook was about to become another victim.

Adrenalin pumped through him. He shoved open the door and fell into the street as a car drove slowly by, barely missing him. The driver slammed his hand onto the horn. Jerry didn't notice. He was on his knees in the street. Trying to steady himself as this latest vision obstructed his eyesight, he went around the car and ran a weaving, drunken trail up the sidewalk to the front door. Breathing hard, he leaned against it, hoping his brain would clear. It didn't. Finally he slammed his hand against the bell. Then, remembering that the bell was broken, he banged on the door. "Ann!" he yelled. "Christ, Ann, open the door. Open the door!" He turned the knob, Locked. "Shit!" he breathed. He went to the picture window. Through the killer's eyes he could see her move closer. Impossibly, there was a vacuous yet somehow involved look on her face. She stood in front of the couch. The television was on, as was a table lamp to her left. He tried to see through his vision, past the curtain. He couldn't, not entirely. All he saw were two shadowy forms, each without substance, indeterminate as to killer or victim. But his vision, his view through the killer's eyes, allowed him a remarkably detailed view. She turned away from him. He saw a whale on television. "Ann! Ann!" he screamed. Nothing. He ran around to the side of the house and threw open the screen. The side door was open. In his vision she grew closer. Her hair was bright then dark, changing as television light changed. Then, suddenly, and just as sharply as she had earlier, she turned on her heels. In her green eyes he saw fear and anger and denial. Panic stabbed at him. With a small squeal, an expression of fading hope, he burst into the hallway between the kitchen and the basement and then ran up the short flight of stairs to the kitchen. Another door, through and into the dining room. A swinging door. He pushed it open, ran into the dining room and then into the living room and stopped, numb with surprise.

Harry was there, bent over Ann Cook. And although it was difficult to tell, their bodily arrangement made it appear that he was actually biting her. Harry, aware of his brother's presence, stopped suddenly and, still bent over her, turned and looked at him. A grin shone through the blood that ran sluggishly down his mouth and chin. Jerry could only stare, mouth agape, brain numbed, while behind Harry, on television, a whale broke the surface and blew water through its blowhole. It was Harry, yes, but a too-perfect version, like a retouched photograph. His skin was poreless and lifeless, like a doll's skin. Why? How? Jerry remotely wondered. Harry was supposed to be in Los Angeles. Harry casually turned away, siphoned what was left of Ann Cook's blood, stood, wiped the blood from his mouth with the heel of his hand, then took a few steps toward him. For one short, chilling moment, Jerry saw himself, saw the disbelief on his face through his brother's eyes. Strangely, Harry did a slow circle of his brother and then stopped in front of him. Then, and in a voice tinged with fond reminiscence, he said, "Remember when we were kids and you caught me with Tonto?"

Tonto had been the family cat. One night when their parents weren't home, Harry put him into the toilet and shut the lid. Hearing the cat's death screams, Jerry ran to his rescue, but just as he opened the bathroom door, the cat's wails abruptly stopped. Then and now Harry's eyes were like glass.

"Harry, God . . ." Jerry said.

"God?" Harry interrupted. "Now there's an un-original utterance if I've ever heard one. But walking in

227

on this kind of thing could leave a person kind of addle-brained, I guess. Least till you get used to it."

"But why? I don't understand!"

There was look of real puzzlement on Harry's face now. "Why?" he said. "Jesus Christ, Jer, there is no why! You gotta eat, I gotta eat. It's that simple. That goddamn simple! Why? That's pretty lame, Jer. Christ, you even wrote a book about vampires, didn't you? Never got it published but you hacked it through."

Jerry felt like an observer in a nightmare.

"But you know," Harry continued, "it really feels great to be without a conscience. Even with Tonto there was this little soprano-voiced bastard telling me some shit about how I shouldn't do that, how God was gonna make life a real bitch for me. Tonto, for chrissake! Tonto was just a fucking cat!" He turned and looked at Ann Cook who was past looking back. Then he looked again at his brother. "But you know, Jer, you know what really gets my blood churning. It's not that my writing is so much better than all you other hacks. No, I don't give a rat's rectum about that anymore. What I like is, well, there is no other way to put it I guess: I like having dominion over those I create. The undead, you see, Jer, really have no memory, only a compelling need to please their creator." He grinned broadly yet ungenerously. "And I will only be pleased when my revenge is complete, when the tables are turned." He spoke conspiratorially. "And very shortly, dear brother, that revenge will be realized." He looked beyond Jerry as a loud banging began on the front door. "For now though I think I'll leave you to your fate." He started to go, turned back. "Oh, yeah, almost forgot. If my instructions were carried out, then Tad, my nephew, your son, a blood relative, should by now be my guest. Oh, your wife's probably frantic. Mothers get that way when their kids are taken from them. Anyway, if you can break loose I'd love to continue our little chat later. And we got a lot to talk about. Isn't that right, Jer?"

Jerry said nothing.

"Just as I thought, cat's got your tongue. Just as fleet of thought as you always were. Twin brothers, shit! If I had your brain I'd . . . Sorry, Jer. I told myself I wouldn't get nasty."

With that said, he ran out the side door, trailing laughter like a train whistle behind him.

Still Jerry couldn't act. Couldn't move. Cement filled his legs. The truth had been sledgehammered at him. Too much truth. His brother a murderer, a . . . vampire!

Behind him the front door suddenly slammed open, the hardware exploding. Jerry turned slowly, still imprisoned by his brother's lingering presence, and watched as Guy Henry stepped into the room, cautiously appraising the situation. He was smiling, although he didn't realize it, and he had his gun drawn. He looked beyond Jerry at Ann Cook. "Jesus!" he said. "What the hell'd you do to her, anyway?"

Jerry's eyes widened. He chanced a glance at the body. "No, I didn't . . ." he managed.

Guy Henry looked like he was about to laugh outloud. "Sure, pal, sure," he said. "Just raise your hands high, real high. I'm takin' you in."

By now Jerry fully realized what had happened. He saw the gun, a 38, pointed at his belly. He remembered his brother leaning over Ann Cook and he also realized that Guy Henry was about to arrest him for a murder that he certainly did not commit. He made a quick move and Guy Henry made a quicker one. For a short, stocky, middle-aged man, the sheriff was surprisingly agile. The butt of the gun fell onto Jerry's skull wickedly, drawing blood instantly. Pain blossomed in his head. He grabbed at it, winced. Groaning, he fell to his knees.

"I got bullets, too," Guy Henry whispered, eyes narrowed. "Real bullets! So you just put your hands behind your back and be a good boy. You understand?"

"I didn't . . . my brother," Jerry mumbled through a haze of pain.

Cautiously, Guy Henry moved behind Jerry and pulled his bloodied hand off his head. Then he slapped a cuff on, pulled the other hand down and finished up.

"Get down on your stomach," he said. "I'm gonna call this in. Go on, get down."

"Christ, I can't, I can't break my fall!" Jerry pleaded.

"So what?" Guy Henry said. He put a boot into Jerry's back and pushed. Jerry went down like a sack of bricks and mashed his face against the hardwood. Pain exploded in his cheek.

"Prize buck," Guy Henry said. "Yes sir. Gonna mount this one."

Tad looked up. Light spread in all directions, but it was only faint and spotty as if he were standing in the middle of a weakly lit carousel—certainly not enough light to see, not yet, not until his eyes adjusted. Where am I? he thought. He tried to remember what had happened. He remembered walking into his dad's dark study. He even looked behind him at Mr. Norville and his mom. They were both looking in his direction, but they couldn't see him. He was still in the dark. Then they looked away, probably because they couldn't see him, and just as he reached for the light switch, he felt a hand over his mouth. Immediately he kicked and tried to yell, but nothing would come out, only a deep sound that didn't go very far at all, at least not into the living room, where his mom and Mr. Norville sat watching TV. He also remembered that no matter how hard he tried, he couldn't get away. In the kitchen, just before she opened the cellar door, he had tried to kick a chair as a signal, but all he could do was rock it a little. He knew it was a she because she had whispered something about how fighting wouldn't help. And it had sounded like Mrs. Griffin, too.

She had closed the cellar door, leaving him in the dark. But she still held her hand tightly over his mouth and he still tried to get away. At least until he heard her say,

"Dammit!" Then he felt a sharp pain in the back of his head and he passed out.

He rubbed his naked arms as a chill raced through him. And the odor, pungent enough to make his eyes water even though it was cool, was highly reminiscent of the aroma that had wafted into the Silver Spoon, only much stronger. And now that his eyes had adjusted, he could see a wagon wheel of tunnels, each curving slightly so its ultimate destination was not visible. Small candles had been placed every ten feet or so. Their number seemed much higher because of the curving design of the tunnels. The overall effect was like that of a mirrored funhouse lit by rows of low-wattage bulbs. But although this maze of tunnels seemed endless and confused him tremendously, he also sensed that one of them would take him back into his cellar. It had to. The last thing he remembered was going into the cellar, so . . . His skin suddenly tingled. His breath quit. He backed against the earthen wall, felt some of the dirt give way as he tried to scrabble upwards. Earlier, before his eyes had adjusted, he had glimpsed shapes, solid and perfect, yet fuzzy, suspended from the ceiling. Now, with better sight, he saw what they were. Coffins, their edges penetrating the tunnelled ceiling. These tunnels, he realized now with dawning horror, had been built beneath the cemetery! Fear glowed in his belly like a ball of live wires. With a shrill scream of terror he pushed himself to his feet and just ran, choosing the closest tunnel. Candles, only inches from him, flickered as he ran past. He leaned as the tunnel leaned and ran upright as it straightened. It was a trip that to him lasted an eternity. In reality, however, only ten or so seconds passed, just enough time for him to reach the end of this particular tunnel.

He saw it as he rounded a gentle curve, not more than three feet away—a stinking, rotted coffin leaning against the wall, ghostly lit by flickering candlelight. Rot and the length of the fall had caused it to pop open, but only enough to reveal one thin, skeletal arm, palm up. A gold

231

ring glittered dully in the feeble glow. His fears had been realized. He screamed and turned to run, but he was suddenly hoisted high into the air like a baby. He looked down into Sharon Griffin's white, smiling face.

"Your uncle will be here soon," she said. "Wouldn't want you disappointing him by running off, now would we?"

Where it came from he didn't know. Tears should have streamed from his eyes, pleas from his mouth. But neither happened. Inspired by fear or maybe even acceptance, bald and focused, Tad simply spat.

Enraged, Sharon cupped his small head in her hands and squeezed.

In what he now thought had been a career-ending mistake, Guy Henry had taken his prisoner away from the scene of the crime before the local police arrived. But at the time only one desire burned inside of him. He, Guy Henry, pissant town sheriff, had caught a murderer, a murderer who had eluded a much better-equipped and supposedly better trained police force. Had he waited at the woman's house, he would probably have had to turn him over to them. And all the while he waited, some hundred yards away, while Jerry Matheson himself waited for what he probably thought would be the right moment, he could only think of the look on Aman's face when he brought in the killer. Sure, he had left a note, he had told them something about how his prisoner had been injured during a short chase, but once they checked the hospitals they'd find out the truth. Maybe the best thing to do would be to actually take him to a hospital, have him looked at then come back. He could call the nearest precinct house, just to keep them informed of the whereabouts of their killer. He looked into his rearview mirror. Jerry Matheson lay dazed in the backseat, his head bobbing about as the car cornered or found a pothole. "Dammit," Guy Henry said. "I sure fucked up

232

this time! Instead of getting pats on the back I'm gonna lose my goddamn job!"

He glanced around. He knew Rochester only moderately well, but he did know that he wasn't far from Ridgeview Hospital. He saw a sign indicating hospital to his right. He took the turn and a short while later pulled into the parking area of the emergency room at Ridgeview General Hospital.

Maria stood at the edge of her property and shone her flashlight into the cemetery. "Tad?" she called desperately, as light slanted off tombstones. He wasn't out here and he wasn't in the house. They had even gone to Walker's house. Nothing. Now they were grasping at straws, the last of which would be the basement. They had opened the door and yelled, but no one answered, so they looked elsewhere. But Tad was nowhere to be seen or heard. And the pieces were coming together. If Tad had seen a woman in the kitchen, a woman who had been in the basement, then there was something else down there, something they couldn't see with just a flashlight. A hidden room, maybe. Something. Anything. But why would someone want to kidnap Tad? They weren't poor, but they weren't rich either. And now Walker Norville had spoken the unthinkable, something to do with the undead and vampires.

"I don't want to alarm you needlessly," he had begun. "But we probably should look at this thing from all angles." Then he told her what he knew, how much Christine had changed before her disappearance, about what he had learned about vampires, etc, etc. He didn't want to alarm her needlessly, huh. Well, she was alarmed all right! She was bordering on frantic. And where the hell was Jerry? He hadn't even called.

But Jerry had tried to contact her, at least in a round about way. Guy Henry had tried to call while Jerry was having his face looked at. But as circumstances would have it, both Walker and Maria had been out of the house. Guy had let the phone ring ten times before he hung up. Maria heard it on the seventh ring, as she drew closer to the house, but by the time she picked up the receiver, all she got was a dial tone.

When he got no answer at the Matheson's, Guy Henry called the nearest precinct house. "Listen," he said to the dispatcher, a woman with a level, official tone, "I called earlier, reported a homicide . . ."

"Hold, please," she said immediately.

After a very long wait a man took the line. His skepticism was not very well masked. "Sheriff Henry?" the man said.

"Yes?"

"You reported a homicide at ten fourteen P.M. Is that right?"

"I guess, I didn't . . ."

"Where are you now, sheriff?"

"Well, like I said in my note . . ."

"Note?"

"Yes, my prisoner sustained an injury . . ."

"You shot him?"

"No, I didn't shoot him! Christ. What the hell . . . ?"

"Sheriff. We found no body at the address you gave. We found no note either. We found absolutely nothing."

"But that's impossible!"

"Look, sheriff, if you really are a sheriff. There are laws against falsely reporting a crime. And penalties are quite severe . . ."

Before he quietly hung the phone back up, cutting short the desk sergeant's warnings, a thousand thoughts pushed through Guy Henry's brain. Only a few shone through. And they were these: without a victim, he had no crime. Without a victim he also had no criminal. It would be his word against Matheson's. He'd have to let him go. He wouldn't do that. He was an elected official

234

whose job it was to enforce the law and he had witnessed a murder. Now some goddamn technicality was going to deprive him of his rewards. Well, there was obviously only one thing to do. Until this thing was cleared up he'd have to detain the suspect. There was no other way. He'd disappear if he released him, then when they found the body . . . No, he really had no choice at all. Of course, he couldn't tell Matheson. He'd just lock Matheson up till they found the body then produce him. Sure. But he wouldn't let him go. No way. He'd killed a woman tonight and chances were damn good he had also killed Tom Smith and Len Griffin. And any further conversation with the man on the other end of the line had been unnecessary.

He led Jerry back to the car and started toward Naples Falls.

Chapter Twenty-Five

There was a cancer on Naples Falls. It attacked and withdrew, then attacked again. It customarily attacked at festival time.

As a patient Naples Falls had, at one time, been a willing participant in the patient-doctor relationship. It stood strong and proud against the disease that coursed through its veins, that attacked its vital organs. But it did so only because the disease itself was comparatively weak and confined, almost merciful. In check. In remission. "We'll take a wait and see attitude," the doctor might have said. "We'll give it five years, the customary length of time for a disease of this nature to show signs of regeneration. If the disease does not reassert itself then we consider the patient to have a fifty-fifty chance of survival. But," the doctor might have continued, "at times a patient, open to suggestion, you might say, is a prime candidate for an even more diabolical and less merciful disease. His will has been undermined, his zest for life tested to its limits. Very often terminal disease occurs when a patient is mentally as well as physically impaired."

And so it was with Naples Falls. Greta and her flock were, certainly, a disease coursing through the veins and arteries of the town, but, almost in cooperation with the town, they remained somewhat subdued, almost passive

236

in their ubiquity. Such was not the case with Harry Matheson. As Greta had guessed, his was a more traditional vampire philosophy. Which was: conquer and reign. If that is not possible, then destroy.

She had always had faith, Maria told herself. She hadn't practiced that faith, sure, not since she had married Jerry, but that was only because his beliefs were so damn strong. Then maybe my faith hasn't been as strong as his beliefs, she thought. I shouldn't have been swayed so easily. True, she had taught Tad on the sly, without Jerry knowing. But at least she had given him a basis for choice. Jerry hadn't even done that.

But she had chosen to closet her faith, to secure it tightly behind a door labeled "family harmony." They had argued, oh yes, each at one time or another yelling to be heard, but he was so damned close-minded. He took the intellectual approach, the rhyme and reason of it all. The show-me attitude. She chose a simple blind and obedient faith. If the scientific and philisophical mysteries were so unexplainable, then why couldn't simple faith explain away biblical enigmas? The universe, she told him once, was as vast and as complicated as the atom itself. It was foolish to think that explaining its existence would be easy. And now, at least according to Walker Norville, faith was vital. Without it they were pretty much unarmed. Of course, she didn't know what they should arm themselves against, but anything—anybody—that stole children during the night was not a godly being. Devil maybe, but not a god.

They were about a hundred yards from the house now, on their way to Father Monroe's church. There were others, rival denominations, but they, both Walker and Maria decided, were probably not as firmly entrenched, as willing to listen to a story like theirs. And Catholics had been fighting demons for a long time.

They were walking because the streets were crowded

with festival goers and snarled traffic. From here they looked like a thousand writhing snakes. Walking would actually be quicker than driving, and Walker didn't know if his car would start anyway. (Jerry had taken the wagon). She looked behind her, at the house. Why were they doing this? she wondered suddenly. Tad was back there, in the house somewhere, probably in the basement. Why weren't they looking there instead?

You're panicking, Maria. There are right ways to do things and wrong ways. If you rush into that basement, you're doing the wrong thing. If Walker's right, if there are . . . vampires down there, then . . . Her vacillation caused her to stop suddenly. Walker walked on, unaware, then stopped ten or so feet further on.

"This is crazy," she announced, hands on hips.

He regarded her for a moment, then, "Yeah, I know that. Crazy as anything I can remember. But so's Tad just disappearing like that, right from under our noses. And the dog! The dog's still hidin' under the dining room table! What'd he see, Maria? What's gonna make a dog react like that? Didn't even whimper. And what about Christine . . ."

"Okay, okay. You made your point. Let's just do it. Let's get whatever advice we can get and get on with it, if he doesn't just laugh at us."

Walker came back to her and took her hands in his. "Look, Maria, I got a feelin'. A hunch. I think Tad's okay. I really do. Don't ask me why, I just do. I think somethin's been building to happen in that house, maybe for years, I don't know, but I don't think it's time yet. I think we still got some time to arm ourselves and maybe rescue the boy. But I do think we gotta go through that basement."

Suddenly a festival goer in clown face stopped, blew up a balloon that said NAPLES FALLS FESTIVAL and popped it loudly on his hand. Then he skip hopped back toward town, laughing like a maniac. Maria put her hand to her chest and caught her breath. Walker cussed. It was a

238

moment that underscored their plight, the madness of the moment, of this night. And, strangely, it also refortified them. They pressed on, elbowing away rowdy revelers or ignoring them entirely. The garishness of the whole affair, Maria thought, was amazing. And now there were more than a few pockets of sexually explicit attractions. Now the disease had spread like gangrene. Woman wore huge oversized brassieres, flaunting them openly. The crotches of the men, many men, bulged obscenely. In doorways and alleyways couples groped and moaned and struggled for pleasure. Maria glanced at Walker. His expression betrayed his disgust. Maybe there was something in the air, she thought. Something you breathed in. Or maybe it was in the water, water was always a good scapegoat, boil your water now, or you'll turn into some sex-crazed sleazoid. She took Walker's hand and found herself taking air in short gulps. Just in case.

For a couple of reasons she let go of Walker's hand and stopped at the Silver Spoon because she remembered Tad's face as he described the odor. And reason number two—the building was totally dark, the only dark building on the street. Even the pet store was lit like a Christmas tree. She pressed her face to the glass and cupped her hands over her eyes. Inside she saw only a stationary orange-red glow. An alarm light? she wondered.

"Maybe we oughta get movin'," Walker said.

She backed away from the window. She saw the NO PETS sign and thought about Prince. Then they continued walking.

Shirley Wise lifted the cigarette to her mouth, drew in a lungful of smoke, and exhaled it through her nose. *Who was that?* she wondered. A lot of people had pressed their face to the glass, but they had been part of the festival. The woman and the old man weren't part of the festival.

Al lay dead behind the counter, his heart pierced by a shish-ka-bob fork. She had really had no choice. He had found something he shouldn't have. She recalled the look of complete surprise on his face as she skewered him, a look that had saddened her.

Behind her she heard a noise. Seconds later, the ash burned down to her fingers. Her skin sizzled.

Approaching the little white Catholic church, Maria had expected to feel somehow relieved, and comforted. To a small degree, she did. But there was something else lingering, as if she had allowed a vagrant to sleep on her porch. Regardless of size, she expected God's house to offer mental and physical sanctuary. But walking up the steps to the wide double doors, she felt anxious. As the doors closed behind them, leaving them in the un-paralleled silence of the church, she attributed that anxiety to other things—the festival, the possibility that they'd be laughed at, or even worse, that they wouldn't.

They stepped through the archway into the nave. In what was a purely mechanical movement, Maria dipped her fingers into the holy water encased in a marble font and then crossed herself. Candles had been lit on either side of the altar. On the right, above the candles, she could see the hymn numbers for the next mass. In the front right pew, seemingly in prayer, they saw Father Monroe. They moved forward slowly, reverently, genu-flected before entering the pew, and sat behind him and to his left. They listened while he prayed. His words were mumbled, the same words he had mumbled for the last fifty or so years. His attention didn't waver, although he sensed someone behind him. Watching him, Maria suddenly longed for the religious fervor of the Latin mass, not today's watered-down version. This compro-mise, she thought, had been a mistake, done solely to attract parishoners. As she perceived it, mankind (in its immensely shallow vision and wisdom) could never conceive a ritual too elaborate or too drenched in awe and wonder to accommodate a being capable of producing life. As far as she was concerned, replacing the Latin mass had been a giant step backwards. Especially now, when they needed all the religious mystique and majestic reverence they could summon. They needed a cannon, not a cap gun.

Slowly, Father Monroe made the sign of the cross and turned to greet them. His face was wan and drawn, as tired a face as either could ever remember seeing. Walker was reminded of Harriet's face toward the end, when her pain had entirely drained it of joy, of the zest for life. Father Monroe's face was like that. As if he had been told of something terminal.

His first words, spoken with a tired certainty, caught them by complete surprise. "You want my advice on what to do about vampires, right?"

The preliminaries, the attempts at persuasion, had not been necessary. The subject had been broached with the transitional abruptness of a dream. They could only nod.

"Then come with me. I will not speak of such things in God's house. I will not defile His glorious name. Come with me."

Facially he appeared to be hazardously close to death's door, just as he had looked the night he came to visit Sharon. But he walked upright and with a briskness that was astonishing. They followed him outside and to a round redwood table behind the church. A totally idyllic spot for a picnic.

"How did you know?" Maria asked.

"How did I know? Well, Maria, there's been a parade of concerned citizens. They've all got these very graphic tales about loved ones that sleep the day away, who don't reflect in mirrors, who are then, 'beset by evil.'"

It seemed that he spoke with a touch of sarcasm.

"And you don't believe them?" Walker said.

There were more questions, yes, many more. They didn't know that the entire town had been affected. But they left those questions unasked, preferring to be more specific about their own needs. And now time was more an enemy than ever. They couldn't let this old priest ramble. They needed his advice and his blessing and they needed to return to the house.

"I believe in evil. And good," Father Monroe continued. "As a rational, thinking man I can no sooner believe that vampires have invaded Naples Falls than I can believe that the sun rises in the west. But I am also a priest. And before being a rational, thinking man I am first that." He almost seemed to smile at the irony. "So I will give you my blessing. I will send you on your way as fully armed as possible. That's all I can do. I can only protect you. I know you're Catholic, Maria. What about you, Mr. Norville . . . I don't recall . . ."

"I guess I am, too," Walker replied.

"It doesn't matter, I'd hear your confession anyway. You see you've got to go into this thing . . . clean, without evil, something for the beast to hold onto."

He believes us, Maria thought triumphantly.

"And I'll give you holy water. It's blessed. Only where evil is pure can it do harm. And when evil is pure, there's no hope. You've got to purge it. Do you have crosses?"

"Yes, a small one," Maria said.

"Father," Walker interrupted, "I don't understand why you don't ask us about . . . details."

Father Monroe stood and walked to the edge of the lawn where hedges described a dark and tall border. He faced away from them, his hands clasped together behind his back. "The less I know of you as mortals, the better it will be," he said. "You're going to fight a being who is the devil's pawn. That some say is the devil himself, doled out in small portions to each of the undead. There's a chance . . . At any rate, I'm safe here, I know I'm safe here. I see no need for particulars. I can only do what I'm trained to do. Bless you, hear your confession and offer you the protection of the church. Beyond that I don't want to know. In the morning I will have mass. The

242

congregation will be far smaller, I know that, but I'll hold mass anyway. Eventually, there will be no one and I'll be transferred. I'm just a priest. There's only so much I can do."

Maria stood abruptly, her eyes burning with rage. "Just a priest!" she yelled. "Just a priest! You're not a priest, old man, you're a fake. How dare you send us out there to fight this thing without the full blessing of the church! And you would, you know. You would. By disclaiming yourself, your interest, your belief that evil can be conquered, you might as well send us out unarmed. Oh, you'll hear our confessions and you'll bless the water, but it won't do any good. Why? Because you're weak, Father. You're weak!"

With that said, she turned to go.

"Wait," Father Monroe said.

Maria stopped, turned. "What for?" she answered. "I have nothing to say to you. Confessing to you would be like confessing to that bush."

Father Monroe turned and walked toward them. Stopped. "I'm a weak man, I know that. That's why I was sent here. But I'm also a conduit to the saviour. Regardless of my personal failings, I am at least that. If I bless you, you are blessed by Him. If I hear your confession, then you have confessed to Him. God will hear your prayer through me. Believe me."

He was persuasive.

"Then you do believe us?" Maria asked.

"Yes. I do."

She was skeptical. "That simple? Yes, I do?"

He paused, then, "I hesitate to tell you this. I don't really believe it myself." He paused once more, appraising them, their sense of purpose more than their veracity, a sense of purpose detailed closely in Maria's condemnation. Still, he needed further proof if he was to tell them what he had told no one. Looking closely, he saw that their faces revealed more strength than fear, unlike the others he had spoken with. Convinced now, he cleared his throat, set his jaw firmly. "Have you ever heard of a town called Hunt? It's not far from here, eighty or ninety miles."

"Of course I have. There were a series of murders . . ."

"Yes, murders. I had a friend, Father Unu. He was a victim. No body was found, but he was a victim. He visits me every now and then. He comes to my window. When a man of the cloth, who has given his life to God, falls to evil, there's . . . great confusion. I see that on Father Unu's face. Even now, as one of the undead, he still wanders the path, unsure of which fork to take. One minute his face radiates love and piousness, the next, evil and a hatred so ugly you could cry." He stopped then, his lower lip trembling. He regained his composure quickly. "And so, yes, I do believe you," he continued. "I have seen them, too. The face of evil is not unknown to me."

Maria and Walker realized now why he had chosen to remain somewhat clinical. A look of great sadness had filled the old priest's face as he spoke of Father Unu. But it was an admission that fired both their resolve and fear. Tad was in mortal and spiritual danger. That had been verified by a priest, as unimpeachable a source as any.

Maria took Walker's hand. "Do you want to hear our confessions inside?" she asked.

A trace of a smile appeared on Father Monroe's face. "Yes, inside," he replied. "Everything inside."

Chapter Twenty-Six

10:38 P.M.

Noise came out of Guy Henry's mouth, just noise. Every now and then Jerry made out a word, but only because the sheriff raised his voice when he tried to hammer home a point. Mostly he seemed interested in making Jerry confess. Jerry's head ached dully and Guy Henry's ramblings didn't help.

They were approaching Route 5, points south. Naples Falls was still over forty miles away. Businesses clustered only infrequently as they neared real country, some open, most not. White fluorescent dominated, which gave everything a black and white dream quality. This is all a bad dream anyway, Jerry thought. Soon I'll hear Maria's soft voice and I'll wake up and go downstairs and have some coffee with honey in it and Tad will ask me if he can do something he probably shouldn't do. Then Maria will give me that look she gives me when she has an opinion and doesn't want to voice it and I'll have to tell Tad no and he'll look dejected, but only for a little while because he doesn't really mope around, not really. He's not a moper. He's too filled with the joy of life to be a moper.

With this time given over to transient thoughts, Jerry opted then for the past, to his childhood and two separate incidents that had lain dormant in his storehouse of workable thoughts until now.

And only now did he realize exactly when those incidents took place: right around their birthday, the 30th of October.

Incident number one: Halloween, 1956. A dreary evening, as is generally the rule for Halloween in the Northeast. A light drizzle, with what appeared to be stationary droplets of moisture, no wind whatever. A funereal pall lay over everything, highly appropriate for the date. Their treasure bags were filled to bursting, and indeed probably would have burst had their mother not foreseen that possibility and replaced paper with plastic. They were in the house now, smiles all around. As was always the case, the brother with the heaviest bag also received the most attention, as if some higher level of intelligence or charm had been the reason. On this night, Jerry's coffers were slightly more prodigious, a fact that was dutifully, almost religiously noticed by the assembled adults: parents, uncles, grandparents. Competition, then and now, was of vital importance, the cornerstone of life.

Some time later, after all the candy had been heaped onto the kitchen table, Harry and Jerry decided to sample their booty. The usual fare stared back at them, twinkies, Baby Ruth bars, a few donuts, all in a pile.

Harry spotted an apple, "I'll trade," he said. Even the thought of apples made Jerry's mouth water. "No way," he answered. Harry reached for the apple, but Jerry snapped it up and immediately took a bite. He chewed vigorously. An apple, after all, wasn't like fish. You didn't eat apples with some special care. In retrospect, he realized he probably should have. The pain was crisp and tightly focused. Blood trickled down the bitten part of the apple and onto his wrist. His eyes ballooned in horror. He looked at Harry, at the disbelief on his face, (yes, disbelief, he told himself now. No other reaction had fought through that thick layer of disbelief.) Thinking about it with clearer vision now, only one conclusion could be drawn. And one simple fact made that conclusion undeniable. Traversing the dark, slick and shiny streets together, chorusing their trick or treats, they should have received like rewards. And for the most part, they had, save for the few added candy bars and popcorn garnered by Jerry, who sometimes loitered if the sweets were sweeter. But he didn't remember the apple, the large red delicious. And he would have noticed it; apples made your bag sag. Later he found out that the blade was a fresh Gillette double edge, the kind their dad used. At the time everyone thought that was just coincidence. No other explanation was possible.

Incident number two: November 2nd, 1960. Fall was breathtakingly early. A riot of color, almost running the visible spectrum, rimmed the sand pits, a large chew out of the earth worked by local construction firms. The sky was a glaring light blue, the air dry and brisk and stimulating. Harry and Jerry were prone on the rim, peering down into that yawning chasm, their attention drawn to a parade of trucks whose sunken backs were filled with earth as they weaved in and out of this fresh new scar upon the earth. Harry looked at Jerry wildly as one of those trucks belched in their direction and then stopped directly below them, some sixty feet away, ugly, black diesel smoke pouring out of its stack. "Hell of a target," Harry said.

Jerry gave him a quizzical look.

"The truck!" Harry added.

"Sure, I guess," Jerry said, "but maybe you shouldn't, Harry. Someone could get hurt. Maybe killed."

Harry was deaf to Jerry's argument. Once his mind was made up, he rarely changed it. He picked up a fist-sized stone, stood and lofted the stone as high into the air as he possibly could, thereby increasing its velocity on impact. It struck the right windshield of that belching behemoth squarely, shattering it in spectacular fashion and producing a sound not unlike a shotgun discharging. Curses fouled the air as the driver got out, first to inspect the damage, and then to see what or who had caused it. As the driver scanned the rim, Harry stood, looked down at him, then ran into the surrounding woods. Jerry followed.

The sand pits and the area surrounding them had been a natural playground. Some months earlier they had shoveled out a subterranean hideout, covering it with dead branches and grasses. During their retreat they passed within ten feet of that hideout. Harry stopped, looked back, and said, "Go on, hide in there. Go on."

"What about you?" Jerry asked. "What are you gonna do?"

"I'm gonna distract him. I did it, didn't I? Wouldn't want you catchin' shit for something I did. Go on."

Reluctantly, Jerry did as Harry asked, he slid down into the hole and waited in the dark.

Only minutes later he heard mumbling, the shuffling of feet in the weeds, then nothing. Blood pulsed high in his arms, his head throbbed. All of which preceded a thick, angry laugh and then the sensation of being buried alive. And had more earth been heaped upon the roof, death very well might have claimed him.

Looking back it seemed obvious what had happened. Harry had somehow marked their hideout. And in so doing, he had almost caused his death.

Today's events had pulled those incidents into his thoughts. There was a truth evolving. All these many years, during which Jerry had looked upon Harry with awe, Harry had flatly refused to acknowledge their twinship. Hell, he'd done his best to end it. Was his ego that huge? Could he so vehemently deny his twin? Jerry wiped the sweat from his face and decided that yes, he sure could. Most definitely. That truth was neon bold and etched in the hardest granite. Their twinship was a lie. Somewhere during the genetic coding, they had coupled, sure, but something had altered that coupling. Harry, if druthers were possible, would druther have been a single. Not a double. The sheer weight of that realization made Jerry feel as lonely as he had ever felt in his life.

*   *   *

248

They stopped for a traffic light at the intersection of routes 5 and 20. The light changed but the two old ladies ahead of them, apparently engrossed in conversation, remained at a standstill long after the light turned green. In the back seat a young boy about Tad's age expressionlessly peered back at them, as kids are shamelessly wont to do. "Christ Jesus!" Guy Henry said. He threw his hands into the air, cursed and slammed the palm of his hand onto the horn. The other car moved slowly forward then, but the boy continued to stare. Seeing him, a wave of parental concern washed through Jerry. He imagined his son and Harry in some hideous embrace, as Harry had embraced Ann Cook, and then he imagined Harry turning with agonizing slowness and lapping up the blood on his chin, his son's blood, his eyes ably reflecting the depths of his pleasure. And Harry obviously had Tad, or one of his "creations" had him. Those he had "dominion" over. But what could he do? Not a goddamn thing. Sure, his hands were free, but so what? He was trapped inside this car; no door handles, a goddamn chain link fence between him and Guy Henry. He could worry all he wanted and it wouldn't do him any good. The car lurched forward like a frightened cat, the road ahead clear now because the old woman had turned. As they picked up speed, a sigh of utter hopelessness worked out of Jerry, a hopelessness as profound and complete as that of a man washed overboard in midocean. Times past ushered rudely into his thoughts and the car was suddenly a subterranean hideout, crushing in on him, seeking his life.

Walker Norville's gnarly finger stopped about mid-page. "Here," he said to Maria, the word spoken with quiet acceptance. They were in his kitchen now, chairs drawn close. For the very first time, Walker Norville smelled old to her, like slightly rancid cabbage. "A vampire," Norville went on, still speaking softly, "can be killed only by these methods." He listed them: Fire, decapitation, sunlight, which was tantamount to fire, or a stake through the heart; ash preferably. It went on to say that death by the use of an ashen stake was best accomplished by a mortal who had, or did still, love the immortal in question. Again Walker thought of his vow. But now, with that moment drawing ever so near, he wondered loudly if he was capable of that. His seed had, in joyous harmony with Harriet's, given Christine life. Could he renege on that? Was he capable of looking her in the eyes and then taking back what he had given her? But then he remembered what else the books had told him. If she was immortal, she was already dead. And even worse, she was the devil's pawn. It was his duty—his obligation as a loving parent—to do something about that. But until he saw her glaring at him like some source of fresh food and not as her father, he would hold on to at least a slim hope.

"I have some firewood," he began. His dentures clicked.

Maria put her hand on his in gentle reassurance.

He smiled miserably. "It'll only take a half hour or so," he said and got up.

Maria watched him go out the back door and, with what was unusual calmness and clarity, wondered if maybe he shouldn't make a small one, too.

10:53 P.M. IN THE WOODS
BEHIND THE SILVER SPOON

There were ten deer in all: six bucks and four does munching contentedly on grass and leaves. The air, sapped of energy by the furiousness of the passing storm, was afoul with wild smells, deer mostly, one of which had an open wound. Maggots, just part of the healing process, clustered there like a ball of animated rice.

The deer moved about quietly, their hooves whispering in the tall grass. They ate with abandon and without fear, which, to an onlooker might have seemed highly unusual, because the deer were not alone. On a log, in the center of the herd, sat what looked like a man. An enemy. But their sense of smell, an integral part of their defense mechanism, told them differently. Although slightly blood-tinged, this human gave off an odor that was not unlike other odors in the forest. Not unlike their own. So there was no reason for fear, just a simple curiosity between feedings.

For the last ten minutes they had allowed the pseudohuman to sit and watch. But in the future they would remember this human who didn't smell like a human. They would remember the blood urge upon the moist night air.

In what was a purely random selection process, the pseudohuman stood and started toward the closest deer, a young doe who rolled her eyes toward him, grass arcing from her mouth, her expression one of modest interest. And even when the man quickly closed the distance between them and plunged his teeth deep into her furry neck, she only continued to chew. The pain, you see, was minimal, and the bark of a gun had not preceded his attack. But when her legs began to weaken from loss of blood, she panicked. A susurrating appeal left her mouth and her eyes grew wide with fear as she tried to run, but she was already too weak for that. She made even more sounds, but there was little strength for that as well, and slowly her sounds diminished to inaudibility. Only she knew she was making them. Finally her legs wobbled and she pitched straight forward, the man still at her throat, and simply lay there because there was really nothing more that she could do. Again her eyes rolled to the man, who continued to drain the life out of her. And for a few horrified minutes, she just watched. Only a few nearby deer turned their heads to witness her death.

The slightly sweet, mealy taste of the blood of wild things was a pleasure he had denied himself for too long. As he drank, his mind filled with vicious pleasures: thousands of mindless vampires ravaging whole towns while he commanded them, the innocents of the world, the children, suffering unspeakably violent deaths, priests and nuns and all clerics subjected to bizarre sexual explorations, and then, when that was done, disembowelment or castration or both. It was oh so provocative, oh so stimulating. But it was also, unfortunately, intellectually draining. For many minutes after he would be useless, able only to lie there, both physically and mentally exhausted. It was not something to be done often. Only occasionally. In preparation. Like now.

11:25 P.M.

Because the blood of wild things always provoked the same response, Harry let go with a ululating wail that coursed through the town. Even above the din of merrymaking it could be heard and the town as a whole stopped and wondered from where it had come. They even looked to the eastern sky, as lightning slashed harmlessly into the far-off mountains.

Seconds later, as each, in some quiet, entrenched understanding, resumed the pursuit of some hideous or libidinous pleasure, Harry Matheson dematerialized almost completely and slipped brazenly through the keyhole in the back door of the Silver Spoon.

Out front, meanwhile, in the still-dark restaurant proper, Shirley Wise lit yet another cigarette and remotely wondered about immortality.

11:27 P.M.

Without realizing it, Walker Norville prepared his weapons with consummate skill and care, pointing them precisely, sharp enough to draw blood with even the slightest pressure. If one of these stakes was going to puncture his daughter's heart, he wanted it to happen

252

quickly and with as little pain as possible. He could give her that much at least.

He made ten stakes in all and after that was done, he fashioned a large wooden cross, three feet tall and two feet wide, securing it with shoelaces from a discarded pair of Reeboks. In the wood surrounding the center he carved out the initials IHS (In His Service). Satisfied that they had prepared as well as they could, both spiritually and physically, he took his weapons back into the house and held out his hand. Together, they left the house and crossed the road.

Chapter Twenty-Seven

11:28 P.M.

This is what Tad saw: people walking past. At least he thought they were people. Every now and again one would stop in the doorway and he would see a face lit by the candles on either side. They'd look at him funny, as Christine Norville had looked at him, but then they'd look like they remembered something and they'd just leave. Even then it looked like they didn't know which way to go. He thought they were like the street people in the city who had no place to go, and nothing to do, who sometimes asked for a quarter for a cup of coffee or maybe a drink. He had always been with his mom or dad when he saw them. But he wasn't with them now. He was alone now.

Sharon stood beside the carved-out entrance. She's probably a guard, Tad thought. Every now and again she looked at him like the others did, but she hadn't moved. Looking at her, Tad wondered about how strong she was. He remembered light flickering in his forehead when she squeezed him after he had spit on her. Not too smart, he thought. She could have squashed my head like a tomato. But Tad realized something else was going to happen. One of those "people" was going to come all the way into this small room. What then? What would happen to him then?

Guts. That's what they called it. Guts. Hell, Sam Wilson thought, I ain't got none left! Sam, a retiree with a penchant for cognac, had spent the evening at his sister's playing guts, a two card poker game. Sam's card-playing abilities diminished in direct proportion with just how many shots of cognac he'd had. Tonight he had lost thirty-five dollars, give or take. All on a ten cent ante game. And he had drunk close to a half bottle of very expensive cognac.

The left front head lamp of Sam's pickup truck was out, shattered by a rabid raccoon days earlier, so the truck looked like a motorcycle as it rolled down the highway, first hugging the shoulder then the center line, then again the shoulder. Lambent moonlight, cast from a quarter moon just now cresting the hillside on Sam's left, shimmered off the bumpers and the large stag hood ornament. The muffler, joint-rusted and mottled, grumbled noisily. The low rumble traveled along the valley like a snake. Now, behind the wheel of the white 83' Ford, and an unwitting player in the events as they were about to unfold, Sam Wilson felt sick, almost violently so. Even worse, considering he was driving, he felt as if he were going to pass out. It was all he could do to keep his eyes open, and his stomach bubbled like a hot pool of lava. Asked his opinion, Sam Wilson would probably have likened his condition to that of fresh, steaming dog shit. Never again would he drink that much cognac. No sir! Suddenly the bile pressed into his throat and stomach gas escaped stingingly through his nostrils. His bloodshot eyes fogged. Cresting a hill only a quarter mile from home, Sam Wilson finally realized that he was going to lose both the cognac and the burp-inducing tacos he had

255

had for supper. He slowed the truck down and stuck his head out the window, one eye on what was being jettisoned from his mouth and one eye on the solid white center line. The cool night air revived him somewhat and he was glad for that, but in leaning out the window, he unconsciously turned the wheel to the left. His half, as the saying goes, was being taken out of the middle. Accordingly, Sam Wilson, who would have been sixty-six on his next birthday, had only a microsecond's notice before the collision. His head, still leaned out the window, took the brunt of the impact. It slapped onto the side window like a struck punching bag, instantly snapping his neck. The truck, unguided now except by God, did two quick, tire-squealing circles, then flipped onto its back like a turtle. For a few seconds the only sound on the seldom-used highway was the whirring sound of spinning tires. Seconds later, however, the relative silence was violated by a tremendous explosion. The accompanying fireball, fueled by a fresh tankful of 93 octane, was visible for miles.

Sam's wife, jostled from a light slumber by the explosion, knew of Sam's wish that he be cremated—something to do with waking up in his casket and discovering the tightness of his quarters. Cremation now, however, would be redundant.

11:34 P.M.

"Saints above, I found it!" Walker said.

Maria was on the other side of the cellar. She froze. Secretly, she hoped they wouldn't find anything, and she would be able to forget this nonsense. A bubble seemed to grow in her throat. Speech was impossible. She started toward him. Light fell onto his suddenly old face. He raised his hand a little and she lowered the flashlight's beam.

"Trap door, looks like a trap door!" Walker continued

with rising excitement.

But although this discovery was certainly important, Maria wondered if what preceded it, their avoidance of that corner of the basement, might not have been just as important. A cloud of palpable dread had followed them into this stinkhole of a cellar, and for a long while they had simply roamed the basement like volunteers tromping a dark woods looking for a missing person, each wondering what they'd step on next. In what at the time seemed unimportant, she had even watched Walker stand perfectly still, his flashlight illuminating the spot he was at now, before turning away and continuing his search elsewhere, even wandering into previously explored sections. Without realizing it, she had done the same. It was Walker who, his words garbled, as if issued through cotton, had finally remarked, "Over there, did you check over there?"

She brought her flashlight to bear on that spot. She didn't answer at first, she couldn't. Walker asked her again. With a huge effort, she shook her head. "Me, neither," he said flatly.

Immediately they realized what might have happened. They had been misdirected. Through some far-flung psychic gymnastics they had been mentally prodded to look elsewhere, to avoid that particular spot entirely. And it had taken the combined power of their obviously lesser intellects to first recognize that attempt at misdirection, and then do something about it. She thought of Jerry. He had come down here alone. Maybe the same thing had happened to him. Maybe he had been misdirected. Her optimism nosedived as the inferences of this first line of defense became clear. Whoever—whatever—had taken Tad was both physically and intellectually overpowering, its power perhaps drawn from its essence, cultivated early in its immortal development and then slowly strengthened over the years. It was a line of thought that made her heart thud dully, that was more draining than Father Monroe's blessing was inspiring. It was a very sobering and chilling preview of what was to come.

Before he moved slowly to that spot, Walker chivalrously directed her to another corner.

Within ten seconds he had found it.

They looked at each other now, then at what looked like a piece of hardwood with attached O-ring. Maria crossed herself and felt a coldness that seemed to start from within. Walker hesitated briefly, pushed the dirt aside, then curled his fingers under the O-ring and pulled upwards. Nothing.

"What's wrong?" Maria asked.

"Don't know. Locked on the other side, maybe, I don't know."

He tried again, with both hands. It moved, but barely an inch.

"I can't do it," Walker said. He gasped for breath. "It's too damn heavy. Must weigh a ton!"

Maria placed the flashlight on the floor. "I'll help," she said.

"Yeah, maybe," he said.

Each took half and after they had sucked in a deep, lung-swelling breath, pulled with adrenalin-laced strength. Their muscles protested loudly, but, inch by agonizingly slow inch, the trap door opened. With each inch they both felt that their strength would fail them, that the other would be left alone to bear the weight. But that didn't happen and somehow they managed to push the trap door to a vertical position. It rested there for just a second, before Walker kicked it over. The resulting concussion of air filled the basement with a loud *WHUUMP*.

11:37 ON ROUTE 5

Guy Henry's face was a puzzle of skin and bone and blood. He had been thrown through the windshield. He

258

lay on the hood now, half in the car and half out. His legs were drooped over the steering wheel and his arms were at his side, palms up. His right cheek rested on the hood, although, given the severity of his injuries, right or left was difficult to determine. There was the suggestion of an ear, but it looked more like a wild, red-tinted mushroom than an ear. A sort of collecting bowl had been formed where his head first contacted the hood. A congealing pool of blood had gathered in it. Sam Wilson's truck continued to burn behind the patrol car, but there was only a trace odor of burning rubber, most of it masked by the more powerful and rancid smell of burning flesh. Bernice Wilson, Sam's wife, had left the house a couple of minutes earlier. From a little less than a quarter mile away, she could easily see the bonfirelike flame. She walked slowly at first, but as her fears grew, stoked by years of watching her husband waste away, a slave to the bottle, she moved faster. Eventually she was actually running. At an eighth of a mile away she could see that it was Sam's truck ablaze. With that knowledge she dropped to her knees and cried.

The sabering pain in Jerry's right arm was intense. He lay on the shoulder of the highway, having been thrown from the car at the moment of impact. For a short while after contact with the ground he had lost consciousness. In minor shock now, he could only stare at the burning hulk and Guy Henry's body pitched onto the hood of his cruiser. But even through this horror, Jerry realized one additional fact; he was free. And although Guy Henry and someone else had paid for that freedom with their lives, there wasn't a lot he could do about that now. Or ever. His main concern now was the living—hopefully living. Specifically, Tad.

While Bernice Wilson watched, he pushed himself to his feet and started to walk south, toward town. His legs felt disconnected, just dream legs moving through sucking mud. But within seconds, bolstered by the possibility that he could save his son, he broke into a trot.

A minute later he had increased that trot to a dead run. The house, he calculated, was about two miles away. He had run two miles in less than ten minutes in high school. But he wasn't in high school now, and he was hurt. His arm might even be broken. It hung limply at his side, throbbing with each step. Twenty minutes seemed more like it, if he could do it at all.

"God, the stench!" Maria said. She pushed herself backwards in a furious crabwalk, turned onto her hands and knees, and threw up.

Watching her, Walker thought he'd do the same.

Maria wiped her mouth with her sleeve and they looked at each other. They shared the same thought, the same revulsion. What they smelled was human flesh, decayed and decaying human flesh, trace amounts of which had sometimes found its way into her kitchen. Not only would they be facing horrors the likes of which they could barely imagine, they had the vilest of odors to contend with as well. Maria considered quitting. The odds were enormous. And Tad was probably dead by now. More odds on that. Good ones.

"Maybe we'll get used to it," Walker said. Immediately he realized how stupid that sounded.

Maria crawled to the edge and shone the flashlight into the darkness, her eyes slit from the almost unbearable stench. Yes, she thought, Tad could be dead—or worse. That's very possible. But he could just as easily be alive, waiting to be rescued. How can I even live with myself if I don't at least try? Would I want to live?

"C'mon," she managed. "Let's do it!"

Walker put a hand on her shoulder. "I'll go first," he said. "You got everything?"

She checked her weapons cache closely. Five stakes, all in her belt, the holy water blessed by Father Monroe in her jeans pocket. A cross. Yes, she told him, she was ready.

Walker lowered himself into the area beneath the trap door and explored this macabre foyer with his flashlight. The walls on either side were only inches from his shoulders, and in front of him, at neck height, was the forty-foot-long tunnel most recently used by Sharon. With a surge of excitement, he pushed his flashlight into the opening. The beam pierced through to the end, illuminating nothing except regenerated spider webs.

"There's a tunnel," he whispered. His breath kicked up dust from the tunnel.

"Well don't go in yet, let me come down first," Maria said.

Perhaps because his nephew had been a tunnel rat in Vietnam, the word boobytrap suddenly wandered into Walker's thoughts. He stepped slightly away from the tunnel and like someone performing exploratory surgery moved the flashlight slowly over the entire circumference. Best described the tunnel looked and smelled like a large, vacant intestine. Satisfied that crawling through it wouldn't result in sudden and hideous death, he steadied the light on the other end. Suddenly something moved across the entrance like a bird flying quickly over the face of the moon, and just as suddenly disappeared.

"Tad?" he said, above a whisper.

Maria was almost down.

The shape stepped into the opening and Walker's skin tingled icily.

"Daddy?" he heard. "Is that you, Daddy?"

The voice, tear-filled, choking, pleading for help, was Christine's, but not as an adult. The voice that traveled that tunnel was that of a child.

Just as Maria dropped down, Walker, driven now, pulled himself into the tunnel.

Christine coaxed him. "Please, Daddy, please help me. I'm so scared!" she said.

On all fours Walker played the flashlight beam into the opening. There was no one there. "Chrissy?" he said hopefully. "Is that you, Chrissy?"

Maria touched his foot. He turned, shone the flashlight at her. "Chrissy," he said excitedly, "I heard Chrissy!"

She felt the beginnings of hope, but before she could respond further, a wolf spider as large as a rat suddenly dangled down to eye level. It yoo yooed up and down on its web, its heavy legs working sluggishly, as if burdened under their own weight. She fell back against the wall and froze instantly. Unaware, Walker turned the flashlight back into the tunnel and started crawling away from her. "Chrissy?" she heard him say, "Are you there, honey, are you there?"

Maria's strength left her. Dangling at eye level was the largest wolf spider she had ever seen. It was the strongest and most vexing of nightmares. But prodded by her desire to rescue her son, she suddenly envisioned herself brushing it away, of casually dismissing it. But she saw this only in her mind, her muscles simply wouldn't react; and Walker was moving steadily away from her. He would be out of sight soon. Again she saw herself brush away the spider, but this time her arm twitched. Maybe, she thought, the pure force of her will, her desire to rescue her son, was helping her overcome her deeply rooted fears. Finally, as Walker reached the end of the tunnel, she convinced herself that the spider just couldn't be real. She was imagining it—or maybe, she thought, it was just another hallucination. She stared at the thing. It looked back. It certainly looked real—it was so detailed; but it was impossible. Molten anger suddenly bubbled inside her. Her eyes widened. "Fuck you!" she seethed. "Just fuck you!" She made a fist and clenched her jaw, and with a mighty, concerted effort, swung at the spider. Her fist hit nothing but air. The spider disappeared.

As Walker stepped out of the feeding tunnel, he saw three vaguely curved tunnels. He swung his flashlight from left to right. Nothing. He swung it back and forth again. And stopped. It couldn't be—how could he have missed . . . Christine, drenched in shadow, stood in the tunnel to his left.

Joy surged through him, but he had to be cautious. "Chrissy?" he said. He took a step toward her.

A giggle, light and wispy.

He took another step toward her, but she took a quick compensatory step backward, almost as if they were playing a child's game. He took another, she did the same. He stepped faster, to no avail.

Walker stopped. "Chrissy, please, why are you doing this to me?" he said.

She giggled and skipped away. He chased after her.

"Daddy, please, Daddy, help me, please," she cried. Walker stumbled and called her name. "Stop, Chrissy, please stop," he said. "You can't stay here, Chrissy." Behind him every now and then, he heard Maria yell to him, but he pressed on, moving faster with each glimpse, each spoken word, each plea for help, doggedly pursuing a being that could only harm him, a simple fact he might have realized had he had his wits about him.

The weariness in his legs now was hard to deny. His breathing was labored and raspy. He stopped, leaned over, put his hands on his knees. The air was clogged with dust motes that ate into his lungs and deprived him of oxygen and fogged his vision.

"Why, Christine?" he said in a tortured voice. "Why don't you stop? Please, please stop."

He heard her giggle again. The sound rose through the dust with foghorn clarity. But then, and with absurd nonchalance, he heard her say, "Okay."

She was about ten feet away. She had her hands clasped in front of her. She could have been at her first communion, as lovely a ten-year old as had ever been born. Walker's face drooped with sadness. He knew this wasn't Chrissy. But that didn't mean he couldn't bask in her remembered glow, in the newness and fragility of childhood. His hands came together as if in prayer.

"Chrissy," he said, almost in supplication. "Dear, dear Chrissy." She smiled coyly and he thought there should have been a sun down here because her skin shimmered and her hair sparkled. She was radiant, absolutely radiant. With one exception. Very notable. Her eyes were like lead. Flat and colorless. Completely non-reflective.

"Mommy's dead, did you know that, Daddy?" she asked. Her head nodded that truth.

She looked so pretty in her pink dress and her black, patent leather shoes.

"Yes, yes I did know that," Walker answered.

She smiled, and in an even, noninflective tone, designed to relay fact and not childlike wonder, she said, "She's got funny bugs in her mouth and eyes. You know, the big flat ones with spines? Those kind? They like Mommy! They'll like you, too, Daddy. When you're dead. When your skin turns to leather and your balls turn to marbles." She sighed deeply. "Won't that be nice, Daddy?"

Walker stood tall and took another step in her direction. She held out her arms and smiled even more broadly. "Christine," Walker said, his voice as fragile as snow.

"Daddy."

The distance between them grew shorter.

"Christine?"

"Daddy. Dear Daddy."

Without realizing it, Walker dropped his hand to his weapons.

She seemed to alter rapidly between what she was now and what she had been thirty years ago, as if she hadn't yet made up her mind. Then a more adult smile came to her face and her leaden eyes opened wider still. She opened her mouth into a huge o and the rancid whiff of tombs returned in a wave. The air was thick with it, each dust mote laden with it. Breathing was difficult and Walker sweat profusely; his shirt clung to him like

264

Handi-Wrap clings to warm liver.

But even though his senses were being assaulted and his eyes flooded with tears, he still tightened his hand around a stake.

She was on him now, glaring, smiling, hungry.

She bent to him, and for a moment Walker almost submitted, almost allowed her to take him rather than do what he had vowed to do. But the moment passed and he said, "I love you," and an instant before she could sink her teeth into him, he raised the stake and drove it into the flesh between her breasts. He felt it penetrate the skin there and then actually vibrate as it lanced her devil heart.

Her leaden eyes reflected surprise and the air fouled again, this time with an odor that seemed drawn from the center of the nearby pile of rotting flesh.

She grabbed the stake and stumbled backwards, her eyes questioning, burning, dying, her dark red blood flowering out around the stake and over it, cold blood, thick as oil, spilling out of her center. "You killed me, Daddy!" she said with real surprise. "Why? Why did you kill me?"

Walker thought his own heart would burst. There was pain enough for that, sudden and sharp, and even though he had wielded the instrument of death, he couldn't help what he did next. He wrapped the stake with his hands and with his daughter, tried to unseat it. "Don't die, Chrissy, don't die," he screamed. "Oh, God, please don't die!"

She reverted then. She snarled and cursed and tried to bite him, succeeding twice, but he was oblivious to that. And, of course, once in, the stake could not be removed. There was no King Arthur roaming these tunnels.

But Walker refused to stop trying; even as her cheeks began to crumble like sand structures, even as her eyes fell into their sockets and disappeared like marbles into a well, even as her full red lips disintegrated. Finally her skeletal structure devolved into crushed chalk, leaving

265

only her clothing, at which he could only stare in disbelief, only remotely understanding that he had carried out his vow, that his dear daughter was now at peace. But now there was pain. Such pain. So mercifully waving into him . . .

"Walker!" Maria whispered. "Where are you, Walker?"

Her flashlight moved jerkily from side to side, through the mazelike structure of tunnels. Dust roiled in the beam, but she wasn't sure whether she or Walker had raised it. Panic was definitely becoming an alternative, it circled in her periphery with vulturine persistence. Ahead now, the beam detailed three more tunnels, two to the right and one to the left. She heard what she thought was mumbling. She stepped quickly in that direction. The tunnel on the left drew closer. The mumbling became what sounded like crying. Tad? She stopped just in front of that tunnel and listened.

"Mr. Norville?" she heard. "Please, Mr. Norville. Wake up, please wake up!"

She took a deep breath, stepped into the tunnel opening and brought her light down. "Tad?" she said. Then, as he looked at her, "Tad! Thank God!"

Then she saw Walker Norville, and beside him what looked like women's clothing.

"He's dead, Mom! He's dead! Mr. Norville's dead!"

She ran to him, wrapped him in her arms. He's cold, she thought, so cold! God, please let him be okay. Please! "It's all right, Tad," she said to him. "Everything's going to be just fine."

She looked at Walker Norville's body. He looked dead, but how? He was on his stomach, the left side of his face exposed, his eyes and mouth open. She wondered if she hadn't had some kind of precognitive episode earlier, when he smelled like rancid cabbage, and when his face seemed older than it ever had. She lightly touched his

266

face. She wanted to take him out of here, both he and Tad, but there wasn't time. There just wasn't time. Later maybe, and with Jerry's help, she would come back for the body. But for now, her only concern was the living. She felt sadness and joy; sadness that her friend was dead and joy that she had found her son. She pushed Tad to arm's length and looked into his eyes. They were so listless, so indifferent. He had to be sick. "We'll come back, I promise," she said. "But we've got to get you out of here now. Are you okay? Can you run?"

He wiped his eyes, nodded.

"Good. Very good. Now let's go."

She tried to remember where she had gone as they ran, but she couldn't. Why hadn't she marked her trail, why?

Behind her, she heard, "To the left, Mom, the left."

She went that way.

"The right now, I'm sure of it, the right!"

She turned right.

Some time later she saw it, the feeder tunnel.

She stopped, caught her breath.

"Go on, you first," she said.

She lifted him. God, she thought, where's my strength? Even Tad feels heavy. He crawled quickly, she followed.

Once into the cellar, she took his hand and ran for the cellar door.

But as they reached the bottom of the stairs, his hand seemed to suddenly grow in size. She stopped. A chill crept into the area behind her eyes. Then she heard:

"He's . . . dead, Mommy."

Weakness cascaded over her. It was Harry. She was holding hands with Harry! And she was positive it was Harry. She had always been able to detect the slight difference in the twin's voices; she was the only person that could. She let go of his hand. He laughed. With dull realization, she understood the turn of events that had preceded this night, events that allowed only one final and inescapable conclusion: Harry Matheson, her

267

husband's twin, was a vampire. Again anger swelled within her, and, in what was a purely reflexive action, she pulled out her ampoule of holy water, uncapped it as quickly as possible, while he laughed raucously. She threw the whole bottle into his face. Each drop found its mark immediately, provoking a keening of pain that filled the cellar to capacity. She could only cover her ears and watch as he brought his hands to his face, as smoke ushered between his fingers. He backed away drunkenly, screaming obscenities, cursing her to all the beasts of hell. I've killed him, she thought. Thank God, I've killed him! Please let me have killed him. But that hope died a quick death. He suddenly stopped his drunken gyrations and stood passively by, as if collecting his thoughts. She pointed the light at him. His face was literally gone, leaving only the flat white of bone and eyes dancing merrily in their huge sockets. His teeth, like those of a German shepard, dripped spittle and a long shank of hair fell over his huge white forehead.

"Look what you've done!" he said, gesturing. The words gurgled from his throat. "Someone's gonna pay for this. Oh, yes!"

He started for her. She backed away and started up the stairs. "Stay back!" she warned. "Stay back! I'll do it again. I will, I'll do it again!"

He walked faster.

A squeal of fear worked out of her. She turned and ran up the stairs, threw open the door. And burst into Jerry's arms.

"Maria!" he said.

She shook loose, slammed the door closed. "Harry," she managed. "He's down there, down in the cellar!"

She eyed the cross to the right of the door, snapped it up, held it against the door. At the same moment a pounding began.

"Jesus!" Jerry said, backing away.

"Get a nail!" Maria ordered. "Something, get something, dammit!"

Jerry rifled the kitchen drawer, came up with a nail and hammer. The pounding continued.

"Quickly, Jerry, quickly," she said.

He took the cross and with one grand swing, nailed it to the door then backed away. The pounding subsided, then stopped altogether. Seconds later, in the same gurgling voice, they heard, "Tad's gonna visit his uncle for a while. Don't expect him."

Then, after the laughter retreated, the house again fell silent.

Chapter Twenty-Eight

"Tad," Maria gasped, "he's got Tad."

The wooden cross, tied together with shoelaces and carved with the initials I.H.S., stared back at them like a dead end sign. Certainly going back into that basement, then into the maze of tunnels would be tantamount to that.

Maria had reacted well during the crisis, but now, with time to more fully understand what had happened, she collapsed emotionally. Her eyes pleaded with him. Tell me how to get my son back? they seemed to say. God, please tell me! Jerry did his best to project quiet strength and confidence but Maria wasn't buying. She had been in the belly of the beast; sanity in an insane, almost incomprehensible situation seemed impossible. Chances were very good that Tad was going to die. And everything considered, that might very well be a blessing. The voice of calm spoke to her from someplace far away.

"Maria! C'mon, get a hold!"

(There's danger. Tad's in danger, dammit!)

Jerry shook her.

(And you're certainly not going to help him in your condition!)

"Maria!"

Somehow she found a reserve of strength. She shook away.

270

"What happened, Maria? Tell me what happened."

She told her story calmly and efficiently, sparing no detail. She told him about the tunnels, about the trap door, about Walker Norville's death and the mind games. She told him about the spiders and how Harry had assumed Tad's image. And she told him that Walker Norville had run off after something that wasn't real. Just like Tad hadn't been real.

There was another problem, too. But as Jerry looked into her eyes, he realized that with all she had witnessed, he wasn't about to compound the situation by telling her about his Jekyl-Hyde tug-of-war. That was something he would have to do battle with alone. On the way to the house, while he ran through the streets of Naples Falls pushing aside stuporous, and seemingly drug-crazed revelers, he asked himself this question: what if I find Tad alive, waiting to be rescued, and I'm confronted by what might be my true nature? What then? But not trying, he told himself, would even be worse than that. And he couldn't even imagine himself killing his son, anyway. No, he thought, he wouldn't take his son's life. He couldn't.

Hopefully his love for his son was stronger than his own private demon.

Prince whined. They turned and saw him standing in the kitchen doorway, listless, puzzled, frightened.

Seeing the dog, Jerry became even more aware of his own angst. He slammed his fist against the wall and cursed as pain shot through his bad arm. "What are we going to do?" he asked no one in particular. "What the hell are we going to do?"

Now he needs *my* help, Maria thought. But for now she was more concerned with his pain. She touched his arm delicately. "What happened, Jerry, what the hell happened?" she asked.

Jerry ran his fingers through his hair. There was no time for a lengthy explanation. "It's not important," he said. "Shit, there was an accident. Nothing we can do

271

now, though."

She looked into his eyes, saw the pain. "It hurts bad, doesn't it? Oh, Jerry, how can you do anything like that?"

Jerry only shrugged, "I'll manage," he said. "No big deal." Yet another macho display. This time Maria allowed it.

Then it dawned on him. Hope shone in his eyes. "There's got to be another way in," he said. "If I'm right, he's got his creatures down there with him! How'd they get there? Not through here!" Suddenly his hope dulled. "But where?" he said desultorily. "Christ, where the hell do we even begin to look?"

The words came out of Maria's mouth slowly, like the dawn. "The Silver Spoon," she said.

Jerry looked at her questioningly.

"The what?"

"The Silver Spoon," she repeated, enunciating with perfect clarity. "Tad blurted out something about the Silver Spoon, how bad it stunk. Jerry, those tunnels stunk. It's got to be, it's just got to be!"

Jerry remembered some of the things Guy Henry had said, something about Tom Smith and Lenny Griffin being seen in the area of the Silver Spoon. "What'd you do?" he had asked, "Kill 'em then send em' off to get you a burger?"

"Walker and I were there earlier," Maria continued. "I saw something in there." She thought a moment, her face lit up. "Jerry, the festival—everything's open, everything. The whole town—everything except the Silver Spoon."

Jerry mulled it over, caressed it. It just . . . felt right. That and they had nothing else. He took one of her stakes, then her cross and the flashlight. Before he left he kissed her, but only quickly, like he was leaving for work. Finally he told her to stay away from the cellar door, far, far away from it.

Watching him run down the driveway, preternatural

272

weapons in hand, she felt a blanket of gloom settle over her. Would she ever see him or Tad alive again? Would any of them live out the night? These questions tugged at her, and it wasn't very long before she decided that she wasn't doing anyone much good by guarding a door that seemed impervious to attack anyway. A few minutes later she locked the door behind her and set off into the darkness in search of her husband.

11:58 P.M.

Afraid, yet strangely intrigued, Tad watched as Sharon turned only her head and peered intently to her left, into the tunnel outside his prison. Whatever was out there had her full attention. Tad could only think of Prince being drawn by the ultra high pitch of a dog whistle. Her attention was diverted for no more than ten seconds before she looked back at him. But this time she didn't look like some stone-faced guard. It almost looked like she was pleading with him now. He even believed he saw her hand come up and reach out to him. But that passed fast enough to make him wonder if it had happened at all. Then she left, slowly, purposefully. She simply walked out the door and left him unguarded. But like his dad, Tad wasn't given to action without thought. He didn't run as soon as she left. Instead he thought about his situation. It could be a trick, he decided. He could make a run for it only to make it as far as the door. But he probably wouldn't get a better chance than this. He had to do something.

He fumbled with alternatives. But before he could choose one, the light from the candles began to dim; as if each candle was being snuffed out one at a time. Soon, he realized with building horror, there wouldn't be any light at all. He got to his feet as more candles went out, and pressed himself against the earthen wall. Now he thought more seriously about running, before it was too late. But

273

before he could, the two remaining candles on either side of the door were snuffed as if an eddy of wind had found its way into the tunnels. Darkness, as complete as that known to the blind, quietly reigned. Tad felt his heart thump in his chest. His ribs seemed to bend from the pressure. Without knowing it, he dug his fingers into the wall.

Seconds later he felt a presence, and in his mind he even imagined someone standing in the doorway, watching him through the darkness. Something that wasn't afraid of the dark, maybe even made stronger by it. So it really didn't surprise him when he heard; "Come with me, boy. Every execution needs a witness."

Although he couldn't hear it, he thought the man moved closer. Tad backed up as far as he could—he wondered how thick the wall was. Maybe he could dig through, into another room or something. Then he felt a huge, cold hand encircle his arm. Screaming, he was guided through the darkness.

By the time they stopped, Tad's throat was so swollen from screaming he had lost his voice. A match was lit. Tad covered his eyes against the sudden glare. After his eyes adjusted, he looked to his left. Beyond the glow he saw only a skeleton with inhuman eyes. Match light danced over flat white bone and teeth that had no business in the mouth of a human being. Its hair was tangled about its head like the thread of an old, sparse mop, some of it was dry and singed. The eyes that looked at him were round and pointed with blood. It looked like they were suspended in midsocket. Tad could only stare in disbelief. It was the worst of images, considering what he had seen earlier, the open casket, the hand. He tried to scream; nothing came out. He tried to pull away, but he couldn't do that either.

"What's the matter?" Harry said. "Don't you recognize your uncle?"

Harry turned a little to reveal a fleshy ear, the only part

274

of his head that hadn't been touched. "Look," he said, pointing. "Look over there." He held the match out in front of him. It went out. He cursed, lit another.

The gang of miscreants were gathered against a wall: Sharon and Lenny Griffin, Tom Smith, Ann Cook, David Warner. Through the stench of the dead, Tad faintly smelled gasoline. Behind his uncle, he saw the glint of metal. Gasoline cans. The match went out. Harry lit another. "They're confused, Tad. See how confused they are," he said joyously. "You see, I made them in my image, immortal, but because I made them, I can do what I want with them. You know, like having your own toys."

His creatures did indeed look confused, and, although they were apparently free to go, they clung to each other like frightened children. With paranoid eyes they gazed into each corner of this large room, inspected every inch; but not once did they look at Harry, their creator. Their master.

Harry spoke like a teacher now. "You know, Tad, revenge is never sweet unless you can share it with someone, remember that. That's why I brought you here. Tell you what you do, pretend I've taken you to a ballgame and the home team has just won the game with a ninth inning homer. The crowd roars! Women and children faint, grown men hug each other and cry openly. Glorious, glorious day! And then—fireworks. Everybody loves fireworks!"

With that said, he threw the lit match into the air. Tad watched as it arced, its flight imprinting onto his eyes. The conflagration was immediate, the heat instant and almost unbearable. The fire rose a few feet off the floor and beat a hasty path toward Harry's creations. Their eyes widened in disbelief as death approached. Sharon tried to run, but she was too slow. Fire surrounded them at first, but only for a split second before their gasoline-soaked clothing gloriously ignited.

Harry backed away and pulled Tad with him. And had

Tad been watching his uncle rather than the ghastly show, he would have seen his bone actually stretch into a smile.

To their credit, they at least screamed like immortals. The death screams of five burning humans would have reached only a fraction of the screeching intensity attained by Harry's creations. Tad covered his ears, but the sound probed through the flesh of his hands like a steel rod being forced into his skull. All he could do was try to scream along with them, but he couldn't even do that. He still didn't have his voice.

Jerry stopped. He had heard something about a hundred yards away and to his right, something beyond the garbled crowd noise and the revelry of the festival. He turned, shone his flashlight in that direction. Tall weeds waved in a gentle wind. The noise suddenly stopped, but he decided to investigate anyway. He walked about fifty yards, stepped up to the fence and shoved the light into the cemetery. Halfway up the hill he saw a cluster of five random size tombstones. The largest, a huge stone cross, was over ten feet tall. He could barely make out the name: LEONARD. From this cluster of tombstones he saw smoke rise, not fog or calcium deposits that mimicked ghosts, but smoke. Something was burning beneath the ground, beneath the caskets. But how was that possible? What could possibly burn beneath a cemetery?

Beside him then, frightening him, he heard, "Weird, man. Fucking weird!" He turned sharply and saw a couple of festival goers, a young man and woman. Their arms were draped over the fence, apparently oblivious to anything but the smoke rising from the cemetery.

Jerry backed away and continued on toward the Silver Spoon.

Chapter Twenty-Nine

On the way to the Silver Spoon, Jerry was stopped by Father Monroe. His eyes were crazed and he screamed nonsense about visits from the undead and other priests who scratched at his window. "Tonight," he said ponderously. "Father Unu was here tonight! Tell Maria. Please, please tell Maria!" He attached himself to Jerry, as if he was the only one capable of understanding. *There's no time for this,* Jerry thought. He pushed Father Monroe aside, just as he had other festival goers. But Father Monroe wasn't easily dissuaded. He stopped a few more people and tried pleading with them, but they weren't as gentle as Jerry had been. The last he saw of Father Monroe, he was on his back in the street.

Jerry reached the Silver Spoon about five minutes later. As Maria had said, it was dark inside; which was highly unusual considering the fact that virtually every other light in town was on. He tried the front door. It was locked. He shone the flashlight through the front window. For a moment he thought he saw something. He looked closer. Nothing. He went around to the side, to an alleyway. Muffled by the closeness of the buildings, the sounds of merrymaking faded as he moved further into the alley. He stepped out of the alley and shone his flashlight into the woods behind the Silver Spoon, then stepped onto the small back porch and tried the door. It was locked, too. He shone the flashlight into the back window and saw the stairway into the basement. He stepped off the porch to a side window and illuminated a hallway and doors on either side, the johns, he thought. After one last look into the alleyway, just to convince himself that he was alone, he broke the window with his good elbow. The sound of glass breaking sounded cacophonous, easily loud enough to alert anyone inside the restaurant. But no one was in there, or in the living quarters on the second floor. He was sure of that. He waited a few moments. Hearing nothing, he cleared away the shards of glass that were left and swung a foot inside. But as he swung his trailing leg in, his foot caught on the broken window. He fell heavily to the floor—glaring white pain surged through his bad arm. But through that pain he thought he saw someone. His muscles tightened—he saw a thin flash of light. A moment later his upper thigh erupted in pain. He grabbed at it, felt something cold and hard slip through his fingers, cutting them with the crisp, focused pain reminiscent of a razor cut. Vaguely, he saw an outline, that of a large woman towering over him. He could only watch as she first muttered something about "intruders" and then raised the knife high over her head. Instinctively, he kicked upwards with his good leg as the woman started the knife on its downward arc. In what was a natural movement, he slanted his foot during the execution of the kick, just enough for it to fit into Shirley Wise's wide and meaty throat. Her larynx collapsed instantly. The knife fell from her hands and clattered onto the linoleum beside him. He rolled out of the way as she fell precisely onto the spot where he had lain. He got to one knee, shone the flashlight at her. Her hands were at her throat like she was trying to strangle herself, and her eyes had rolled almost completely, leaving only the whites. He knew there wasn't a thing he could do for her. Within a minute or so her huge body just went limp and her hands fell to her side.

He examined his leg. It was bleeding profusely, as were his fingers. Somehow he had to stanch the bleeding. He tore off a few pieces of the woman's skirt, an effort that

278

further aggravated his wounded arm, and wrapped the cloth tightly around his wounds. He couldn't worry about tourniquet damage now, his main concern was to limit the blood loss.

His way was clear now, but he seriously doubted if he could even walk down the cellar stairs. He tried anyway, mimicking very well the halt and lame. His right leg, he guessed, was about fifty percent, and it wouldn't get any better quickly. His left arm was like cooked spaghetti.

Walking through town, he had pictured a long and exhausting search for the entrance into Harry's domain. That was not the case. The woman, he decided, had probably been a guard. With a guard Harry didn't have to hide his entrance very well.

Toward the back of the cellar, crowded with the detritus of the restaurant business, booths and old refrigerators, he found one thin piece of plywood covering a very small hole cut at about a forty-five degree angle. He moved the plywood away, hesitated a moment and then lowered himself head first into the tunnel.

Although he felt a hunter's anxiety, he hadn't yet experienced the psychic, almost magnetic pull he thought he would. He thought of the kid's game, warm and cold. Well, truth was, he felt cold, and not simply because he was underground. He continued on quickly, not at all afraid of what might be ahead, just beyond the next curve in the tunnel or in one of the many rooms. With a kind of twisted reasoning, he wanted to be more afraid.

12:15 A.M.

Maria saw Father Monroe first, and she was thankful for that. *He's gone over the edge,* she thought. Maybe their talk had had something to do with that. Maybe something else. Whatever it was, she didn't want to talk to him, not now. So she became part of the crowd. She pretended not to see him and continued on to the Silver Spoon. She arrived just as a fight broke out near the pet store. She watched the fight for just a second and then tried the front door. It was locked. She went around back via the same alleyway Jerry had used earlier.

She knew he was in there. The window was broken—he had to be. She stuck her head inside. "Jerry?" she said. "Where are you, Jerry?" She saw the dead woman. But she had seen a lot worse tonight. She was only mildly startled, certainly not frightened enough to make her run. She avoided the body as she stepped inside. Then she stood over it. She felt some vague moral duty to see if the woman was dead or not, but even in the dark, it was plain to see she *was* dead. Death had a certain look. Kind of a still, almost photographic look, she decided. As she wondered about the cause of death, she heard movement outside, in the alley.

Someone was walking toward her.

Jerry had expected this. Walking through these tunnels, the putrid smell had grown steadily more intense, even palpable. Now, as he brought the light to bear upon the bodies that had been mindlessly thrown into a shallow room, he felt his stomach rumble acidly. He covered his nose and took in breaths through his mouth. He chased back his gorge. Then he trained his light on the dead. Some appeared to be tourists, as evidenced by the cameras still draped over their arms and the moldy, insect-eaten pie tins near the body. Their ages ran the spectrum, an obvious random selection. Harry's choices. He, Jerry thought, was probably the first mortal to see this—unless . . . unless Tad had beaten him to it.

He saw something with his mind's eye, but only for a second. Tad? he wondered. He saw it again. Not as fleetingly. It *was* Tad. Jerry squinted. Sleeping? Is he sleeping? He saw something over his head . . . photographs, maybe? Then the image was gone. But that image stayed with him as he stabbed his light into various size

280

rooms, and down long, undulating tunnels, again searching for the paranoia that might signal that he was at least getting close. But he still didn't feel any more a psychic connection than he might have felt in Carlsbad Caverns. And that worried him. He wanted this ended, one way or another.

12:22 A.M.

He saw a pile of loose earth in front of a wall. This, he told himself, was probably where the burning took place. He scooped up a handful of earth and let it slide between his fingers. Bits of clothing and charred skin mixed with the dirt. His skin tingled. Someone *had* been cremated here, Jesus, maybe a lot of people.

Some minutes later he found the feeder tunnel, similar to the one beneath the Silver Spoon, only larger.

As he crawled into it, he saw another vision. It was Tad again, but there were booths around him. Restaurant booths! Then he understood what he was seeing. Harry and Tad weren't in these tunnels at all. He hadn't felt any psychic connection down here because there was none to be felt! They were at The Silver Spoon! They were seated at a goddamn booth at the Silver Spoon! He worked his way through the tunnel. Luckily, the trap door was open. It took a lot of effort, considering his injuries, but he finally managed to climb into his cellar. He hobbled to the stairs and pushed open the door. "Maria?" he yelled.

No answer.

"Goddamnit, Maria, where are you?"

Still nothing. He looked at the cellar door. The cross was still there. And she hadn't been in the tunnels or the cellar. "Christ," he said. "She followed me."

12:30 A.M.

His old football coach would have been proud. His pain

281

was enormous, but he still made it back to the area of the Silver Spoon within five minutes. But it was as if the restaurant were able to transmit some deadly contagion; no one stood near the windows or even on the sidewalk out front. People walked through the street, but everyone purposely avoided the area, apparently without realizing it. And as he approached, brushing past partiers, he began to feel the psychic pull he had wanted to feel in the tunnels. He stepped cautiously toward the streetlamp lit window and let his flashlight probe the interior. He saw the bar first then the booths. Harry and Tad were seated in the very first booth, facing away from him; Harry in the middle and Tad on his right, toward the wall. Without turning, Harry raised his hand and waved him in. Jerry didn't hesitate, and this time the front door was open. He entered quietly, feeling somewhat foolish about that. After he had stepped around the booth, he raised his flashlight first to Tad and then to Harry. Harry greeted him with a wide smile. The sight of his brother's grotesque, seemingly acid-gouged face, made Jerry shudder. "You still wanta be twins?" Harry asked. He gestured to his face with his open hand. "It can be arranged."

Tad lay very still. But because Jerry hadn't yet witnessed his death, he thought he was only unconscious. He stepped toward them while Harry raved on.

"Here's what I got in mind, Jer. Works like this." His skeletonized head moved in stuttering phases while he talked, as if the musculature had faded, leaving only burned ligaments to do the job. "I make you immortal—you'll like that part—then you make Tad immortal, then Maria, then maybe her mother." Again he smiled.

Harry pointed at the stake in Jerry's hand. "You weren't gonna use that on me, were you, Jer?" he asked.

Stunned by the sincerity of Harry's tone, Jerry didn't answer.

"Christ," Harry added, "You'd treat your own kin like that—drive a goddamn stake through his heart? I'm

282

hurt, Jer, deeply hurt! Do you actually for one minute think I like this adversarial arrangement? Do you? Jer, you're my twin, my very essence. I love you, Jer!"

For a moment he actually sounded sincere, but when he laughed as delighted a laugh as Jerry had ever heard, the truth was revealed with all the clarity of a desert sun.

"You tried to kill *me,* Harry, twice that I can remember," Jerry said matter-of-factly.

Harry shrugged. "Oh, that. Well, what can I say? You were a nuisance. Always were, you know. I really hated having a mirror image. God, what a drag! And then you decided to be a writer, too, just like me. And you know, Jer, you can't write a lick. Not a lick. Oh, I took a look at some of the stuff you wrote after you moved into the house, and I have to admit, it was pretty decent. But, Jer, that was all my doing. You were just transferring to paper what I supplied you. So you see, you're still talentless. All you can do is mimic."

Harry gestured to the seat across from him, then he tried to smile. This time it was a rictus grin at best. Jerry remained standing.

"You see, Jer, if you really wanna write, you've got to have some evil on which to draw. You've got to be willing to go that extra mile. You never were evil. Not really. You're just a nice guy who can maybe get some things published in newspaper magazines. And until you become immortal, Jer, you will never know the real meaning of evil. Then you'll forever be relegated to mediocrity. Sorry, pal, that's just the way it works."

Seconds later Jerry sat down across from him. His hand tightened on his weapon. Harry seemed intrigued by Jerry's attempt at stealth.

"What you gonna do, bro?" he said. "You gonna shove that thing into my heart? Is that what you're gonna do?"

Jerry leaned forward, his face within inches of his brother's. With a certain amount of difficulty he looked him square in the eyes. "Something like that," he said.

Enraged, Harry's eyes narrowed. He grabbed his

unconscious hostage by the hair and pulled his head back as far as he could without snapping his neck. Tad's windpipe pressed rudely against his skin. Jerry's breath caught in his throat. "Like a twig, Jer. Just like a twig," Harry seethed. "And oh what a pleasure it would be!"

Again Jerry saw himself through his brother's eyes— as if he were the target all along, not Tad. Harry let go of his hostage and stood. Tad moaned.

"Tell you what I'm gonna do," he said, gazing out the window. "I'm gonna give you a sporting chance. You always were a sporting man. I'm gonna take Tad outside, you know, with the partiers. Then I'm gonna stand in the middle of the street and tell everyone that I'm going to make him immortal." He looked back. "I know, what sport is that? Well, the way I see it, evil is really powerful. Good is, well, not as powerful. That's the way I see it. I'm willing to bet my 'life' on that. It's gonna go down like this. All those inherently evil revelers will just go about their business. They'll just let me do it. Why? Because my soul, my essence, has permeated this town. It's mine now, every goddamn one of these people is mine. Oh, sure, they're still mortal, still able to determine right from wrong and all that garbage, but they'll choose wrong. Just like I have. Just like you will. You just watch and see."

"And if they don't?"

"Stay with me, Jer, stay with me! That's where the sporting chance comes in. If they don't, if they tell me no, then I won't. That simple. I'll just leave. Fair enough?"

"What choice have I got?"

"You know, you've got a point there. Now, fair enough?"

Jerry paused, then, "Yeah, okay. Fair enough."

With the bargain struck, Harry grabbed up his hostage like an old coat then moved to the front door, pulled it open and stepped out onto the sidewalk. Jerry was right behind, his stake at the ready.

Jerry watched the crowd, the assorted beasties: the

kids in pig masks and the werewolves and the aliens and a few amorphous demons. None of them took notice of the bizarre creature watching them. From the pet store and above the crowd noise, Jerry heard dogs yapping, dogs of all sizes, soprano barks, tenor barks, a few deep bass barks. A man wearing only his underwear had climbed a light pole. He hung there by one arm and drank from a liquor bottle. The brand was indeterminite. A more traditional vampire strolled past. He seemed Transylvania-inspired, right down to the red velvet cape and the chalk-white face. He was tall, commanding. He moved slowly yet with athletic grace. He was the only one that turned in their direction. Harry seemed to find that amusing. The moist night air bore the smell of festival foods well: pizza, sausage, pies. Again the scene was charged with blatant sexuality. Some costumes were laughable: a woman wearing a bulldog mask and a plastic body mask with a set of canine nipples; a man wearing a tutu and a long, black, thickly veined dildo. Lust and debauchary seemed to have arrived at an equal footing with the original theme of the festival, demonism.

Again Tad moaned, shifting Jerry's attention. Maybe he'll come out of it, he thought. Maybe when he does . . .

Harry suddenly moved out into the street and lay Tad down. "Listen up," he said conversationally. He spoke barely loud enough for Jerry to hear, hardly, Jerry thought, a call to order. But within ten seconds the crowd grew quiet and formed a circle. Jerry stood about twenty feet away, his stake still clutched tightly in his hand.

A breeze came up. In the distance lightning flashed. A filigree of clouds passed over the moon. A few people stepped in front of Jerry. He allowed it.

Within another minute or so, the street was as quiet as it had been loud. Harry seemed pleased. He spoke casually, as if asking for directions. "Would anyone object to my, uh, taking this boy?" he asked. "By 'taking' I mean turning him into an immortal."

A few titters, then again, silence.

He gave the crowd a moment, intently peering into

285

each face for an answer. Much to Jerry's disbelief, people stirred, but no one voiced an opinion.

Harry gave him a skeletal gaze, his teeth reflecting the light. Again he addressed the crowd. "Then I take it no one would raise a hand to save this boy?"

Still nothing.

"He's got it coming anyway."

Murmuring.

"Last chance. Just a simple no."

Behind him then Jerry heard a quiet "Yes." He turned to see who had spoken. The traditional vampire smiled at him. A few more people said yes, then a few more until finally the street echoed that response, up and down its length, deafening to hear and impossible to understand.

"No!" Jerry shouted above it. "No, for God's sake, no! Can't you see he's not kidding—that's not a costume for chrissake, he's really a vampire! God help us, he's really a vampire!"

Harry looked at him and said, "Evil, dear brother, wins again." Then he took up the crowd's chant like some macabre and hideously ugly cheerleader. "YES, YES, YES!" the chant continued. Harry looked at his brother. "Yes," he breathed. "Yes!" Then he lifted Tad into his arms and hugged him. His teeth flashed in the streetlight glow. Jerry pushed, but the crowd wouldn't let him past. "YES, YES, YES," they chanted maddeningly. The flow of those words passed through the town like a tidal wave. It's going to happen, Jerry thought. Good God in heaven, a whole town is going to stand idly by and let this evil thing happen! Tears welled in his eyes. He screamed for his brother to stop. But his pleas for mercy, as he knew they would, fell on deaf ears. Harry lifted Tad high into the air. He shook him playfully and laughed as his limbs ragdolled.

"NO," Jerry yelled. "For God's sake, NO!"

For the very first time in his life Jerry had actually considered God's help. It was a realization that shot him first with wonder then renewed strength. He gripped the stake firmly and stepped toward his grinning brother, who was too engrossed in triumph to notice. But his way was blocked. He tried to push the blockers aside, but he couldn't. Harry drew Tad closer still. Jerry pushed on the crowd, it budged, separated slightly. Harry's teeth were on his son's throat now, beginning the final pressure. The crowd parted. Jerry charged, his stake raised high in his good arm, his slashed leg pleading with him and splashing blood onto his makeshift bandage, his face contorted with rage and fear. No time, he thought. God, there isn't enough time!

And there wasn't. There was too much distance between them. He could see his son's skin strain against the pressure. Then, no longer able to ignore the pain in his leg, he fell. Sobbing now, he began to crawl. Out of the tail of his eye, Harry watched with amusement. Still the crowd chanted wildly, feverishly. In seconds his son would not just die, he would be reborn into evil. "NOOOO!" he screamed. "NOOOO!"

Then, abruptly, the crowd stopped chanting.

Concentrating fully on the entertainment, no one saw it happen. They only saw the aftermath. With a suddenness that was astounding, Harry's chest was impaled by yet another stake, one that looked very much like part of a fence. The last foot or so dripped his dark blood; inches separated it and Tad. Harry, as surprised as he had ever been, again snapped viciously at Tad's throat. But in his severely weakened condition, he could only drop him to the ground. Finally, cursing wildly, he turned. Maria, Father Monroe behind her, stood her ground. She looked Harry in the eye and said simply, "No."

Within minutes Harry Matheson died—again. But he did not go quietly. His body quivered and shook violently. He thrashed in the street like a wounded dog and the air fouled again with the odor of death as he cursed everyone and everything. Finally, having no choice really, he gave up. His body simply disintegrated, puffing bits of skeletal powder into the air, until all that was left was his clothing and the weapon of his

287

destruction slanted across his shirt. A wind sent by the approaching storm rose and scattered the pile of skin dust to the farthest corners of the town. The crowd was stunned. They had partly believed that what they had seen was all just part of the festivities. Harry, they thought, had donned some grand and very convincing costume. Or maybe not.

"Go home, all of you, go home," Father Monroe said.

They balked at first, but Father Monroe simply nodded and that seemed to convince them that they should. They left slowly, in groups of twos and threes. They removed their masks as they walked and they talked lowly about what they had seen, if they had seen anything at all. Within a few minutes the streets of Naples Falls were again empty. The noise of merrymaking was just a memory. Festival litter blew about with the approach of the storm.

"I'll get a doctor." Father Monroe said. "He's going to need one." On his way, he wondered about the size of tomorrow's congregation. And tonight, he thought sure, there would be no visit from Father Unu.

Jerry felt Tad stir then wake fitfully. He woke terrified, but Jerry hugged him and whispered to him that it was over. Finally over.

Maria knelt beside them. Jerry tried to put an arm around her, too, but he couldn't raise it high enough.

"I'm sorry," she said as she put her arm around him. "I'm so sorry."

"Don't be," Jerry said. "Please, don't be."

Lying in the street, his family close, Jerry felt conflicting emotions: happiness, anger, loss. But through these emotions he sensed a spiraling loneliness, perhaps inspired by the fact that he was no longer a twin.

Or, more to the point, that he had never really been one.